Clutches
and Curses

Books by Dorothy Howell

HANDBAGS AND HOMICIDE

PURSES AND POISON

SHOULDER BAGS AND SHOOTINGS

CLUTCHES AND CURSES

Published by Kensington Publishing Corporation

Clutches
and Curses

DOROTHY HOWELL

KENSINGTON BOOKS
http://www.kensingtonbooks.com

KENSINGTON BOOKS are published by

Kensington Publishing Corp.
119 West 40th Street
New York, NY 10018

Library of Congress Card Catalogue Number: 2011922118

ISBN-13: 978-0-7582-5330-9
ISBN-10: 0-7582-5330-3

First Hardcover Printing: June 2011

10 9 8 7 6 5 4 3 2 1

Printed in the United States of America

To David, Stacy, Seth, Judy and Brian

ACKNOWLEDGMENTS

The author is grateful to the many talented people who have supported her efforts in writing this book. Some of them are: David Howell, Stacy Howell, Judith Howell, Seth Branstetter, Brian Branstetter, Anita Beckenstein, Dorit Berger, Eric Berger, Martha Cooper, Chelsee Glover-Odom, Sheila Lowe, Linda Saunders, Mark Saunders, Bonnie Stone, Suzanne Stone, and William F. Wu, Ph.D. Many thanks to Evan Marshall of the Evan Marshall Agency, and to John Scognamiglio and the talented team at Kensington Publishing for all their effort and support.

Clutches
and Curses

CHAPTER 1

"It's b.s.," Bella grumbled. "You ask me, it's b.s."

"Yeah . . . ," I said, flipping through *People* magazine.

Bella sat across the table from me in the breakroom of the Holt's Department Store where we were both employed—notice, I didn't say *worked*. Around us, other employees came and went, clocking in or out, getting a snack from the vending machines or microwaving their dinner.

Bella had been on a rant since we'd sat down. Now, twenty minutes into our fifteen-minute break, she was still going strong. I'm not sure what she was talking about. I drifted off.

How could I not? I hadn't seen this week's *People* and I was way behind on my celeb news. Plus, it was their fashion issue and I absolutely had to know what was coming up for fall.

It wasn't just a simple need to know. It was way more than that.

I, Haley Randolph, with my print-worthy dark hair and my long pageant legs, had teamed with my very best friend in the entire universe, Marcie Hanover, and started a purse party business. In a matter of months, we'd gone from crazed, obsessive, twenty-something white girls to full-blown successful handbag businesswomen.

It helped that the brains behind our archrivals had been murdered—I mean that in the nicest way, of course.

Anyway, the purse party field was wide open now, and Marcie and I were taking full advantage. Marcie said we should keep our regular jobs—she's almost always right about things—so here I was still pulling down a whopping seven bucks an hour in a midrange department store with ungrateful customers, supervisors who insisted we actually work, and a clothing line that's greatest contribution to the fashion world would be making the "Don't" column in *Glamour.*

Of course, enriching the lives of deserving women through the sale of knockoff handbags and toiling away at one of L.A.'s least respected department store chains wasn't the sum total of my contribution to the world. I also attended college.

I'd cut-and-pasted my way to a B in my English class and pulled an A in health—thanks to the girl in front of me who never covered her paper—and finished up the spring semester in good shape, academically speaking.

I saw no need to overstimulate my brain by attending the summer session. Honestly, I didn't like college. There had to be a way to get a high-paying job where I could carry expensive purses and wear great clothes and make everybody do what I said, without slogging through semester after semester of school—and hopefully I wouldn't need a college education to figure it out.

"So, are you going?" Bella asked.

"Yeah . . . ," I said, turning another page.

"What?" Bella exclaimed.

I glanced up. Bella looked at me as if I had antennas coming out of my head and an anal probe in my hand.

Okay, so maybe I should have been paying attention.

"But it's b.s.!" Bella exclaimed.

The whites of her eyes shone in her dark face. Bella was black, tall, and probably close to my age, twenty-four. She

worked at Holt's to save for beauty school. In the meantime, she practiced on her own hair.

I guessed she was experimenting with the celestial
phase. Tonight she'd fashioned two spheres atop her head.
It looked like a solar eclipse—or maybe a lunar eclipse. I
don't know. I hadn't taken astronomy yet.

"What's b.s.?" Sandy asked, sitting down at the table
with us.

I'd known Sandy since I started working here last fall.
Like me, she was a sales clerk. We'd hit it off right away.
Sandy was white, blond, and cute and had a boyfriend
who routinely wiped his feet on her. She didn't seem to notice—that's how nice she was.

"*That's* what's b.s.," Bella declared and pointed to the
bulletin board beside the refrigerator.

In foot-high red letters was a sign that read EMPLOYEE
NOTICE, and an equally large red arrow pointing down to a
typed memo.

Jeez, how had I missed that?

Maybe if they'd put stuff like that by the time clock I'd
notice.

"Holt's is opening a new store in Henderson—that's
right next to Las Vegas—and they're asking for experienced employees to work there for a few weeks to get the
store set up," Sandy said. "I think it would be so cool to
go there."

"I think it's b.s.," Bella told her.

"Holt's is paying for us to stay in a hotel," Sandy said.

"Some place off The Strip, I'll bet," Bella said. "What
kind of trip is that? Sending us to Vegas but not letting us
get close to the action?"

"Plus, they're paying us extra," Sandy said.

"How far do you think that little dab of money will go
in Vegas?" Bella asked. "How are we going to see a show
or eat at the buffet or gamble?"

"It's not a vacation," Sandy said.

Bella shook her head. "It's bs. That's what it is."

"Are you going?" I asked Sandy.

"I already talked to my boyfriend," she said. "He told me not to go. He said he might need me here. He says I'm his muse."

"He does tattoos," I said.

"It's art, Haley," Sandy said.

"The guy's a loser. He treats you like crap. You should dump him," I told her.

I give great advice. I should have my own talk show.

Sandy ignored my words of wisdom—what was up with that?—and asked, "What about you, Haley? Are you going?"

I was with Bella on this one. Staying off The Strip in some midrange hotel, eating at diners and working at Holt's—to say nothing of missing out on all the great shopping—was not my idea of a Vegas trip.

Before I could say anything, the breakroom door swung open and banged against the wall. Judging from the sour look on everyone's face, I figured that Rita, the cashiers' supervisor, was about to spoil everybody's day.

"Break time's over, princess," she barked.

I knew she was talking to me, though I didn't give her the satisfaction of turning to look at her. I already knew what she'd have on—stretch pants and a top with a farm animal on it—and that she'd be scowling.

Rita hated me. I hated her, too. Plus, I'd hated her first and then I'd double-hated her.

She'd jacked Marcie's and my purse party business idea and, thanks to her brainy partner, crushed us.

A few weeks ago, Rita had gone missing—long story—but she'd shown up again. Things hadn't turned out so well for her partner, so Rita was out of the purse party business.

I think she double-hates me back now.

"You're supposed to be serving Bolt." Rita stomped over

to our table and pointed to the bulletin board. "Didn't you read the schedule? You're supposed to read the announcements."

I smiled up at her. "Why should I when I've got you as my P.A. to remind me?"

"Go out on the floor and relieve Grace," Rita barked, then stormed out of the breakroom.

The room emptied out—Rita had that effect on people—so I followed along with the crowd and found Grace in the children's department. Grace usually worked in the customer service booth, which was frequently my little corner of retail purgatory, too. Grace was young, went to college—she actually liked it, which was really weird—and always did the coolest things with her hair. Tonight it was spiked up and the tips were Martian green. She really pulled it off. Grace didn't like Holt's any better than I did, so, naturally, we were instant BFFs.

"What the . . . ?" I murmured when I spotted her.

Grace had on a bright yellow bibbed apron with a blue cursive *H* on the chest that matched the Holt's sign out front. A tray was strung around her neck by a strap. She looked like one of those cigarette girls you see in black-and-white photos who prowled the nightclubs back in the day. Except, instead of smokes, the tray held little paper cups of some kind of blood-red juice.

"Bolt. Holt's newest product," Grace said, pointing to the sign on the front of the tray showing a bottle of energy drink with a lightning bolt going through it. She set the tray aside and took off the apron. "We're giving out samples to customers. Didn't you see the memo?"

There was a memo?

"Just hand them out to customers and tell them they can buy a bottle at the checkout registers." Grace gave me a sympathetic smile. "Have fun!"

She walked away and I stared at the tray. Jeez, how much humiliation was I supposed to endure for minimum wage?

At least I didn't have to wear a hat.

I put on the apron and slung the tray around my neck. The juice sloshed around in the cups.

Oh well, I decided. This was better than actually waiting on customers. I headed down the main aisle toward the back of the store.

The first two customers I passed eyed my tray but I kept walking. Hey, if they wanted a sample, they would have said so, right?

As I passed the housewares department, I glimpsed a woman from the corner of my eye heading toward me. She had on khaki pants, a floral print shirt, and an I-need-help look on her face. I recognized it immediately and, thanks to many months of providing my own brand of customer service, kept my eyes forward, ignoring her with ease.

"Excuse me? Excuse me?" she called behind me.

I didn't inherit much from my mom. She was a beauty queen. Really. My one and only resemblance to her was my long legs, which made me an enviable five-foot-nine. Tall enough to be a model, had any of my mom's other genes not given up on me in the womb.

So I glided away from this customer as quickly and effortlessly as my mom had glided the moment she'd crossed the stage to claim her Miss California crown. And as she had when she'd accepted third runner-up in the Miss America pageant, still displaying grace, beauty, charm, and a fervent wish for world peace—even though she must have been disappointed enough to snap the heads off each and every judge, with no thought to sustaining cuticle damage.

"Excuse me," the customer called again. "Can you help me?"

She appeared next to me, panting and out of breath, forcing me to stop. She looked as if she could use a shot of Bolt, but I didn't offer it. Really, people should speak up if they want something, shouldn't they?

"I'm trying to find the—"

"I'm only here to distribute the drinks," I said.

"Oh."

I walked away.

Okay, so maybe handing out this Bolt stuff wouldn't be so bad.

I changed my mind a moment later when I saw Rita bearing down on me. She planted herself in front of me and glared at my tray.

"You haven't given out a single sample, have you?" she declared.

"Of course I have," I told her. "I gave out all of them and just refilled the tray."

Yeah, okay, that *could* have happened.

"Are you telling the customers where to find the bottles?" she demanded.

If I bothered to speak to a customer, I would tell them. Maybe.

"Are you telling them how much it costs?" she asked.

Jeez, how much was this stuff, anyway?

"And that they can charge it to their Holt's accounts?" Rita asked.

No way was I doing that.

"How about the nutritional facts?" Rita asked. "Are you telling them the nutritional information?"

There was nutritional info?

"Of course," I told her.

Rita narrowed her eyes at me, like she didn't believe me or something. Jeez, what nerve.

"Okay," she said, "so how much sugar is in a serving? How many carbs? How many calories?"

"Look, Rita, if you don't know this stuff, I'm not going to stand here and tell you. Read the brochure yourself," I told her and walked away.

At the end of the aisle I glanced back. Rita was gone. I

ducked through the double doors near lingerie and into the stock room.

I love the stock room. Aisles and aisles of fresh new merchandise stacked on shelves up to the ceiling. The place is huge—two stories—with a mannequin farm, janitor's closet, returned-merchandise area, and receiving section where the big rigs backed in and the truck team unloaded boxes.

Since I worked evenings, it was almost always quiet back here. The trucks arrived during the day and the ad-set team didn't show up until after the store closed. As usual, tonight I had the place to myself.

In the domestics section of the stock room, I took off my tray of Bolt and pulled two Laura Ashley bed-in-a-bag sets off the shelf. I arranged them on the floor, then sat down.

Oh, yeah, I was liking this Bolt stuff more by the minute.

I settled back and got comfortable, then pulled my cell phone from my pocket. Holt's employees aren't supposed to have phones on the sales floor, but, oh well.

I saw that I had a text message from Marcie. I expected info from her about our next purse party, but instead she was asking me about my date tonight with Ty Cameron.

Ty had been my sort-of boyfriend for a long time, but since we'd finally done the deed, he was now my official boyfriend.

Not that much had changed about our relationship.

Ty was absolutely gorgeous. Tall, athletic build, light brown hair, terrific blue eyes. He's the fifth generation of his family to own and be totally and completely obsessed with running the Holt's Department Store chain—yes, the very same department store where I was sitting on Laura Ashley bed-in-a-bag sets, checking my texts while I was on the clock, and slaving away at minimum wage.

It's a long story.

Anyway, we've had our ups and downs—maybe a few

more than other couples. Neither of us could explain our attraction to each other—though I wish Ty would put a little more effort into trying—but, for some reason, we're crazy about each other.

I guess it's a chemical thing.

A few weeks ago, Ty asked me to move in with him. I didn't give him an answer that day—he'd been in Europe for a while and we were busy doing the deed like rabbits—and he hadn't mentioned it again. Until yesterday. He'd asked me to go out for dinner tonight and said he wanted to talk about it.

I glanced down at the tray of Bolt drinks. The stuff didn't look so good, but I grabbed a cup and took a sip. Not bad. I chugged the rest.

In her text message, Marcie offered to come to my apartment tonight and help me pick out what to wear for the big are-we-moving-in-together date. I texted her back that, of course, I wanted her help.

I tossed down another Bolt.

A few minutes later my phone vibrated. Another message from Marcie, this one telling me what time she'd be there.

I took another shot of Bolt—jeez, this stuff wasn't half bad—and sent her a text asking for her thoughts on what I should wear.

While I waited, I knocked back another Bolt. Wow, this stuff tasted pretty good, after all.

Marcie messaged me, I drank another Bolt. I messaged Marcie again. I had another Bolt. We went back and forth, both of us suggesting outfits for me to wear. It had to be perfect. This was a big night.

Finally, Marcie texted that she had to go—she was at work and actually had to go do something for her boss, which was majorly inconvenient—so I put away my phone and shoved the bed-in-a-bag sets back onto the shelf.

One cup of Bolt remained on the tray. Jeez, how had that happened?

Well, no use carrying just one. I gulped it down and headed out onto the sales floor again.

As soon as I'd cleared the lingerie department, a customer popped up from behind a rack of bathrobes.

"You help me," she said.

The woman was old, sort of hunched over, with long black hair she'd tried—and failed—to put up in a bun. She had on a shapeless gray dress and about a dozen odd-looking necklaces. Her skin was dark and she had a funny accent, like she might be Eastern European. Romanian, maybe. I don't know. Is Romania still a country? I haven't taken geography yet.

She pointed to a rack of bathrobes. There was a creepy looking bump on the end of her finger.

"You help me. I need robe," she told me.

"I'm just here to serve the drink," I said and gestured to my tray.

"Drink? You serve drink in store?" she demanded.

She looked kind of squirrelly—not fun-at-a-party squirrelly, more like kill-you-in-your-sleep squirrelly.

I took a step back.

"I'll get you a drink," I said. "I'll be right back."

"No!" The woman waved her gnarled hand. "You American girls, you have *everything*. You give *nothing!* You're *selfish, selfish, selfish!*"

I had no idea what the heck she was talking about, but I wasn't going to hang around and find out—not for seven lousy dollars an hour.

"Look, I'll get someone to help you with the bathrobes," I said. "I'll be back in a—"

She leaned in, bared her teeth, and snarled at me. I froze, too stunned to move.

"I *curse* you," she hissed, waving her finger in front of

my face. "I call on the power of the universe and *curse* you!"

She poked her fingers at me, snapped her teeth together, and left.

Sandy appeared out of nowhere, eyes wide, mouth open.

"Oh my God. That old woman just put a curse on you," she said. "I can't believe she did that. Are you okay?"

I did feel kind of weird—but maybe it was all the Bolt I drank.

"It was just some cranky old lady," I told her. "I don't believe in curses."

"You should," Sandy told me. "You'd better watch out. *Anything* could happen."

"Yeah, right," I muttered.

I headed for the front of the store to refill my Bolt tray. A panel fell out of the ceiling and crashed to the floor right in front of me.

Sandy rushed to my side. "Oh my God. It's happening already!"

Oh, crap.

CHAPTER 2

"She put a curse on you?" Marcie asked, then pulled a yellow blouse from my closet. "How about this?"

We were in my apartment in Santa Clarita, a great upscale area about thirty minutes—depending on traffic—from Los Angeles. Thanks to my diligent and consistent use of a number of credit cards, I'd gotten it fixed up just the way I liked it. I love my apartment.

"He's seen me in that," I said.

She shoved the blouse back onto the rack and started flipping through the clothes again, while I sat on my bed watching her and surfing the net on my laptop. We'd been at this for a while now, sorting through my clothes to find exactly the right look for my are-we-going-to-move-in-together date with Ty tonight.

Wearing the perfect outfit takes hours of prep time. Yet it must look effortless, like you breezed past your closet, selected items while texting your best friend with the news that the girl who stole your ex had a drug-resistant STD, or something cool like that, then threw them on and dashed out the door without even looking at yourself in the mirror.

It's a science, an art—no, it's a gift. Really. It's one of the things I inherited from my former pageant queen mom that my younger sister—Mom's Mini-Me—did not.

You can always tell when someone is trying too hard with an outfit. Like those girls who show up at a Dodger's game in a skirt and pumps. You wonder if they knew where they were going when they got dressed.

The perfect outfit—something that made my butt and boobs look round and the rest of me look flat—lurked inside my closet. All Marcie and I had to do was find it. And we would. We're fearless at this.

While she dug deeper into my closet, I clicked on another Web site, and there before my eyes appeared the most gorgeous handbag I'd ever seen in my life—really, I swear, my entire life.

"Oh my God!" I screamed, hopping up and down on my bed.

Marcie rushed over, as a best friend would, and looked over my shoulder. She gasped, too. Instantly, she knew what I'd found.

"The Delicious," she whispered.

Yes, there it was, pictured on the screen before us in all its buttery leather and beaded glory. We observed a moment of silence befitting the hottest handbag of the season before I spoke.

"I'm getting one," I declared.

Marcie had heard me say that before about other bags, so she didn't remind me of how hard the Delicious would be to find, how few stores would carry it, or how fewer still could keep it in stock—she didn't even point out how expensive it was. Marcie just nodded her acceptance of my vow and went back to my closet.

That's why we're best friends.

"This would be fabulous," she said

I dragged my gaze from the Delicious purse and saw that Marcie had pulled a little black dress from my closet that I'd bought at Banana Republic.

"I can't wear that on a night like tonight," I said. "I got it on clearance."

She understood completely and dove into the closet again.

We both knew how important this date was. Honestly, Ty hadn't been the most attentive boyfriend sometimes. Well, okay, most of the time. He broke our dates or showed up late. He took calls and checked messages when we were together. He was gone a lot.

But he had five generations of the Holt's family riding on his shoulders. Lots of responsibility, pressure, stress. I tried to be understanding—even after our first really hot date when we'd come close to hopping into the sack but hadn't—when he'd told me flat out that his job wasn't something he could ignore.

Apparently, I was.

Still, he wanted us to move in together. That meant something. He wouldn't have asked if he wasn't committed to our relationship. Right?

"So who was she? Just some crazy old lady?" Marcie asked, picking up where we'd left off in our conversation as she continued to search my closet.

I took one long last loving look at the Delicious and closed my laptop.

I'd already heard about how Marcie's day had gone—who'd said what, when, how they said it, and what they had on at the time. And I'd caught her up on what had happened with me—which wasn't nearly as interesting, since Marcie worked in a huge office building with lots of people—who had bad hair and didn't know a Fendi from a Gucci, if you can believe it—that we could talk about.

"Yeah, I guess," I said, and added, "Then a panel fell out of the ceiling and nearly knocked me in the head."

Marcie swung around. "Oh my God. It fell? Just like that?"

I waved away her concern. "It was probably already loose or something."

"And it just *happened* to fall right after that woman put a curse on you?"

"I don't believe in curses."

I'd said those same words about a dozen times to Sandy, Bella, Grace, and everybody else in Holt's who'd seen what had happened, and saying them now to Marcie just made me more sure I was right.

"It was a coincidence," I said.

"Was it a coincidence that your car got hit in the parking lot?" she asked.

Yeah, okay, that was kind of weird. But mostly I was ticked off that, when I came out of the store tonight, I saw that somebody had dinged my fender and hadn't left their name or number or anything.

"And that ticket you got for running a red light on the way home?" Marcie asked.

"That could have happened to anybody," I told her.

"That's a lot of coincidences for one evening," she said, shaking her head. "You'd better take this seriously."

Marcie was almost always right about things, but I couldn't go along with this one. Some wacky old woman waving her finger at me and mumbling a few words couldn't really have an effect on my life. Besides, I refused to believe that someone who dressed as badly as she did had the ability to actually call on the power of the universe to curse me.

That's how I roll.

"Look," I said, "tonight I'm going on a hot date, with a really hot guy, and we're going to talk about moving in together. Could that happen to someone who'd been cursed?"

"Well, maybe not," Marcie said. "But still . . ."

"A few bad things happened to me, but so what? They weren't serious. Just annoying. And they certainly didn't have any real impact on my life. If they did, then maybe—"

My cell phone rang.

Marcie and I both froze and looked at it lying on the bed beside me. We turned to each other again and I knew we were both thinking the same thing—that's what best friends do.

"Is that Ty?" she asked. "Cancelling?"

"No way," I told her, and picked up the phone. I looked at the caller I.D. screen and gasped. Oh my God. It was Ty.

"Sorry, Haley," Ty said when I answered. "I can't make it tonight."

I waited for the usual wave of disappointment to hit me. It didn't hit me.

I heard muffled voices in the background, and Ty said, "I'll call you later."

I waited for the usual anger to hit me.

That didn't hit me, either. Nothing hit me.

"I don't think you should call me," I said. "You're not ready for us to move in together. So I'm giving the offer back to you. Keep it. And if you're ready to extend it again, call me."

I hung up the phone, calm, collected, and stunned.

Marcie looked at me, equally stunned.

Why wasn't I hurt, angry, screaming, crying—something? Why wasn't I rushing to the kitchen for a Snickers bar, or clawing into my emergency package of Oreos?

This wasn't like me, to be completely emotionless. I wasn't acting like myself at all. It was like some weird cosmic force had taken control of me and—

Oh my God. *Oh my God.* Had I really been cursed?

Everybody in the Holt's breakroom was staring at me—which was understandable since I'd walked in a moment ago with a gorgeous Fendi shoulder bag, which I'd stowed in my locker—except, they were all looking at me weird. I was in line at the time clock, waiting for another few hours of my life to chug past in a forgettable blur, and, not only was everyone staring, they were leaning their heads together, whispering and pointing.

Had I missed a meeting?

"Everybody heard about the curse," Sandy, behind me in line, said quietly.

"I'm not cursed," I told her, loud enough for everyone to hear.

"Nothing bad has happened to you—other than that panel falling out of the ceiling, nearly killing you?" Sandy asked.

Everyone in the room stared harder.

Yeah, okay, my car had been hit in the parking lot and I'd gotten a traffic ticket—not to mention that thing with Ty and my weird reaction to it—but none of that meant I was cursed.

I saw no need to mention them.

"Well, you know, things happened—but things always happen," I said.

Everybody glared harder at me now.

The line moved forward. The time clock *thunked* as the employees ahead of me fed their time cards into the slot.

"You have to see a psychic," Sandy said. "It's the only way to find out how to break the curse."

"I'm not cursed," I insisted, as I stuck my time card into the machine. "I don't believe in—"

The lights in the room went off, leaving us in pitch black. Gasps and moans rose from the employees. The time clock made a loud grinding noise. Sparks flew out of the top.

The lights flashed on again. Somebody screamed and pointed at the floor. My time card lay in black, smoldering pieces at my feet.

"Great," somebody in line behind me complained. "The time clock is toast."

"How are we going to get paid?" somebody else asked.

Everybody groaned, then turned and again glared at me.

"Thanks a lot, Haley," someone snapped.

"Yeah. Now all of our paychecks will be late," another person added.

"It wasn't my fault," I told them.

"See a psychic, Haley," Sandy insisted. "Please, for all our sakes."

I left the breakroom feeling a little shaken. Yeah, okay, a few weird things had happened, but I was just having a run of bad luck. I mean, those things could happen to people all the time. Right? I wasn't really cursed, was I?

Grace stood in the customer service booth as I approached. Six customers waited in line

"You're supposed to be in the meeting," she said.

A meeting? Again?

Maybe I was cursed, after all.

"Nothing you can do here, anyway," Grace said, waving her hands around the booth. "When the electricity blinked, all the registers went wacko. The inventory computer is jacked up, too. Even the phones aren't working."

Since, apparently, it was impossible to perform any task whatsoever, it sounded to me like a perfect time to work the customer service booth. But, instead, I had to go to a meeting. Damn.

I headed down the hall past the store managers' offices and into the training room. About a dozen employees were already seated in the rows of chairs that faced the front of the room. The screen wasn't pulled down, which meant no PowerPoint presentation to suffer through—always a good sign.

I took my usual spot at the rear of any gathering and found a seat behind the big guy from men's wear so I could nod off, if necessary, without being noticed. The two employees I'd sat between gave me stink-eye, then got up and moved.

Jeanette, the store manager, came into the room a few minutes later. She was in her mid-fifties and, for some reason unknown to even the greatest minds of the universe, always dressed in Holt's hideous clothing. She wasn't doing the line any favors. Jeanette had a cylindrical shape, which wasn't attractive under the best of circumstances, but lately she'd put on, to be generous, I'll say a *few* pounds, which had widened her midsection considerably.

Tonight she wore a neon white pencil skirt and button-up jacket. The designer, in what I can only think was a moment of supreme optimism rather than a career death wish, had given the jacket a ruffle at the bottom.

She looked like Saturn.

I wondered why she was in here conducting a meeting when everything electronic in the store had gone haywire. But she'd probably made phone calls on her cell to whomever at Corporate handled this sort of problem, and was waiting for someone to show up and fix things.

Jeanette started the meeting and her words quickly turned into *blah, blah blah,* and I drifted off.

Why hadn't Ty called me? I mean, I'd told him last night *not* to call me until he'd rethought this whole moving-in-together thing and was ready to actually discuss it, but still.

What did it mean? Was he just busy? Ticked off at me? Did he really not want to move in together? Was he glad I'd given back his offer so he wouldn't have to tell me he'd changed his mind? Had he found somebody new? Did he have another girlfriend, someone he really wanted to move in with?

I threw out my mental stop sign, bringing my runaway thoughts to a screeching halt. No sense in making things up. I re-centered my thoughts and imagined a different—that's code for *better for me*—scenario.

I'll be somewhere way cool—the handbag department at Nordstrom maybe. I'll turn and see Ty standing next to me—I'll be wearing a V-neck sweater and a demi-cup bra—holding two dozen roses and a fabulous piece of jewelry that's just short of gaudy—no wait, better still that Delicious handbag *plus* the jewelry. Then he'll turn toward me with that smoking-hot smile of his, confess his eternal love, then take me outside and point to the heavens where a skywriter has written *Please move in with me* in big puffy letters. Then he'll take me in his arms and—

My cell phone vibrated in my pocket, bringing me back to reality. Jeanette's words reverberated through the room, something about needing experienced employees in the new Holt's store opening near Vegas. I checked the caller I.D. screen and nearly gasped aloud.

My mom. She'd sent me a text message.

Since when was she willing to risk breaking a nail to send me a message?

I read her message: Mother–daughter week at spa. Your sister cancelled. You're coming with me. Leaving tomorrow.

A knot the size of a Prada satchel formed in my stomach. No, no, this couldn't be happening. I read the message again, hoping, praying that I'd somehow misread it. But no, it was true.

My mom wanted me to go on her annual spa-week trip with her coven of former beauty queens and their beauty queen daughters. A week of talking tiara placement, runway strategy, double-sided tape, and Vaseline tricks. The mothers would recall every step they'd taken down every runway, what they'd worn, what they'd said, what everyone had said about what they'd worn and said. The daughters would brag about the pageants they'd been in, which ones they'd won, which ones they planned to enter next. All of them would go on and on about their "talent," who made their costumes, how they'd rehearse, *where* they'd rehearse, and who would surely comment about how and where they rehearsed.

And I wouldn't be able to say anything. Not one word.

For an entire week, I'd sit there like a dork, nodding and pretending to smile, because I'd never been in a pageant in my life.

Not that my mother hadn't attempted to force me into her footsteps down the runway. From a very early age, I'd taken tap, ballet, modeling, piano, voice, absolutely every kind of lesson imaginable. She hadn't let me quit until I set fire to the den curtains—it was an accident, I swear—twirling fire batons.

But the truth was I couldn't sing, dance, or play a musical instrument—I wasn't even all that interested in world peace—so no way would I fit in with this group.

My mom knew this, of course. She was only asking me to go because my sister—who loved this crap, thankfully—had cancelled on her, and she couldn't show up at the mother–daughter spa week without a daughter.

Okay, this was awful. No, it was beyond awful. It was terrible and horrible and—

I gasped aloud and sat up straighter in my chair.

Oh my God. Was it true? Did this confirm it? Was I really cursed?

If so, I wasn't going down easy.

I shot out of my chair and screamed, "I'll go! I'll go to Vegas! I can leave tonight!"

"You're late, okay?"

For a minute I thought I was having a Rita flashback.

I'd just walked through the front door of the new Holt's store near Vegas—technically, it was Henderson—and a Rita wanna-be had stomped over. She looked nothing like Rita—rail thin, fortyish, with long gray-streaked hair—but she had that same I-love-being-a-bitch look on her face.

"I'm Fay, the cashiers' supervisor, okay, and you're late," she said again.

She had a deep, nasal voice, like she needed her tonsils

and adenoids removed—or maybe she'd already had them removed. I don't know. I haven't taken anatomy yet.

"We start work at eight sharp, okay?" Fay said. "Just because you're out of your usual store, don't think you can take advantage, okay?"

I didn't say anything.

She didn't seem to notice.

"Check in at the office, okay?" Fay said, gesturing toward the back of the store. She pointed to a flip chart on an easel near the front door. "Look for your name and your department assignment on the chart every day when you come in, okay? At eight. Don't be late."

Fay was, apparently, totally unconcerned that I looked like absolute crap. And I was about to point that out, but she walked away. No doubt I'd find time to tell her later. Already, I could see it would be a long day.

It had sure been a long night.

Jeanette hadn't hesitated to approve my temporary reassignment to the Henderson store—which might have hurt my feelings, or at least made me suspicious of something, if I hadn't been so desperate to get out of town—so I'd dashed home to pack. Marcie met me at my apartment, as a best friend would, promised to get my mail and keep an eye on the place, and had even found an old high school classmate on Facebook now living in Henderson that I could hook up with. I'd fought it at first—the girl, Courtney, and I were not exactly BFFs back in the day—but Marcie thought I should know somebody in town, especially with this whole curse thing hanging over me, so I'd agreed.

The five-hour trip had taken twelve hours. Traffic was miserable. Apparently, there was an octogenarian convention in Vegas and I'd gotten trapped at the end of the convoy.

A tire blew somewhere in the vast expanse of desert, stranding me on the side of the road in the dark, in the middle of nowhere, with no cell phone reception. Hours passed before a highway patrol car spotted me and stopped. More hours passed before the auto club guy got there to change my tire. Luckily, the provisions I'd packed—I'd gone with an all-chocolate theme—and the mental image of the Delicious handbag, the totally hot, fantastic, gorgeous purse that I absolutely *had* to have, helped pass the hours.

The mental image of the Sinful handbag—the *last* totally hot, fantastic, gorgeous purse I'd absolutely *had* to have—had also popped into my thoughts for a few seconds. After an all-out search of every department store and specialty shop in Southern California a few weeks ago, I'd all but given up on finding one. Then, out of the blue, I got one. But no way did I want to look at that bag and be reminded of the guy who gave it to me. I was done with him—forever, hopefully. So I'd given it away. Without a second thought. *That's* how much I didn't like that guy.

By the time I made it to Henderson, I was already late, so I went straight to the store instead of checking into the hotel the Holt's employees were staying in. Only to be treated like crap when I arrived. Guess I shouldn't have been surprised. It was, after all, Holt's

No one at Holt's knew I was dating—and possibly moving in with—the owner of the chain, and of course I didn't want my personal business to be common knowledge—unless it benefited me, of course. Like now.

I was exhausted, cranky, hungry, and I probably smelled bad, and I wanted to crash at the hotel. I was sure that once the manager on duty heard my story—and got a whiff of me—I'd be out the door right away.

I headed for the rear of the store. The place looked huge without the merchandise. Beige carpet had been laid. Heavy manila paper was taped over the tiled areas of the floors. A few display shelves and racks had been installed.

People ran around like farm animals. Workmen were busy hammering, sawing, drilling things, dragging power cords, climbing on ladders into the ceiling, making all kinds of racket. Employees pushed U-boats and Z-rails full of merchandise, unloading and stocking shelves. Empty boxes were everywhere. A couple of janitors ran vacuum cleaners. A half-dozen employees huddled around a bank of cash registers.

As I passed what would eventually become the women's clothing department—all Holt's stores were laid out the same, as if customers wouldn't have sense enough to read the signs—I noticed a dark red stain on the carpet at the entrance to the dressing room. I recognized it immediately. Bolt.

Jeez, I sure could use a hit of that stuff right now. Just the energy boost I needed to make it to the hotel.

The trail of Bolt that darkened the carpet led into the dressing room. I followed it and I knew without a doubt that the employee I'd find on *break* in the dressing room drinking this stuff would instantly become my new BFF.

Or maybe not.

Whoever it was had really gone nuts with the energy drink. It was splattered up and down the walls and on the carpet of the narrow hallway that ran alongside the changing rooms.

The place smelled weird.

I got a weird feeling.

At the end of the row, I pushed open the door of the handicapped changing room. A young woman lay sprawled on the floor, blood covering her neck, chest, right shoulder, and arm. Dead.

CHAPTER 3

"Hi. I'm Haley Randolph. I'm from the Santa Clarita store," I said.

I was standing in front of the store manager's desk in his office at the back of the store. It was in a little suite of offices—exactly like in every other Holt's store—just past the customer service booth and the employee breakroom, outside the training room.

Preston, the store manager, looked up and smiled.

"Yes, indeed you are Haley Randolph," he agreed, then tapped his computer screen. "I received an e-mail from Jeanette, your store manager, advising me that you'd arrive this morning. And here you are!"

I figured him for maybe mid-fifties, dark hair, balding, and kind of soft, like he should have spent a little less time at his desk and a little more time at the gym. He had on a white short-sleeve shirt with a necktie, a look that screamed I'm-single-and-I-dress-myself. Preston seemed a little too chipper to have been a store manager for very long.

"I've got some bad news," I said.

"Oh, no, no, no," Preston said, still smiling as he wagged his finger at me. "We don't accept bad news at this store. I won't allow it!"

Yeah, he'd just made store manager, all right.

There's no easy way to tell someone that you've found a

dead body—I know this from experience—particularly that someone who will ultimately be responsible for juggling cops, detectives, crime scene people, the media, distraught employees, and, of course, the corporate office. So there's no need to waste mental energy trying to think up a way to sugarcoat it, or waste time easing into the topic. It's best to just say it.

"I have your time card right here," Preston said, selecting it from one of the neat stacks of papers on his desk.

Okay, so maybe the news could wait. After all, that girl in the dressing room wouldn't be any less dead two minutes from now.

I took my time card, walked to the breakroom, punched in, and returned to Preston's office.

"There's a dead body in the women's dressing room," I said.

He just looked at me. Then, slowly, his brows drew together.

"A . . . what?" he asked. "A dead—*what?*"

"Body," I said.

Preston gazed across the room at nothing, then turned to me again. "But that's—that's just not possible."

It takes awhile for this sort of news to sink in, but I had my doubts that Preston was going to come to terms with it anytime soon. So what could I do but take over?

"Get the supervisors on duty to cover the exits. Don't let anyone in or out of the store. Get on the P.A. and tell all the employees to come to the training room. The detectives will want to question them," I told him. "And you need to call nine-one-one."

Preston still just looked at me.

"Now." I clapped my hands together. "Let's go. Move it."

I guess my decisiveness spurred him into action. He rushed out of the office and down the hallway.

I probably should have gone into the training room

where all the other store employees would assemble, but I didn't want to. I headed into the breakroom instead.

Two Snickers bars, a Milky Way, six miniature Almond Joys, a bag of peanut M&Ms, the current issues of *Marie Claire*, *Vogue*, and *In Style* later, the breakroom door swung open and Preston came in.

"There you are," he declared and plastered his hand on his chest. "I've been looking for you. I couldn't find you."

Considering that he hadn't even known there was a dead body in his store, I wasn't surprised.

"These detectives want to talk to you," Preston said, gesturing behind him.

Two men followed him into the room. Homicide detectives. I knew their kind.

They'd probably already checked out the crime scene and done all the things homicide detectives do in a situation like this. Since I had the dubious distinction of finding the body, I knew they'd get to me sooner, rather than later.

Talking to homicide detectives—or anyone in law enforcement, for that matter—isn't something to be taken lightly. Believe me, I know. So I was ready for them.

Thanks to a massive intake of sugar and caffeine, courtesy of the breakroom vending machines, my brain cells were humming at peak condition, ready to field, deflect, and sidestep their questions, as necessary.

"This is Detective Dailey," Preston said, pointing. "And this is Detective Webster."

At first glance, Detective Dailey appeared to be nearing retirement age, thanks to a full head of white-gray hair; but on closer inspection, I downgraded him to late forties. He was tall, over six feet, with wide straight shoulders and a strong build that made me think he'd been a football player back in the day and still appreciated a good workout. He had on a houndstooth jacket and an okay-looking shirt and tie. Probably the best he could afford on a cop's salary. He looked like the kind of easygoing man you could be comfortable with.

Lots of times I can tell if I'm going to like somebody just by looking at them. It's a science, an art—no, it's a gift—and it had served me well at many an employment interview, party, and bar.

I didn't like Detective Webster the minute I laid eyes on him. Judging from the look I got in return, he felt the same about me.

He was okay looking, in his mid-thirties, only a couple of inches taller than my five-foot-nine height, and probably outweighed me by ten pounds, at most. He had dark hair. He also had a stinky look on his face, like he was trying to prove something, like he was always right, like he was smarter than everybody else.

If Dailey was a shepherd, Webster was a terrier.

I hate terriers.

After pleasantries—such as they were—were exchanged, we all settled at one of the breakroom tables. Preston yanked his cell phone out of his pocket and claimed he had to answer a call. He said it was on vibrate, but I doubted it. I figured he just wanted to get out of the room.

Wish I'd thought of that.

But no sense in delaying this interview. I had nothing to hide, nothing to cover up. No way were these detectives going to cause me a minute's worry. I wanted to get this over with, get to the hotel, and crash before the brain-boosting snacks I'd eaten—strictly to aid law enforcement, of course—wore off.

Detective Dailey got the preliminaries out of the way quickly by asking my name and address and the name of the hotel I would be staying at, and checking my I.D. while Webster wrote it in a little notebook he carried.

"You're here to help with the opening of the store?" Dailey asked.

"Yes," I said.

"From Los Angeles?" he asked.

"Santa Clarita," I said. "It's a little north of L.A."

"And you got here this morning?"

"Yes," I said.

I figured he'd already asked Preston these things and just wanted to hear me say them to make sure the story stayed the same.

No problem.

Still, Detective Webster was writing down everything I said like it was really important. That weirded me out a little.

"What made you decide to drive up here to work?" Dailey asked.

The key to being questioned by homicide detectives was to be brief in your answers. Don't talk any more than necessary. Don't give away much. Don't volunteer anything.

So I saw no need to tell him about the crazy old woman who'd claimed to put a curse on me, my dented fender, the traffic ticket, or my mom's demand to take me to the spa for a week with the beauty queens. Really, none of that was relevant.

"It just seemed like a good opportunity," I told him, pleased that the liberal chocolate coating I'd applied to my brain cells had my thoughts clicking along like stilettos on a New York catwalk.

Detective Dailey looked at me as if that weren't enough of an answer. I pressed my lips together to keep from saying anything else. That's the mistake criminals always made on those detective shows on television. They started blabbing and didn't shut up. No way was I doing that.

"How did you happen to find the body?" Dailey asked.

"I saw the stain on the carpet and thought it was Bolt, so I—"

"Bolt?" Detective Webster shot the question at me like it was a bullet from a 9mm handgun.

"It's an energy drink Holt's is selling," I explained.

Detective Webster wrote that down, for some reason.

"I followed the stain on the carpet into the dressing room," I said. "That's when I found the dead girl."

"Why would you do that? Follow the trail?" Dailey asked. "Why not find the janitor to clean it up?"

Good question. Damn, these homicide detectives were quick—and I doubted they were jacked up on chocolate.

Explaining that I'd planned to take a break and guzzle some Bolt—as I'd done in the Santa Clarita store—might not cast me in the best light. It's not a crime, but still. No need to get too deep into things.

"I just wanted to see how big the stain was so I could tell the janitor what he'd need to clean it," I said.

Okay, that sounded lame. Jeez, had my chocolate-charged superbrain let me down? Already?

"Did you know the victim?" Detective Dailey asked.

"No," I said.

Webster wrote that down. I saw him underline it.

I don't like him.

"Ever seen her before?" Dailey asked.

"Never," I said.

Webster wrote that down, too. He underlined it twice.

Now I really don't like him.

Detective Dailey leaned back in his chair. "Come to Henderson often?" he asked.

"Vegas a few times a year," I said. "I always stay on The Strip."

Dailey nodded and rose from his chair. He looked a little tired, slightly weary, as if he'd hoped I could give him more info, help him solve this crime.

A murder in a department store that catered to families wasn't good for business, wouldn't draw the hordes of Vegas shoppers out to Henderson. I figured Detective Dailey was under some pressure to solve this murder quickly.

"Thank you, Miss Randolph," he said and left.

Detective Webster followed him out of the room. At the door, he looked back and gave me a stinky look—for a second, I thought he might put another curse on me—then left.

I silently clicked him over into my mental I-hate-you category. I expected Webster got that a lot.

I left the breakroom, more than anxious to put Dailey, Webster, the Holt's store, and the murder victim in my rearview mirror. I was coming down from my chocolate high and needed to get some sleep.

Of course, I could have found Preston and told him I was leaving or, at the very least, hunted down Fay and let her know. But I didn't want to take the chance they'd give me a hard time about it. I was too tired to argue. So I clocked out and left.

The Holt's store was located in a shopping center on Valle Verde Road, just off the 215 freeway. Some other store had once occupied the building, gone under, and left Holt's to snap up the property. Lots of smaller stores were in the complex—a nail salon, real estate office, gift shop, dry cleaner, café. Across the parking lot was a Pizza Hut restaurant.

I took Valle Verde Road south, then hung a right on St. Rose Parkway, where the motel that Holt's had booked for its employees was located. St. Rose Parkway, was huge, ten lanes wide—more lanes than the road to get to Vegas—as if the Henderson gods of commerce had big plans for the place.

And they were getting their wish, obviously. A zillion stores, shops, strip malls, restaurants, gas stations, condos, and housing tracts lined the highway with acres of empty lots in between awaiting future development. Off to the right, in the distance, stood the huge resorts and casinos that line The Strip.

I caught sight of the big sign on the left side of the highway that rose above the Culver Inn Motel, my home away from home for the next couple of weeks. I swung into the parking lot and pulled to a stop in the check-in lane.

All I could think was that, thank the stars above, I'd gotten here. I was mentally and physically exhausted, and wanted nothing more than to crash for a millennium or two.

I passed through the automatic doors into the lobby. Holt's had not, by any stretch of the imagination, booked us into the kind of glitz and glam hotel Vegas was known for. This place looked as if the set dresser for *That 70s Show* had retired to Henderson.

It was decorated with sturdy industrial furniture in shades of burnt orange, brown, and avocado green that showed signs of wear. The registration desk was off to the left, and on the right was a small furniture grouping—the Culver Inn's idea of a lobby seating area, I guess. Beyond that were a dozen small tables and chairs, and along the back wall a continental breakfast buffet was laid out. A couple of people sat eating and sipping coffee, reading the newspaper and pecking away at laptops.

The place didn't look so hot, but I was glad to be there, and it was a relief to realize that everything that could possibly have gone wrong today already had. I mean, jeez, I'd found a dead body, how could things get any worse?

The woman behind the registration desk smiled when I walked up—which was a shock given the orange, brown, and green uniform she was forced to wear. I gave her my name and told her I had a reservation. She smiled brighter and tapped the computer keyboard in front of her.

Her smile soured a bit. "I don't see anything under your name," she said.

My sleep-deprived brain took a minute to react. Jeanette had told me last night, as I was running for the door, that she'd call right away and have the Culver Inn hold one of the rooms Holt's had blocked off for the employees.

"I'm with Holt's," I finally said. This was, of course, something I never admitted to anyone. But I needed to get to my room right away. If I stood there any longer, I'd probably pass out on the lobby couch.

The desk clerk nodded, as if this explained everything, and clicked a few more computer keys.

"Okay, here we are," she said, then nodded again confidently. "Yes, yes, I see this now. And no, no, we absolutely don't have a room for you."

I just looked at her for a few seconds, my mind taking its time to comprehend this.

"Okay, so you don't have a reservation for me," I said, managing to sound calm as I mentally plotted my revenge on Jeanette for not taking care of my accommodations as promised. "Just give me any one of the rooms Holt's reserved."

"No, no, those are all taken," the desk clerk said. "Sorry."

"So give me another room," I said.

Okay, that sounded a little harsh, but come on. This was a motel. What was the big deal?

Apparently it was a majorly big deal, because the clerk just looked at me with her smile frozen on her lips.

"Any room," I said. "I don't care."

She gave me a tight smile. "There are no other rooms available."

"None? Not one room?" I demanded. "Are you telling me that this entire three-story motel, with hundreds of rooms, miles and miles from The Strip, with questionable furnishings and accommodations, is full up?"

"I don't understand it," the clerk said, shaking her head and managing to look convincingly bewildered. "This never happens. Never. It's as if something very odd hit us—completely out of the blue."

Like maybe a curse? I wondered before I stopped myself.

"Look," I said, "there has to be something you can do. I need a room. Will you please call the motel manager and see if—"

Movement off to my left caught my eye. I turned and saw Detectives Dailey and Webster walk through the door, heading straight for me.

Oh, crap.

CHAPTER 4

I crossed the lobby to meet Detectives Dailey and Webster—no way did I want the desk clerk to overhear our conversation. If she claimed she couldn't find a room for me now, I knew she wouldn't go to any extra trouble if she knew I was being questioned by homicide detectives.

People are just strange like that.

"Find the killer already?" I asked, managing an encouraging smile.

I read somewhere that if you want something, you just had to say it aloud, put it "out there," and you'd receive it.

From the look on Detective Dailey's face, I hadn't said it quite loud enough.

"We need to speak with you," he said, and nodded toward the lobby doors. I saw what had to be his plain vanilla, police-issued car parked outside. No way was I going out there.

"Let's chat here," I said.

I didn't wait for his response, just walked to the little seating area in the lobby. Dailey and Webster followed, as I knew they would. Men always follow if you walk away. It's some sort of hunting–tracking instinct left over from a couple million years ago—either that or they just wanted to look at your butt.

I sat down and they pulled up chairs. Detective Webster

made a show of taking out his notebook and clicking his ballpoint pen.

I still don't like him.

"We just need to cover a couple of things with you again, Miss Randolph," Detective Dailey said. "You told us you didn't know the victim. Is that correct?"

I hesitated a few seconds, waiting for him to get to the point, but he just looked at me.

"That's right," I said. "I don't know the girl who got killed."

This hardly seemed important enough to cause two homicide detectives to stop in the middle of an investigation, drop what they were doing, and rush over. But what did I know? I haven't watched *Law and Order* on TV in a while so maybe I was behind on my crime scene investigation techniques.

Detective Dailey let my answer just hang there for a moment, then said, "And you told us you'd never seen her before. Is that also correct?"

I looked back and forth between Dailey and Webster. They both watched me intently, waiting for my response.

Okay, so maybe they don't watch *Law and Order,* either. Maybe they do things differently in Henderson.

"I've never seen her before," I said, and since they were making such a big deal out of it, I asked, "So who was she?"

"Courtney Collins," Detective Webster snapped, like I should know who she was.

I got a bad feeling in my stomach—and it wasn't from all the chocolate I ate in the Holt's breakroom.

"So do you *still* claim you didn't recognize her?" Webster demanded.

Maybe I should stop eating so much chocolate.

"That you didn't know her?" he asked, narrowing his eyes.

No, maybe I needed *more* chocolate.

I glanced at the breakfast buffet at the back of the room. Did they have something chocolate there? A muffin or, better yet, a doughnut? Some Cocoa Puffs, maybe?

"Miss Randolph?" Detective Dailey said, leaning to his right to block my view. "Do you want to reconsider your answers?"

Okay, I'd had about enough of these two. I was tired, hungry, slightly nauseous, and it looked as if I was going to have to sleep in my car. The info I'd given them wasn't that complicated. There was no reason—no reason that would benefit *me*, that is—they should need to go over it again and again.

I stood up. They stayed seated. It was kind of cool looking down on them.

"Look," I said. "I have no idea who this Courtney what's-her-name is. None whatsoever. I just got to Henderson this morning. I don't know anybody here. So unless you've got something else to ask—"

"You contacted her last night," Detective Dailey said. "On Facebook."

Oh, crap.

I sat down and flashed back to my apartment when Marcie was helping me pack. She'd used my Facebook page and contacted that girl I went to high school with. Oh my God. It was Courtney Collins. I'd forgotten all about her.

"That was Courtney?" I asked. "In the dressing room? Dead?"

"It was her, all right," Detective Webster said. He swaggered a bit in his chair. "So why did you lie to us? Why did you claim you didn't know her? Or recognize her?"

Jeez, I could hardly take it in. The dead girl on the dressing room floor was Courtney Collins, that girl I'd gone to high school with?

I desperately needed something chocolate.

"You can't hide that sort of information from law enforcement. Not these days," Webster said, barking the words at me like an annoying little dog. "First thing we did was look at her computer, cell phone records, e-mail account."

Right now I'd settle for chocolate sauce and a straw.

"We know you contacted her on Facebook last night," Webster said.

Actually, that was Marcie doing me a favor, trying to find me a friend here. No way was I going to throw Marcie in front of the bus.

"We talked to the manager of the Santa Clarita Holt's store," Detective Dailey said, sounding a little more composed than Webster. "She told us you were insistent about coming to Henderson. You left immediately. You practically ran out of the store."

Yeah, okay, I'd done that, but only because I didn't want to go to spa week with my mother. How could I explain that to the detectives? Since they didn't know Mom, no way would they understand.

I decided to take another tactic.

"I hadn't seen or heard from Courtney since high school," I said.

"Which makes us wonder why, suddenly, you decided to come to Henderson and why, suddenly, you contacted her," Dailey said.

Was this a good time to explain about the old woman who'd put a curse on me? A curse I didn't even believe in, myself?

I didn't think it would help my cause.

"So here's what it looks like to us." Detective Dailey mellowed his voice and leaned in a little, like we were best friends and he was imparting some confidential info. "It looks as if you contacted Courtney Collins, lured her to the Holt's store, then killed her."

"That's crazy," I said. "Why would I do that?"

"That's what we intend to find out," Webster told me. He stood up and threw a nasty look at me. "Don't leave town."

Oh, crap.

I sat there in the lobby watching as Detectives Dailey and Webster left the motel, got into their dull, boring police car, and drove away. For a moment, I considered running after them, volunteering for a night's stay at the jail—just so I'd have a place to sleep.

Jeez, what had happened to my life? Going to jail had suddenly become a *good* thing?

And where was my official boyfriend in all this? For weeks, Ty had been after me to move in with him. It was *his* idea. Now I hadn't heard from him in two days.

Yeah, okay, I'd given him that ultimatum about withdrawing his request for us to move in together, but that's no reason for him not to call me, one way or the other. Now, of all times, when he could get me a suite at the Bellagio, the Venetian, or the Wynn—not to mention bail money.

Then it hit me. Maybe he'd called me last night when I was stuck on the side of the road with a flat tire and no cell service.

Oh my God. That was probably what had happened. There was a message—no, wait, a dozen messages—on my cell phone from Ty begging me to move in with him.

The scene played out in my mind. Ty telling me how wrong he'd been to put his work ahead of our relationship, how stupid he'd been to make me think he didn't value me above all else.

I pulled out my cell phone and put it to my ear, ready to hear Ty's apology repeated over and over in numerous voicemails.

I had no voicemails.

Huh. Okay, well, that didn't mean Ty still didn't feel awful about what he'd done. And to prove it, he'd get us the most fabulous penthouse in Vegas so we could—

Oh, wait. Ty didn't know I was in Vegas.

I punched in his number on my speed dial. Of course, it didn't suit me to call him, not with the whole ultimatum thing hanging unanswered between us, but what else could I do, under the circumstances?

I put the phone to my ear and readied myself for his heartfelt apology, his fervent thanks that I had called him.

His voicemail picked up.

Crap.

"I'm in Vegas. Call me," I said, glad that I hadn't sounded desperate or anything.

I dropped my phone into my purse and sat there stewing. Even thoughts of the Delicious handbag couldn't cheer me up.

I dragged myself out of my chair and went back to the registration desk. The same woman was there, in the same hideous uniform that made her look as if she'd been side-swiped by the Partridge Family touring bus, clicking the computer keys. I doubted she was still looking for a room for me.

My first thought was to leap the counter and force her—I don't know how, exactly; my plans often have big holes in them—to find me a room. The last chocolate-charged brain cell in my head melted and, instead, I was left with only enough emotional strength to be nice.

"Look, Amber," I said, after glancing at her name tag, "I drove in from L.A. last night. I haven't slept since yesterday. I'm completely exhausted. Could you please help me out? I desperately need a room."

Amber looked up and smiled. "Well, certainly I'd love to. But there's just nothing available."

Okay, so much for being nice. I don't know what I was thinking, really—it just shows how tired I was.

Back in the day, I'd worked for the Pike Warner law firm in Los Angeles, one of the biggest, baddest, most powerful, most feared law firms in the history of mankind. Yeah, okay, I'd worked in their accounts payable unit, but still, I knew what the threat of litigation could do.

"I'm seriously tired," I said to Amber. "If I have to drive to another motel, and if I should get into an accident on the way, well, that could mean you and the Culver Inn could be liable."

I had to hand it to Amber, she kept her smile in place and said, "Let me make a quick call to our manager."

She picked up the phone, pushed some buttons, and turned her back to me.

Not a good sign.

I headed across the lobby to the breakfast buffet. If Amber was really calling security, I'd at least get thrown out of the place on a full stomach.

I stopped in my tracks. Oh my God. Everything was gone. The entire breakfast buffet had disappeared. Not a muffin, a sugar packet, or a pat of butter was left. Jeez, it had all been there just a few minutes ago.

This does *not*, however, mean that I'm cursed.

A door at the rear of the room swung open and a young woman walked in. Beyond her, I could see the kitchen. An aroma that smelled vaguely like food wafted out.

She looked to be about my age, kind of short, with dark hair. She had on an apron and carried a broom and dust pan.

"Any chance I could grab something to eat?" I asked as I walked over.

"Sorry, the buffet closed at ten," she said as she swept beneath a table.

She shoved chairs around and whipped the broom over the floor at a frenzied pace. I could see she was in a hurry.

We've all got our own problems.

"I'm starving. I haven't eaten since yesterday," I said,

seeing no reason to mention the chocolate I'd consumed—
strictly to aid in a murder investigation, of course. "All I
need is a muffin. A banana, maybe. Something."

She stopped sweeping and looked at me. Hopefully, I
looked bad enough or desperate enough—or maybe
both—that she'd take pity on me. Her gaze dipped to my
purse.

"Oh my God. I love your bag," she said.

I held it out. "It's a—"

"Dooney and Bourke," she said, walking over. "Their
spring collection. I love it."

Instantly, I knew that not only would I get something to
eat, I'd made a new friend. Purse lovers just find each
other, somehow.

"Check out the lining," I said, and unzipped the bag.

She gasped. I couldn't blame her. You can't beat a great
lining.

"It's gorgeous," she proclaimed, then leaned in a little
and lowered her voice. "Sorry about the buffet. The motel
manager is really strict about his policies."

"He sounds like a real jackass," I said.

She huffed a short laugh. "Like you wouldn't believe."

"I'd believe," I assured her. "I work retail."

She glanced at the registration desk, then whispered,
"Come on."

I followed her through the swinging door to the kitchen.
It wasn't a big, full-service kitchen like most hotels have,
just the basics, since the Culver Inn had no dining room.
The remains of the breakfast buffet had been packed up in
coolers and bins, ready to be carried out.

She dug out a muffin. I wolfed it down.

"So what are you doing in Henderson?" she asked.

"The department store chain I work for is opening a
new store here," I said, nibbling crumbs off the paper.

"Yeah? Which one?"

I don't usually tell people where I work. Not that I'm ashamed of it, but—well, okay, maybe I'm ashamed of it.

"Holt's," I said.

She handed me a carton of orange juice from the cooler. "There're some nice things in Holt's. But the clothes, jeez, they're . . . awful."

Immediately I knew this girl wouldn't simply be one of those people I talk to because their life is so crappy it made mine look better. And we wouldn't be just friends, but BFs *forever*.

"I'm Haley," I said, and put out my hand.

She put another muffin in it and said, "I'm Maya."

I peeled off the paper. "Oh my God. These things are delicious."

"I made them myself," Maya said.

I chugged the juice. "You made them? Yourself? Like from a mix or something."

"It's my own recipe," she said and smiled proudly. "I'm a culinary major at UNLV. I want to start my own bakery as soon as I graduate. One more semester and I'm done."

I gulped down the last of the muffin. She was going to the university? Actually attending classes? Graduation was in sight? And she already knew what she wanted to do?

I hate my life.

"Of course, first I have to get the money for my fall se-mester classes," she said. "I'll manage—one muffin at a time."

Maya wrapped another muffin and a banana in a cou-ple of paper napkins and gave them to me.

"You may as well take them," she said. "The motel pays me a flat fee for catering breakfast, no matter what gets eaten—or what I bring."

"Thanks," I said, slipping the food into my purse.

"I've got to go," Maya said, closing up the cooler. "Guess I'll see you tomorrow for breakfast?"

"I'm supposed to have a room but the desk clerk says nothing is available. She's checking with the manager now," I said.

"Bradley," Maya grumbled. "He's the manager. The guy's a complete jerk. Come on."

I grabbed another muffin out of the bin—just so Maya wouldn't think I didn't like them, of course—and followed.

The lobby was deserted. Amber stood at the registration desk clicking away at the computer keyboard when we walked up. Her wax smile morphed into something friendlier at the sight of Maya.

"Haley really needs a room," Maya said.

Amber threw me a quick glance. "I know. But there's nothing available."

Maya leaned in a little. "You and I both know there's a room available."

Amber squirmed. "I tried to contact Bradley, but I couldn't reach him. And you know I don't dare—"

"Look, Amber," Maya said. "You're in charge here. Just give her a room."

Amber cringed. "You know how he is."

Even *I* knew how Bradley was, and I hadn't even met him.

"Amber, you're running the desk—so run it," Maya insisted.

She fidgeted for a moment, then finally squared her shoulders and said, "Well, okay."

All I could think was thank God Maya and I had bonded over my handbag. Otherwise, I'd be out on the street.

"I need to see some I.D.," Amber said, "and a credit card, in case of damage."

I handed them over. Back at the keyboard again, Amber ran a plastic room key card through the reader.

"Room three-thirty-four. There are only four rooms in that wing. You'll be the only one there," she said.

I started to get a weird feeling.

"Something happened up there and we're not supposed to book those rooms," Amber said.

My weird feeling got weirder.

"What happened?" I asked.

"I'm making an exception for you," Amber said, holding up the key card. "Do you want the room, or not?"

"Yeah, of course I want the room," I said, and managed a weak little laugh. "I mean, it's not like somebody got murdered up there or anything. Right?"

"Enjoy your stay." Amber slapped the key card, my driver's license, and my credit card into my hand and walked away.

Oh, crap.

CHAPTER 5

I wheeled my suitcase out of the elevator on the third floor and headed left toward room 334, my new home away from home. The carpet and wallpaper screamed '70s, just like the lobby.

Honestly, I didn't get it. This whole section of Henderson hadn't been developed back in the day, so just why the decorator had wanted to incite motel guests to throw on some bell-bottoms and dance the bump to *Brick House*, I didn't know. My best guess was that the Culver Inn management had gotten the furnishings from some other bankrupt motel chain at a discount—a whopping discount, obviously.

At the end of the long hallway, I turned left again. Just as Amber had said, only four rooms were in this wing of the motel. I found mine on the left at the end of the hall.

From the look of things, this area hadn't gotten any attention from the housekeeping crew in a while. The place was dusty. Something smelled weird.

Jeez, I hoped that wasn't the scent of toxic mold growing under the carpet.

I stopped outside my door and glanced around. One room next to mine, two across the hall. An exit sign above the door at the end of the corridor flickered in the dim light. It was deadly silent up here.

Maybe a week at the spa with my mom wouldn't have been so bad.

I pushed that thought away, hurried inside my room, threw the dead bolt, slid the security chain, and switched on all the lights.

The room boasted amenities not found in the upscale hotels in Vegas: end tables with lamps bolted to them, pictures screwed into the walls, the TV remote tethered to the bed frame. The bathroom was small, the closet smaller. Orange shag carpet, a silver and brown bedspread, and avocado green drapes completed the bad-acid-trip look the decorator seemed to be going for.

Actually, a week at the spa with Mom might have been okay.

I pulled back the drapes, sending a flurry of dust motes into the air, and looked outside. This particular room wasn't raking in an upcharge for its incredible view.

The Culver Inn was U-shaped, and my room was on one side of the U. Below was a swimming pool, now drained; leaves and mud lay in the bottom. A dozen ratty umbrella tables surrounded by broken chairs completed the patio-from-hell effect.

A couple of large boulders, a half-dozen tall palm trees, and a wrought-iron fence enclosed the grounds and separated it from the motel's service area. There was a small building that I guessed held the pool and maintenance equipment, and some Dumpsters.

Beyond that, the desert stretched for a few miles to a housing tract just visible on the horizon. In between lay piles of rock and construction debris. Seemed the construction companies didn't bother to haul away their leftover crap, just dumped it in an open spot in the desert.

Spa week with Mom flashed in my mind.

I looked down at the swimming pool again.

I thought about Mom and the beauty queens.

Yeah, I'd rather be here.

I took a quick shower, pulled on my pajamas, and yanked back the bedspread. Nothing crawled out. I crawled in.

A really annoying buzzing sound woke me. I rolled over and realized the alarm clock was going off—at two in the afternoon. Not unusual for Vegas. The alarm had probably been set the last time the room was used, back during the Bush administration, I guessed.

Immediately, a hunger pang hit me. I threw on jeans and a T-shirt, stuffed my laptop into an awesome Betsey Johnson tote, and left the room.

Despite the fact that my room was crappier than crap, I was grateful for it. I intended to thank Amber for putting herself out there so I could use it, but when I got to the lobby, she wasn't on duty. Another woman in the hideous Culver Inn uniform stood behind the registration desk. I got my car from the parking lot and hit the road.

Driving was the ideal time to check phone messages, I'd found. Of course, it could be against the law to use your cell phone while driving in Nevada; I didn't know. I was sure some law-abiding citizen would scream at me from the next lane, or offer a helpful hand gesture, if it was.

I expected my voicemail box to be loaded with calls from Ty. It wasn't. The only message was from Marcie, asking me to call her right away. I pulled to a stop at a red light on St. Rose Parkway and punched in Marcie's number. She picked up immediately.

"Are you sitting down?" she asked.

No how-are-you, no what's-up, no oh-my-God-you're-not-going-to-believe-what-happened. This must be big.

"I just picked up your mail, like you asked," Marcie said. "And you got . . . something."

My spirits lifted. Wow, this must be great. Marcie wouldn't have called otherwise. I'd probably gotten a refund or rebate on something. Maybe some rich relative had died—which would be tragic, of course—and left me a wad of money. I could use it. My checking account was on life support at the moment.

"It's from the IRS," Marcie said.

My breath caught. A wave of fear washed over me. Sort of like when you show up at a department store wanting to buy the latest handbag but don't see any in the display cases.

"Would that be the International Refund Service?" I asked.

Yeah, okay, I didn't know if there was such a thing, but there could have been. I mean, I'd been in Europe a few weeks ago, shopping diligently, doing all I could to maintain the international balance of trade. I'd maxed out a significant number of credit cards converting U.S. dollars to pounds and euros and God knows what else. And who knew how that conversion stuff worked, anyway. Maybe they'd realized they'd made a mistake. Maybe they were sending me a massive refund.

Or maybe I'd really been cursed.

"It's from the Internal Revenue Service," Marcie told me.

Crap.

"Want me to open it for you?" she asked.

"No."

"Come on, Haley, you have to face this."

Marcie was right—she's almost always right about things. I hate it when other people are right.

"You did file your taxes, didn't you?" Marcie asked.

I did a quick calculation. I'd filed my taxes electronically on April 14, a full thirty minutes before the deadline—beating my own personal best—and had already received my six hundred dollar refund. That was about six weeks ago. Would the IRS contact me now, after they'd sent me the refund?

The traffic light changed and I drove forward with the line of cars.

"I'm opening it," Marcie said. A few seconds passed, then she said, "Did you get a refund this year?"

"Yeah," I said.

"Well, they want it back," Marcie told me. "Plus penalties and interest. Plus another two grand. Call it three thousand."

"*What?*"

I shot across two lanes of traffic. Horns blew. Tires screeched—and I don't think they were mine.

Then, like a desert oasis, I spotted a Starbucks.

"I'll call you back," I told Marcie, and snapped my phone closed.

I cut off an SUV and whipped into the parking lot, grabbed my laptop, and rushed inside Starbucks.

Chocolate had a calming effect on people, didn't it? I think I read that somewhere. I intended to put that little bit of info to the test—right now.

The guy behind the counter prepared my grandé mocha frappuccino with whipped cream and extra chocolate syrup—no way would anything smaller get me through a crisis of this magnitude—and I found a seat at a table in the corner.

Oh my God. How could I owe the IRS three thousand dollars? And, better yet, how could I possibly *pay* the IRS three thousand dollars?

I sucked down half of my mocha frappuccino, then forced myself to slow down. While chocolate and caffeine had definitely helped solve a number of problems in the past, I couldn't afford brain freeze at a time like this.

I opened my laptop and logged onto my bank account. I needed facts. Then I could proceed calmly and quickly to a solution.

I checked the balance of my checking account and nearly

launched myself out of my chair. Only a couple hundred bucks. I checked my savings account. Jeez, did that "minus" symbol mean I'd overdrawn it? How had that happened?

Maybe I should take an accounting class next semester.

Anyway, no time to worry about that now. I checked the balances on my credit cards and found I had some—not a lot—of available credit on all of them.

I dug a pen and paper from my tote and made a quick list of upcoming expenses and things I needed to buy. I had to get the tire that had blown last night repaired. The fender that had been scraped in the Holt's parking lot had to be fixed, too. There was that traffic ticket I'd gotten. It would be expensive, plus I might have to go to traffic school. I needed to eat while I was here, so I'd have to have money for that, too.

I looked at the calculations I'd made. Yikes! No way did I have enough money to cover everything.

A horrible vision flashed in my head. I was in Vegas, for God's sake. What about seeing a show, or hitting a great buffet? What about shopping?

An even more horrible thought bloomed in my brain: what if I found that Delicious handbag but didn't have enough money to buy it?

Oh my God. This was a crisis of staggering magnitude. Where was my best friend when I needed her?

I drained my frappuccino. I desperately needed another one. But should I spend the money for it?

Immediately, I disregarded the notion. I had a massive problem to solve involving not only basic survival and high finance, but the acquisition of the season's hottest handbag. This was no time to worry about a couple of bucks.

I got another frappuccino and sat down again. By the time I was half finished with it, I felt calmer. Not because I'd come to any brilliant conclusions or flashed on a fantastic solution of what to do. I just decided to forget the whole thing for a while and move on to something else.

Like the murder I was suspected of.

Really, what else could I do?

I Googled my way to my high school's Web site. I didn't even know they had one, but there it was. Good ol' Monroe High, private school to the rich and affluent—and those who could convincingly fake it.

Seeing the photo of the school with its ivy-covered walls, swaying palms, and manicured lawns reminded me of how glad I was to be done with all of that. I'd almost rather face the Iraqi secret police than go back to high school.

My older brother and younger sister and I had all attended Monroe. It was near our house, so most of the students were from our neighborhood.

I didn't know exactly how our family ended up living in the upscale area. Mom's grandmother left the house to her, along with a trust fund. Nobody seemed to know—or was willing to tell—what my great-grandmother had done to get all that money in the first place.

Scholarship kids from other areas of L.A. attended Monroe, too, lest our school might have been considered stuck up and snooty, which, of course, it was. With tuition and fees topping fifteen grand per academic year, what else could you expect?

Attending Monroe High was a lot like surviving in the business world. Networking, who you knew, and who you could meet were important. At private schools, though, most of this was used for evil.

Making connections was often about pretending to be friends with someone just because their family had access to something you wanted—a sky box at Dodger Stadium, an "in" with the casting director at Dreamworks. Social ranking among students was big, based on wearing the latest designer accessories—whether or not they complemented our uniforms. If a student didn't come from a wealthy family, they faked it. "Smart" kids were befriended by "cool" kids just for help with grades.

Not that I had ever done any of these things, of course.

But since we were literally locked behind a gate during school hours, I learned to survive. And, of course, thrive.

That's how I roll.

I scrolled through the Monroe High Web site, seeing pictures of the computer lab, art studio, theater, TV studio, gymnasium, and classrooms, and remembered Courtney Collins.

I hadn't really thought about Courtney since high school. She was one of those girls I was glad to never see again after graduation. Our only connection was some classes we'd had together.

Plus, there was that whole thing with Robbie Freedman.

Courtney had not been my best friend—not even my sort-of friend. Honestly, I'd never really liked her. She didn't seem to know that, though, which was really irritating because she always talked to me and sat next to me in class.

Everything about Courtney annoyed me. First of all, she was really nice. I mean *really* nice. Like, she didn't have enough sense to see what was going on around her and know she should be upset, or mad, or something.

Second of all, the teachers loved her—or maybe they just felt sorry for her. I don't know. Courtney was in my art class and for an entire semester everything she drew, sketched, painted, and sculpted had the same stupid stained-glass pattern. At the school art fair that spring, Courtney's painting got first place—but only because the teacher helped her with it—mine got second. At graduation, she got a couple of scholarships and some awards—not that I thought I deserved them, but still.

Then, of course, there was that thing with Robbie Freedman.

I clicked onto the "alumni" icon. A list of Monroe graduates' names along with their accomplishments filled the screen. Jeez, when did the school start doing this?

I scrolled through a few of the names I remembered from high school. Most people had already graduated college, some were in med school or law school. One guy had opened his own dot-com company and was already a millionaire. A girl—who'd definitely had some work done, judging from the photo she'd posted—was starring in a Broadway play. Everybody was doing big things.

Everybody but me.

Not a good feeling.

Then it hit me. Oh my God, lots of graduates from Monroe had probably logged onto the site, wondering what I'd done with my life. I paged down and clicked my name. Nothing came up.

Jeez, I couldn't let people think I hadn't accomplished anything. Of course, I couldn't let them know what I'd actually done, either.

I set up an alumni account with a password, and paused, my fingers on the keyboard trying to decide what to write. Absolute truthfulness in this sort of situation wasn't required. I mean, half of the graduating class had probably stretched their accomplishments, right?

Then it occurred to me that no matter how far I stretched the things I'd done, nobody from Monroe High School would be impressed. So I typed in that I did undercover work but couldn't disclose anything more, as a matter of national security. Just enough info to be intriguing and make me sound important, without actually entering any facts that might prove embarrassing in the future if some Monroe alumni checked into them and decided to rat me out.

Some things never change, even after high school.

I clicked on Courtney's page on the Web site and was surprised to see the only info she'd listed was her move to Henderson. I'm not sure what I expected to find. Certainly not that she had some big career going. Courtney never struck me as being that bright.

I entered her name into a search engine and eventually found an article about women and small businesses that she'd been mentioned in for the local newspaper. Wow, Courtney had started a fashion accessory business? When did that happen? I kept searching and, half an hour later, I had her address.

I packed up my laptop and left.

CHAPTER 6

My GPS took me to the Bay Breeze Apartments on Warm Springs Road, a sprawling complex in a nice area of Henderson. The buildings were sand-colored stucco with red tile roofs. Lots of pine and palm trees, green belts, plants, and flowers. I wound my way through the maze of driveways and speed bumps and pulled into a parking spot outside Courtney's apartment.

The place seemed quiet. Too quiet. Not much traffic, lots of open parking slots. I sat in my car wondering what was up. I mean, Courtney had been murdered. Where were her family and friends? Everybody congregates *somewhere* at a time like this. If they weren't here, where would I find them?

Only one way to find out.

I left my car and rang the doorbell. I'd done this sort of thing before but still didn't like it. It's not easy walking into a home full of mourners. I didn't top anyone's list of who to call during an emotional crisis. A party, yes, but not something like this.

After a few minutes, I rang the bell again. I was thinking that maybe I'd just leave a note or something, when I heard sounds from inside and the door opened.

A tall guy—I figured him for thirty—squinted down at me. He was thin—too thin, really, which only men can be.

He had black hair, a goatee, and enough tattoos to cause strangers to look twice—and not because they figured he was starring in his own reality show. He wore jeans and a tired-looking T-shirt.

"Yeah?" he said.

He didn't exactly look overcome with grief, but hey, who was I to judge?

"I'm an old friend of Courtney's," I said and introduced myself. No need to get into the whole I-found-her-dead-at-Holt's thing.

He didn't respond. Instantly, I panicked.

What if this guy was Courtney's brother or boyfriend or something, and the cops hadn't notified him that she was dead yet? What if he asked me why I was here? What would I say?

I wished I'd checked Courtney's Facebook page back at Starbucks so maybe I'd know who this guy was. But I'd been afraid to. I figured Detective Webster was monitoring it and would try to make something of it—something that would benefit the cops—so no way was I doing that.

I was ready to make a break for my car when the guy said, "Guess you heard."

I *really* hoped he was asking if I'd heard about Courtney's death.

Just to play it safe, I said, "I heard."

"Detectives were here earlier," he said. "Thought maybe you were them. I'm Tony Hubbard. Come on in."

He walked back into the apartment. I followed.

The layout of the place seemed typical. Living room/dining room combo, small galley kitchen, hallways leading to bedrooms and bathrooms.

From the looks of Courtney's apartment, I figured she hadn't lived there very long. Basic furniture—TV, stereo, sofa, end tables—was in place, but that was about it. No pictures on the wall, no plants, nothing that showcased the personality of the occupants.

It was weird. I mean, why would you not decorate your apartment? Yeah, okay, so maybe she didn't have much money, but who needs money? That's what credit cards are for. Right?

"Want a beer?" Tony asked, as he headed into the kitchen.

"Sure," I said, and followed.

He pulled two cold ones out of the fridge and passed one to me. I cracked it open and asked, "So you're Courtney's . . . ?"

"We've been together for a couple of months now," Tony said, and made a sweeping motion with his beer can. I took that to mean he lived in the apartment with Courtney and they were official boyfriend–girlfriend.

"Does Courtney have family around here?" I asked, glancing around the silent, desolate apartment.

"Nah," Tony said, tipping up his beer. "They're too religious for Sin City."

I nodded as if I completely understood. I didn't, of course. I hadn't known—or cared—anything about Courtney or her family back in high school.

"What did the cops say?" I asked.

Tony grunted. "Nothing. Just asked a bunch of dumb-ass questions—like I was supposed to know what the hell Courtney was doing."

"Do they have any idea who did it?" I asked.

"Cops are idiots," he told me.

I decided it best to keep silent on that and changed the subject.

"I knew Courtney in L.A.," I said.

Tony squared his shoulders. He puffed out his chest like men do when they're mad. It's usually kind of hot, but not this time. This time, all I could think was that I was alone in this apartment with a kind of creepy guy I didn't really know. Nobody knew I was here. Nobody expected me to return.

Not a great feeling.

Tony took a step toward me. "Did Mike send you?"

I took a step back. "Who's Mike?"

"Mike from L.A.," he told me, as if that explained every-thing—and made him madder because he'd had to say it.

I knew a half-dozen guys named Mike, but I wasn't going to admit to it—certainly not at a time like this.

Luckily, I can lie convincingly in a crisis. It's a gift, really.

"I don't know any Mike," I said.

That seemed to make him even madder. "You don't know Mike Ivan?" Tony asked.

I chugged my beer. Since it appeared I might die in the next thirty seconds, I may as well go out with beer breath.

"So who is he?" I asked.

Tony glared at me, as if sizing me up, trying to decide if I was lying or not. I guess I passed some sort of mental test, because he drained his beer and tossed the can into the trash.

"Some lying bastard who's giving Courtney a hard time," he said, and opened the refrigerator. "He won't leave her alone."

"An old boyfriend?" I asked.

He glared at me again, then reached into the fridge for another beer. I decided it best to keep the conversation moving.

"How long has Courtney lived in Henderson?" I asked. "We kind of lost touch after high school."

"Since last fall, I guess," he said, and opened another beer.

Seemed he'd moved in with her pretty quickly. Interest-ing.

Ty flashed into my head. He'd asked me to move in with him but nothing had come of it. And he still hadn't called me.

I centered my thoughts back to the present. This was no

time to get caught up in a why-hasn't-he-called, is-there-something-wrong-with-me mental loop.

I glanced around expecting to see signs of Courtney's fashion accessory line that the online article had mentioned—hats, gloves, scarves, belts, something. Nothing was here. The report was kind of old. I wondered if the company had gone belly-up already.

"So what's going to happen to Courtney's business now that she's . . . gone?" I asked.

Tony tipped up his beer.

"Guess that partner of hers will figure it out," he said.

The article hadn't mentioned a partner, which seemed odd. But maybe the partner wasn't so hot for the publicity.

"Did they run the company here?" I asked, glancing around again.

"Danielle talked her into renting a place," Tony told me. "Some kind of workroom. Eastern something."

I finished my beer and tossed the can into the trash, then fished a pen and slip of paper from my tote. I jotted down my name and phone number.

"Can somebody give me a call about the . . . you know, funeral?" I asked.

Tony shrugged. "Yeah, sure."

I laid the paper on the counter and left. Outside, I noticed a Harley Davidson parked a few spaces down and wondered if it was Tony's. He looked like a motorcycle kind of guy. He didn't, however, look like the kind of guy Courtney would hook up with.

But what did I know? High school was a long time ago.

I got into my car and left.

A lot could have changed for Courtney since I'd known her back at Monroe High. Maybe things had changed with her family, too, but I couldn't stop wondering where the heck they were at a time like this. Surely they knew about Courtney's death by now. Why weren't they here taking care of things?

I turned onto Warm Springs Road. That guy Mike popped into my thoughts. I figured him for Courtney's ex by the way Tony talked about him; that would explain why he was, apparently, stalking her.

Detective Dailey flashed in my mind. He and Webster had been to Courtney's apartment and talked to Tony. Surely they'd learned about Mike and were checking him out.

I got a yucky feeling in my stomach.

Or had they already decided they needed to look no further than me?

Oh, crap.

I pulled to a stop at a red light and looked around. I'd been to Vegas a lot but hadn't often ventured into Henderson. I wasn't sure where I was, exactly, but I knew the Sunset Station Casino was around here somewhere.

I thought about hitting the slots, even though I wasn't exactly feeling lucky lately. But I could sure use the money, if I got on a hot streak.

Marcie had told me not to gamble with that whole I've-been-cursed thing hanging over me, and she's almost always right about things.

I really hate it when other people are right.

When the light changed, I swung into the parking lot of a strip mall and pulled out my phone. I hadn't heard it ring but it might have.

Yeah, okay, Courtney's apartment had been as silent as the vacuum of space, and I hadn't turned on the car stereo, so I'd have definitely been able to hear it ring, but still.

I checked messages. No one (translation: Ty) had called.

At this point, there was only one thing to do—go shopping.

The Delicious handbag bloomed in my mind, crowding out all else, bringing everything into focus.

So what if I was a murder suspect? So what if my official

boyfriend hadn't called me? So what if I'd—possibly, but I still doubted it—been cursed? So what if my financial situation was more precarious than walking in four-inch stilettos?

The important thing was that I wanted that bag. And if I got it—the hottest, hardest to find, most gorgeous bag in the entire world—wouldn't that prove I wasn't cursed?

Yes, of course it would. Then I could call Marcie with my fabulous news, tell her there was definitely no curse on me, and hit the slots.

I accessed the Internet on my cell phone, found the nearest mall, and took off.

Okay, so maybe I really was cursed.

The thought came to me once again as I crawled into bed for the night. I'd combed every store in the mall that might conceivably carry the Delicious handbag, and not one single bag was available.

I still hadn't heard from Ty.

Marcie hadn't called me, either. She was probably out shopping with friends or something, while I was stuck in this crappy motel, helping open a crappy store, because I had a crappy job—which was all my own doing, I know, but still.

Mom hadn't called me, either, which was good, usually. But she'd never said a word about my not going to beauty-queen-spa-week with her. Had she felt obligated to invite me? I was, after all, her only other daughter. Was she secretly glad I hadn't gone?

I've got to get a grip on my life.

I awoke with a start. The room was dark. No light streamed in from around the heavy curtains on the windows. I glanced at the clock on my bedside table. The neon green digits glowed 3:14.

Sitting up, I tried to figure out what had awakened me, though my brain wasn't exactly running at peak performance level.

Bad dream? No, I didn't remember anything. Must have been—

Voices rumbled in the hallway.

Okay, no big deal, I decided, and lay down again. Just a couple of guests coming in late.

I closed my eyes and drifted off to sleep.

CHAPTER 7

I hit the breakfast buffet bright and early the next morning, armed with a hearty appetite and an awesome Marc Jacobs purse. Maya noticed it right away. Yesterday, I could tell we'd be friends. This just proved it.

I didn't see Maya as my absolute-forever-no-matter-what best friend—that distinction still belonged to Marcie—and she didn't seem like the kind of friend you'd call when you were upset and just wanted somebody to agree with you *regardless*. But she'd definitely be one of those friends you knew would have your back if a bitch-fight broke out at a party or something.

"It's fabulous," she said, and rushed over as I helped myself to a muffin. She gave my handbag the moment of silence it deserved, then said, "As soon as I have my degree and get my bakery business up and running, I'm going to get me one of those—maybe two. No, make that a dozen."

"Why stop at a dozen?" I asked.

I wasn't joking.

Maya got a faraway look in her eyes and her lip curled up. I could see her determination growing.

"Yeah," she muttered. "Hell, yeah."

I might have to bump her up to absolute-forever-no-matter-what best friend status.

A dozen or so motel guests were checking out the buffet, filling paper plates, and eating at the tables. Some of them were probably Holt's employees, in town to work at the new store. I didn't recognize any of them.

I grabbed an orange juice and stepped out of the way so Maya and I could continue talking while she kept an eye on the food.

"You're really planning to start a bakery after you graduate?" I asked around a mouthful of muffin.

"And a catering business so I can expand what I've already started," Maya explained as she wiped down the counter. She rolled her eyes. "If I could get Bradley, the jackass who manages this place, to recommend me to the other Culver Inn motels in town, I could do a lot more business now."

"Your food is great," I said, finishing off the muffin. "Why won't Bradley put the word out for you?"

"Because he's a self-centered, thoughtless, self-absorbed idiot," Maya said.

From what I'd heard about Bradley, I couldn't disagree.

"His family, the Penningtons, own the whole chain. They're wealthy like you wouldn't believe," Maya said. "Anyway, I'm going to have to figure a way to get money for my fall classes somehow."

At the mention of money, I mentally shrank back a little. I'd rather not be reminded of my own dismal financial situation. But I pulled myself together for Maya's sake. That's what friends do.

"Have you gotten any scholarships?" I asked.

She shook her head. "Unfortunately for me, I didn't screw up my life at a young age by getting married or having a baby, nor have I been in rehab or jail. Scholarships for people like me aren't easy to come by."

I knew the feeling. I'd been that route myself.

"Can your family help out?" I asked. I knew my parents

would help me—if I asked, which I had no intention of doing.

"Mom's divorced. My dad left us." Maya said. "I've got two younger brothers still living at home, so Mom's got her hands full just taking care of them. I can't ask her for anything. It wouldn't be right."

"So you're doing the student loan thing," I concluded. "I am, too."

I knew she had to be taking that route, same as me. No way could I afford college—and living expenses—any other way. I sure couldn't get by on the pittance Holt's paid me, even with my liberal use of multiple credit cards.

"I've got student loans to Mars and back," Maya said. She sighed heavily. "I'm going to have to bake a lot of muffins to pay all that money back."

We had to pay that back?

Yeah, okay, I knew that. I just hadn't really thought about it. Sort of.

Anyway, no need worrying about that now. Graduation for me was on a very distant horizon.

"I work lots of jobs," Maya said. "There's lots of ways to make money at the convention centers on The Strip. Easy stuff, like handing out brochures and pointing people in the right direction. I can hook you up, if you want."

"Might be fun," I told her.

"Hey, listen," Maya said, "I'm catering a small event next week. I can't hire you, but you should come anyway. It's a handbag club."

My senses instantly snapped to attention. The world stopped rotating for a nanosecond. My heart rate picked up.

Handbag club? There was such a thing as a handbag club? How could I not have known this? How could something this huge have gotten past me?

I've really, really got to get a grip on my life.

"They meet at a cute little shop near Green Valley Ranch. It's such a fun group. You'll love it," Maya declared. She pulled her cell phone from her apron pocket. "Give me your number and I'll send you the details."

I yanked my phone from my pocket at warp speed and we exchanged info.

Oh, yeah, my luck was finally changing.

On the way out of the motel, I checked the registration desk hoping to see Amber. I still needed to thank her for putting herself out there for me yesterday. I also wanted to give her a shout out for booking those guests I'd heard during the night into the room on my deserted wing; it was comforting to know that somebody could now hear me scream.

Amber wasn't on duty, so I went out to my car and headed to Holt's.

My cell phone rang as soon as I hit St. Rose Parkway. It was Marcie.

"Oh my God, Haley, are you okay?" she asked when I picked up.

I could tell right away that she was genuinely worried, but I didn't have a clue what it was about. My IRS bill, my flat tire, my dented fender, my traffic ticket, my official-boyfriend-turned-sort-of-boyfriend?

Jeez, I hope she wasn't calling with more bad news.

Not that things could get much worse.

"I just saw it on the Internet," Marcie said. "A girl got murdered in the Holt's store in Henderson? *Your* Holt's store?"

"Yeah, and get this," I said. "It was Courtney Collins, my friend from high school. The one you found on Facebook."

Marcie gasped. "What happened?"

I saw no reason to get into the whole I'm-a-murder-suspect-again thing with Marcie. Some things even a best friend doesn't need to hear.

"The police are investigating," I said.

Marcie was quiet for a moment, then said, "You're not blaming yourself for this, are you? Because of the curse?"

"Well, jeez . . . I don't know," I mumbled.

Really, I hadn't even thought about it. And now that I was, it didn't feel so great.

Could it be true? Could the curse—which I still didn't believe in, of course—that crazy old lady put on me have somehow caused Courtney's death?

The whole curse thing was starting to be more than a little annoying.

"I'm not cursed," I told Marcie as I changed lanes, cutting off a pickup. "It's all a bunch of b.s."

"Maybe," Marcie said. "But there must be something you can do."

"Sandy said I should see a psychic to find out how to break the curse," I said.

"It couldn't hurt," Marcie said.

Maybe she was right. Marcie was almost always right.

"It might help with Ty," she added. "Have you heard from him?"

"No," I said. "Not yet."

I sped through a yellow light, my phone pressed to my ear waiting to hear Marcie's words of encouragement, her oh-so-logical explanation of why Ty hadn't called, her everything-will-be-fine pep talk.

Marcie didn't say anything.

Crap.

"Think about going to a psychic," Marcie said. "And don't, under any circumstances, gamble."

We hung up as I pulled into the Holt's parking lot. Since it was early, only a few cars were there. I swung into a space near the door, cut the engine, and sat there for a minute.

What was up with Ty? Why hadn't he called? I mean, if he really didn't want to move in with me, the least he could do was say so. It had been his big idea in the first place. You'd think he'd at least—

I gasped and bolted upright in the seat. Oh my God. *Oh my God.* Ty hadn't called because he was coming to Vegas. He wanted to surprise me. That had to be the reason. Why hadn't I thought of that before?

I imagined what our reunion would be like. Ty—looking hot in an Armani suit—swooping into the parking lot in a black limo, sweeping me into his arms, whisking me to the heliport for a romantic ride over the Grand Canyon, begging my forgiveness for not coming sooner, pleading with me to move in with him—the only thing that could possibly make his life complete.

My heart thudded in my chest—sort of like it does when I'm standing outside the Louie Vuitton store—as I realized that Ty actually had another reason for coming to Vegas. Courtney's murder—not that I considered that a good thing, of course.

Ty had personally visited the Holt's stores where three other people had died—long story—to calm the employees and assure us everything would be taken care of. So it stood to reason that he would come here, too.

I gasped. Ty might be in the store at this very minute.

Oh my God. I looked like crap. I had on jeans and a sweater. I looked like I was going to be working all day—which I was, of course, but that wasn't the point. The point was that I hardly looked like the kind of girl who might get whisked away to a romantic rendezvous. I wasn't even wearing a Victoria's Secret bra, for God's sake.

No time to worry about that now. The important thing was that Ty was here, and we could see each other and hash out this moving-in-together thing.

I jumped out of my car and scanned the parking lot. No sign of Ty's Porsche. Okay, that didn't mean anything. He probably flew in and took a cab from McCarran Airport.

I rushed to the store's double doors and stopped in my

tracks. A security guard blocked the entrance. He wasn't there yesterday. Yesterday when I arrived, the doors had stood wide open. Nobody had been in the front of the store checking I.D. or anything.

"Name?" he asked, consulting the clipboard in his hand. I told him and he ran his finger down the column of names, then opened the door for me.

The store looked pretty much the same as it had yesterday. Not much work had gotten done with the homicide investigation in full swing, apparently. Workmen stood around talking. Employees drifted toward the rear of the store, no one in much of a hurry. Guess everybody was still in shock.

I gazed around the store. No sign of Ty.

Fay—the new Rita in my life—wasn't in sight, either, so I checked the easel for today's duty assignment. "*Store manager*" was written next to my name.

This couldn't be good.

Or maybe it was. My spirits lifted as I realized that Ty was probably in Preston's office waiting for me. Yeah, that had to be it.

I struck out for the office suite in the rear of the store, bobbing and weaving around the other employees, then turned down the hallway to Preston's office.

My stomach tingled a little. Ty would be there. Just steps away. Waiting to surprise me.

I paused for a second, ducked into the employee breakroom, grabbed my time card, and punched in.

Ty would want me to get paid for this. Really.

I rushed to Preston's office and burst inside. Preston sat at his desk, the florescent ceiling light reflecting off the bald spot on his head.

"Oh, yes, Haley," he said.

My gaze bounced around the room. Where was Ty?

"Thanks for coming in," Preston said.

Why wasn't he here?

"I wanted to talk to you about yesterday," he told me.

Where could Ty be?

"I talked to the corporate office," Preston said.

In the stock room? Training room? Restroom?

"The big man himself spoke with me."

My attention jumped back to Preston. He had to be referring to Ty.

"What did he say?" I think I shouted that.

"He wanted to come to the store."

"When's he getting here?" I'm sure I shouted that.

My thoughts ran wild. Ty was on his way? He could get here at any moment?

Did I have time to go back to the motel and change my bra?

"I told him not to come," Preston said.

"*What?*" I screamed that.

Preston didn't seem to notice. He shook his head wearily.

"The last thing I need is those folks from Corporate here," he told me. "They're somewhat . . . out of touch, I guess you could say."

I collapsed onto the chair in front of his desk, exhausted.

Preston looked kind of tired, too. His white shirt was a little rumpled, his tie a bit askew. A homicide investigation during his very first management assignment—before the store even opened—had already taken its toll.

I saw no reason to demoralize him further by pointing out that the rough ride had only just begun.

I also saw no reason not to pump him for info while in his weakened condition—strictly to further the investigation, of course.

"What have the cops told you?" I asked.

"Nothing." Preston's already rounded shoulders drooped a little lower. "They keep coming back, looking at things, asking questions."

"Did they take the store surveillance footage?" I asked.

"The cameras aren't hooked up yet," he said, then waved toward the sales floor. "That's top priority today."

"What about the parking lot?" I asked.

Preston looked mildly perturbed. "The complex owners didn't have cameras operating. They hadn't paid the security company, or some such nonsense. It's borderline criminal, if you ask me. We expected certain standards when we took this property and now—"

He stopped talking and took a deep breath to rein in his temper. I couldn't blame him for being angry.

"So, anyway, Haley, I wanted to thank you for handling everything the way you did yesterday," Preston said. He looked a little embarrassed now. "Honestly, I was a bit stunned by the whole thing. I appreciate your jumping in the way you did and pointing me in the right direction."

Not wanting to explain that this wasn't my first murder, I just said, "Glad I could help." It sounded kind of lame, under the circumstances, but what else could I say?

"You're one of our most experienced employees, you know," Preston said.

If that were true, a murder victim in the store was the least of Preston's problems.

"So," he announced, pulling in a breath and squaring his shoulders. "I'd like to do something for the store employees, a sort of reward for what they endured yesterday, and I'd like your input on it."

Doing something nice for the employees always seemed like a good idea to me.

"Sure," I told him.

"Excellent," he declared and rose from his desk. "I'll count on you."

I left Preston's office. Since my department assignment hadn't been indicated on the easel at the front of the store, I figured I'd have to hunt down Fay and ask her.

Of course, it might take me awhile to find her.

As I strolled past the breakroom, two men walking side by side turned down the hallway and headed toward me.

Detectives Dailey and that rat-dog partner of his, Detective Webster.

I froze in my tracks.

They kept coming.

"Just the person we want to talk to," Webster sneered.

"About what?" I blurted out.

They stopped in front of me. Detective Dailey looked down at me.

"Robbie Freedman," he said.

Oh, crap.

CHAPTER 8

Preston ran out of his office faster than teen girls headed to a blowout sale at the mall when Detective Dailey asked if we could use the room.

I guess his appreciation for my help yesterday only went so far.

Webster dragged a chair around to the power side of the desk and sat down next to Dailey. He pulled out his notebook, flicked his pen, and glared at me.

"I guess this means you two haven't solved the murder yet," I said, just to be snotty, as I sat down.

"We're closing in on a suspect," Detective Dailey said.

Jeez, I hope he didn't mean me.

I think maybe he did.

Not a great feeling.

"Tell us about Robbie Freedman," Dailey said.

The first thought that jetted through my brain was to lie. I couldn't help it. It was some sort of natural defense mechanism, I think.

My next thought was to wonder who at Monroe High School had ratted me out to the cops about Robbie.

The third thing that flashed in my head was to wonder if whoever-it-was had also told them I didn't like Courtney back in high school, how I'd made fun of those awful stained-glass windowpane art projects she did over and over again, and how I talked about how stupid she was.

My fourth thought was that I needed a whole new life.

This was not the time, however, to dwell on that. I'd have plenty of opportunity to do that later—hopefully, not in an orange jumpsuit.

Back in the day, I'd made no secret of my dislike for Courtney—though I was surprised the whole thing was memorable enough all these years later that someone would report it to the cops. High school was all about liking or not liking somebody. Guess I was a standout—but not in a good way.

I mentally ditched the thought of lying about Robbie. It's usually not a good idea to lie to detectives—believe me, I know this from personal experience—so why risk it? Besides, the fact that I knew Robbie didn't mean I'd killed Courtney.

Unless you were a homicide detective desperate to solve a high-profile case, that is.

Crap.

"Miss Randolph?" Detective Webster said, making the name sound like *Stupid*.

"I knew Robbie in high school," I said. "But I guess you already know that."

"You bet we do," Webster said, narrowing his beady little eyes.

Somebody should put him on a leash.

"There was a romantic rivalry involving you, Robbie, and Courtney?" Detective Dailey asked.

"Something like that," I said.

Actually, it was nothing like that.

Back in the day, I'd thought Robbie was hot, really hot. So hot, I couldn't get up nerve enough to talk to him. Every time I tried, I got all nervous and jittery, and I knew I'd make a fool of myself. *That's* how hot he was.

I know it's hard to believe I was ever that awkward, but

that was six—or maybe seven, I'm not very quick with math—years ago. A lot has changed since then.

I'd mentioned my feelings for him to Courtney, and the next thing I knew, she and Robbie started going out. It wasn't fair. I saw him *first*.

Anyway, they dated through our entire senior year and I saw them together all the time. Plus, Courtney talked about him to me in class and when she hung around with me and my friends—totally uninvited, of course.

I don't think she did it to be mean—which irritated me even more. She just didn't have a clue what she was doing. She was really weird like that. She never seemed to *get* anything.

"We can talk about this at the police station," Detective Webster barked.

Anger shot through me. Bad enough that I was forced to recall and relive those awful days in high school. I sure didn't like being threatened at the same time—especially by someone who'd probably taken his cousin to the prom.

"I don't know what you're making such a big deal about," I said, none too kindly. "Robbie, Courtney, and I went to the same high school—along with a lot of other kids. Courtney and Robbie dated. I never dated Robbie."

"But you wanted to," Detective Dailey said.

He used that really mellow voice of his, the one that made you want to confess to *something*. No way was I falling for that. Plus, it made me really mad.

"If you think I came all the way to Henderson, got Courtney to come to the store, then murdered her because of some old high school crush, you're wrong," I told them. I stood up and glared at them. "And if that's all you've got, your investigation is in a lot of trouble."

Detective Dailey leaned back in his chair a little. Webster opened his mouth like he was getting ready to say something, but I beat him to it.

"We're done," I told him. I gave them big-time stink-eye for another second or two, then stomped out of the room.

Halfway down the hall, Fay rushed up to me.

"Where've you been?" she demanded. "You're supposed to be stocking in children's, okay?"

I was in no mood.

"I hate children's," I all but screamed at her. "Don't put me in that department again."

"Now, look here," she told me. "You don't get to decide where—"

"*Ever!*"

I walked away.

Like most big companies, Holt's left nothing to chance. Least of all the stocking of their store shelves and the intelligence of their employees—whom they hired—to do it correctly.

I stood in the children's clothing department—which I do still and always will hate—looking at the merchandizing diagram I'd been provided. On it was a grainy black-and-white illustration of the shelving unit each piece of clothing was to be displayed on, along with explicit instructions of where the clothing should be placed on the shelf.

There were also all kind of codes, numbers, and abbreviations which the company's trainers had probably told me about during orientation back when I was hired. I'd drifted off in orientation.

I'd been at this for hours, bringing boxes from the stock room on a U-boat, finding a box cutter—luckily, there were dozens of them in bowls all over the store—opening the boxes, and stocking the shelves, then taking the packing paper and boxes back to the stock room. And, of course, starting the process all over again.

My anger from talking to Detectives Dailey and Webster this morning had worn off a little. I was still disappointed that Ty hadn't been here today and more than slightly put off that he hadn't called yet.

And, it seemed, I really might have to find a psychic.

I glanced at my watch, for about the millionth time, and saw that my lunch hour had finally arrived. Since we were all part-time employees—translation: no benefits—we weren't allowed to work more than a limited number of hours per week. Back in Santa Clarita, that meant I worked four-hour shifts, several days each week. Here, they had us working eight-hour shifts. It made for a very long day—one that included an hour-long lunch break.

Personally, I would rather have had a half-hour break and gone home sooner, but I had no say in the matter. You'd think that because I was doing the wild thing with the big man, as Preston had put it, I'd have a little more pull around here—although I might have if Ty would ever call me.

In the breakroom, I punched out, got my purse from my assigned locker, and left the store.

Since I wasn't all that familiar with the area, I decided to eat at one of the restaurants in the shopping center. I walked a couple of doors down to a little mom-and-pop sandwich shop café next to a dry cleaner.

Vegas was hot—and I'm not talking about the action on The Strip. In the summer—which, technically, was only a couple of weeks away—temperatures routinely shot to over a hundred degrees and stayed there. And all that stuff about it not really feeling hot here because it was a *dry* heat was just a lot of b.s. Living in Vegas was like living in a pizza oven.

I got to the little café just before I started to sweat, got in line, and studied the menu posted behind the counter. I was debating between a double cheeseburger with a chocolate shake or a patty melt with a fries–onion rings combo, when the girl in front of me in line turned around.

"OMG!" she exclaimed. "You're at Holt's! MT! LOL!"

She looked like she was about eighteen years old, short, cute, thin, with blond hair and way too much enthusiasm to suit me at the moment. She was also speaking text. Luckily, I spoke it also. I wanted to tell her to QI—quit it—but I figured she'd think I was JK—just kidding.

"You're at Holt's, too, huh? Yeah, that's laugh-out-loud funny, all right," I said, though the thought hadn't even registered on my internal laugh-ometer.

"This is like my very first job ever," she said, waving her hands and bobbing her head like everything was still LOL funny.

"You picked a winner of a place to start," I said.

It was the nicest thing I could think of to say. Really.

"I'm TH! Let's GF together!" she said.

Translation: she was *too hungry* and wanted to *get food* together.

This didn't suit me. First of all, I was in a crappy mood. Secondly, I didn't like eating with women who were smaller than me. They always ordered a salad, making it impossible for me to order the Trucker's Big Rig Delight, or something equally loaded with fat, calories, cholesterol, and carbohydrates—my four favorite food groups. And forget about dessert.

"I'm Taylor," she said, still smiling, still flapping her hands around and wiggling her head back and forth. "I'm SG to find somebody to eat with!"

I introduced myself and decided that if she was *so glad* to eat lunch with somebody, there was no chance of getting rid of her. I would just have to suck it up and make an effort.

I hate it when I have to make an effort.

We went through the line, ordered salads, and found a table near the window to wait for our food. I got a soda— the kind with the real sugar, not that substitute stuff—and gulped down half of it, improving my outlook somewhat.

"OMG!" Taylor said. She gripped the table with both hands, her eyes huge. "Did you hear the LN?"

"What latest news would that be?" I asked.

"That girl who got killed in our store yesterday?" she said. "They think they know who did it."

Okay, that was weird. Detective Dailey and that annoying mongrel of a partner of his had just been in the store this morning asking me more questions.

"I saw it on the Internet," Taylor said.

That explained it. News on the Internet wasn't always news, more like somebody's opinion.

"Here's the LN," Taylor said, leaning toward me. "That girl who got killed? It could have been her CBF who did it."

"Her current boyfriend?" I asked, just to be sure. Text is a language with many dialects. I wanted to be certain.

"Yes! He's a complete CA!"

"Crazy ass?"

"Yes!" Taylor said again. "OMG. He's like a psycho or something. He's been in prison. Real prison. Not like a little jail or something. It's like a big jail—like prison!"

"OMG!" I shouted.

The waitress brought our salads, and Taylor kept talking about what she'd read on the Internet. I drifted off.

All I could think of was how I'd met Courtney's CA CBF, the charming and oh-so-delightful Tony Hubbard. And not only had I met him, I'd been alone with him in her apartment.

I'd definitely gotten a weird vibe from him—or maybe that's the sort of vibe everyone who's been in *real prison* gave off. I don't know. But something wasn't right there.

Damn. I should have questioned him further while I had the chance.

Regardless of what the Internet was reporting—and I use that term loosely—the homicide detectives were still investigating, evidenced by the crappy mood they'd put me in this morning.

But why were they focused on that whole me-and-Robbie-Freedman thing? Especially if they had an in-your-face suspect like Tony Hubbard?

Taylor brought me back to reality by commenting on my handbag. My mood improved. I figured if she knew a Marc Jacobs purse on sight—you'd be amazed at how many people don't—she couldn't be all bad.

We sat in the café and talked, and I was eyeing the menu, seriously considering getting a strawberry sundae—just so I'd know if I could recommend the place to other people, of course—when a guy walked past our table. He stopped, backed up, stopped again, and stared down at us.

"Wow, man, you look just like Dana Scully," he said. He talked like a turtle, slow and plodding.

Although I couldn't imagine why on earth he'd direct such a comment at me, I had the uncomfortable feeling he was doing just that.

I glanced up. He was mid-twenties maybe, thin, with long wavy brown hair that hung loose to the middle of his back. I figured him for the holder of a GED—the Good Enough Degree—a guy who owned more remotes than shoes. And—yep—he was looking at me.

"OMG!" Taylor said, waving and bouncing again. "Hey, Cliff. What are you doing here? This is SC!"

I wasn't thinking this was anything close to *so cool*.

"Haley, this is Cliff," she said, gesturing to the both of us. "We all work at the Holt's store!"

Cliff didn't seem to think it was so cool, either. In fact, I don't believe he was thinking at all. He just stared down at me with a—pardon the text—CA look on his face.

"Yeah, man, you look just like her," Cliff said. "You're Dana Scully all over again."

"OMG," Taylor said, looking bewildered. "Who's that? Somebody who works at Holt's with us?"

"No, man," Cliff said. "You know, like Fox Mulder's partner."

"From *The X-Files*?" I asked. "That old TV show?"

"Yeah, man," he said. "I love that show."

I liked it, too—who didn't?—but no way did I look like the actress who played the role of Dana Scully. First of all, she was short. I'm tall. She's about a decade older than me in the show. Not to mention the blatantly obvious fact that Dana has flaming red hair, and mine is a warm, touchable, glorious shade of brown.

Maybe Holt's should start drug testing.

Cliff leaned his head back and shook out his hair. "So, like, uh, you want to have lunch or something?"

I pointed to the empty plates on the table in front of us. "We're finished," I said.

"OMG!" Taylor said. "We'd better get back. That Fay person might have an HA or something, if we're late."

Like I'd be so lucky that Fay would have a heart attack—not a fatal one, of course—and not be at work for the next few weeks.

We got up and headed for the door.

"See you around, Dana," Cliff called.

Back at Holt's, several more hours of my life crept past in a regrettable haze and, finally, it was time to leave. I clocked out, got my purse, and left.

In my car, I couldn't stop thinking about what Taylor had said today at lunch about Courtney's boyfriend and his time in prison. He hardly seemed like the kind of guy Courtney would get hooked up with—at least, from the way I remembered her in high school. The whole thing seemed weird.

I backed out of the parking space, but instead of heading for the Culver Inn, I drove to the Bay Breeze Apartments.

The complex seemed just as quiet as it had yesterday

when I was here. I swung into a spot outside Courtney's apartment and got out. The motorcycle I'd thought probably belonged to Tony wasn't there.

Crap.

Then I noticed the door to Courtney's apartment was open. I stepped inside. The TV and stereo were gone. I heard noise from the back bedroom.

CHAPTER 9

This was the part in TV crime shows where the naïve, unsuspecting—translation: stupid—woman goes into the apartment to see what's up instead of running for her life and calling the cops.

I'm neither naïve nor stupid—although I have been accused of not having good sense, from time to time—and this, apparently, was one of those times.

I crept across the living room and turned down the hallway just as a woman stepped out of the bedroom.

She screamed.

I screamed.

We both jumped back.

I sized her up—early thirties, brunette, attractive, well dressed, no designer handbag—and decided she wasn't a threat. I did this in three seconds. It's a science, an art—no, it's a gift.

A gift this woman didn't have, obviously, because she looked like a trapped animal, desperate for escape.

"Look," she said, "I don't know what you want, or what you're doing here, but—"

"I'm a friend of Courtney's," I told her. "From high school."

She eyed me sharply and eased her way around me, out of the hallway and into the living room.

"You're Haley? Courtney mentioned she'd heard from you," she said. "I'm Danielle Shepherd."

"Her business partner," I said.

She looked surprised that I knew this, but there was something else I was reading in her face. Sorrow, maybe? Courtney must have been her friend as well as her partner.

"Where's Tony?" I asked, glancing around.

"You know Tony?" she asked.

"I came by yesterday and talked to him."

Danielle shrugged. "He was gone when I got here. Moved out."

I gestured to the spot where the TV and stereo used to sit.

"Oh my God. Did he take Courtney's things?" I exclaimed.

"Good riddance," Danielle said.

Okay, that was low. To take off with your girlfriend's TV and stereo after she died was lower than low.

Then I wondered about Danielle, why she was here and how she'd gotten in.

"Courtney and I had keys to each other's places," Danielle said, and showed me the big set of keys in her hand. She lifted the tote bag that hung on her arm. "I was looking for some photos of Courtney for the funeral."

Okay, now I felt like a jerk.

Naturally, there was nothing to do but change the subject.

"Where are Courtney's parents?" I asked.

"Turkey. Some spiritual retreat in the middle of nowhere," she said. "I'm trying to locate them."

"When you make the . . . arrangements, would you let me know?" I asked.

I'm not big on funerals, but I thought the least I could do was send flowers.

Danielle dug out her phone and punched in my number.

"Can I get yours?" I asked.

She hesitated for a minute, then gave it to me.

"I was just leaving," Danielle said.

Guess that was my cue to leave, too.

We left together and Danielle locked the door.

"You and Courtney ran a fashion accessory business?" I asked.

"If you can call it that," Danielle said. "It was small. Courtney wasn't really into it. She just didn't understand how to take advantage of a good opportunity, and, you know, life is all about jumping on opportunity. She did the accounting but that was about it."

I paused. "Courtney handled the business end of things? She didn't design the products?"

"I did that," Danielle said. "Look, I've got to go."

She climbed into her van and drove away.

I glanced at the parking space where I'd seen Tony's Harley parked and thought again how awful it was that he'd run off with Courtney's meager possessions. I wondered if Danielle had reported it to the police. Probably not, given that Tony had done jail time, and he'd figure that she was the one who'd ratted him out.

Can't say that I blamed her. Tony Hubbard was definitely not the kind of guy I'd want mad at me.

Maybe I'd call Detective Dailey and tell him myself.

Or maybe not, I thought as I got into my car. I had no proof, and even if I did, it wasn't evidence that Tony had killed Courtney.

My day needed a boost. Casinos and slot machines sprang up in my mind. A huge jackpot would sure give my day—and my bank account—a heck of a boost.

Marcie was right, though, gambling should be avoided. So there was nothing to do now but go shopping. I needed that Delicious handbag more desperately than ever.

I whipped out my cell phone and located another mall on the Internet. The Boulevard Mall looked promising. I set my GPS for Maryland Parkway and started driving.

I couldn't stop thinking about Courtney's death. Why had she been murdered? She didn't seem to have anything worth killing for, judging by the condition of her apartment. I didn't remember anything about her parents from high school, which probably meant they weren't wealthy. If they had been, they'd have been on my mom's radar—so Courtney probably hadn't been living off a trust fund. I recalled that she had no brothers or sisters, or anyone who might stand to inherit if she was out of the picture, even if her family had some money.

So if money wasn't involved, why had she been murdered? And why at Holt's, of all places?

I figured whoever did her in must have followed her to the store. Or maybe the killer knew where she was going.

Tony flashed in my mind. He probably knew. Courtney probably mentioned it to him.

Danielle might have known also. She knew who I was back at Courtney's apartment, so Courtney obviously told her about my Facebook message.

What about that Mike Ivan guy? Tony had told me Mike had been giving her a hard time. Now I wondered if that was really true, or if Tony had said it just to throw suspicion off of himself. But if it were true, I had no way of knowing if Mike was still in L.A. Maybe he'd come to Vegas looking for her.

Maybe he'd found her.

One thing for sure was that whoever had done it had definitely wanted her dead. From the looks of all that blood I'd seen in the dressing room—which still creeped me out to think about it—I figured that she'd been stabbed. The murderer obviously didn't care that lots of people—potential witnesses—were in the store, or that security cameras were humming away—or should have been.

Sounded like a desperate killer to me.

Or maybe a lucky one.

Or one who knew dozens of people were coming and

going from the store, and no one really knew each other well enough to recognize someone who wasn't supposed to be there.

Or someone who knew that the security cameras weren't operational yet.

My head started to hurt. I surveyed the street on both sides, hoping to spot a Starbucks. No such luck. I continued on to the mall.

When I got back to the motel, I still had no idea who'd killed Courtney or why, no Delicious handbag, and no call from Marcie or Ty. Amber still wasn't at the registration desk, which irked me to no end.

Jeez, I was just trying to do a good deed here. You'd think she could come to work so I could thank her.

I did, however, have a handful of shopping bags, courtesy of the fantastic stores I'd visited at the mall.

Yeah, okay, I knew my credit cards were screaming for relief, but how could I walk past all those gorgeous things and not buy something? I mean, in a way, it's kind of rude to go into a shop, wear down the carpet, breath up the air, and leave fingerprints on the merchandise and not buy something.

I'd found a fantastic summer sweater—so fantastic, I'd bought two of them—a couple pairs of capris that cried out for coordinating sandals, and some fun-looking bracelets with matching earrings. I got a raincoat—yeah, I knew it was summer and I was in the desert—but it was on clearance. So, actually, it was an investment—along with the umbrella that went with it.

Up in my room, I put on my comfy clothes, and climbed into bed with my laptop.

If ever in my life I needed a shot of good luck, it was now. As much as I didn't want to admit it, maybe Marcie and Sandy had been right. Maybe I should contact a psychic and find out what I could do to break this curse—not that I believed in it, of course. But something had to change and it was the easiest place to start.

I logged onto the Internet and searched for psychics in Vegas. Wow, there were tons of them.

Psychic readers, palm readers, aura readers, and crystal readers offered advice on love, career, and dreams. Others promised past life regression and astrological chart interpretation. Some would tell your past, present—which I'd think you wouldn't need a psychic for—and future, as well as solve all your problems and provide a view into the mysteries of the universe.

All of this along with Google maps, business hours, payment methods—credit card and PayPal—appointment booking over the Internet, and monthly newsletters.

It was a business, after all.

Even though Marcie had thought this was a good idea, I couldn't bring myself to do it. I couldn't see myself getting reliable advice from a woman who'd probably look like Cher performing "Gypsies, Tramps, and Thieves."

Unless she could provide me with the location of a Delicious handbag.

Maybe I'd think about it.

I grabbed my phone out of my purse and checked the screen. No messages. Hum ... I wondered why Marcie hadn't called—not that I'd given up on Ty calling—but she and I talked almost every day.

My brain clicked over to fashion, for some reason, and I decided to check out the fashion accessory company Courtney and Danielle ran. I was curious to see their line. Danielle seemed like a no-nonsense kind of gal. I wondered what her designs would look like.

I'd considered starting my own line of handbags but never really did it. Who knew? Maybe one day.

I typed every combination of words I could think of into every search engine I could find but didn't come up with anything, other than the article I'd already read.

Guess Danielle had been right. It wasn't much of a business.

Guess I was right, too. Courtney wasn't bright enough to manage the company and this proved it. No Web site, no promo, no Internet presence at all. Not surprising the business hadn't taken off.

I grabbed my phone and hit Marcie's number. Her voicemail picked up. I left a message.

Since my search for Courtney and Danielle hadn't turned up anything—and because I was really tired of the cops bugging me—I decided to try something else. I typed Mike Ivan's name into the search box. I wasn't sure what I expected to find—his name on a terrorist watch list would have been nice—but more like something—anything— that might indicate exactly how he was involved with Courtney.

Nothing came up.

I stared at the laptop keyboard. Not much was going my way tonight. Maybe I should go to Starbucks. Everybody who uses a laptop at Starbucks always looks as if things are going great.

With considerable mental effort, I ditched the idea of Starbucks. A mocha frappuccino—or two—would have me wired and up half the night.

Which might be okay if I weren't here alone.

I could think of only one more way to get info on Courtney's murder. I needed to talk to someone who knew her here in Vegas. Somebody who could give me some insight into her day-to-day life.

Tony Hubbard's info wasn't reliable, and Danielle's only connection that I knew of was through business. Courtney must have had friends in Vegas—since she didn't have sense enough to know when people didn't like her—so I needed to find them.

My first thought was to log onto Courtney's Facebook page and see who her friends were, but since I was still concerned that the cops might be monitoring it, no way was I doing that. I could have asked Marcie to do it, but involving her in a murder investigation was definitely not a best-friends-forever kind of thing to do.

Instead, I logged onto the Monroe High School Web site. A memorial to Courtney had already been posted. Not much info was given, just the bare facts—nothing about how another alumnus had found her dead, thank God—no further info on her life.

A number of people had posted comments. I read through them, surprised to learn that so many former students remembered Courtney from back in the day and had nice things to say about her.

A posting from somebody named Stephanie Holden caught my attention. She stated that she knew Courtney in Henderson, was stunned by her death, would miss her, blah, blah, blah.

I checked out Stephanie and saw that she had a Facebook page—who doesn't these days? I sent her a message. Nothing too deep, just that I was a friend of Courtney's and would like to talk to her. Hopefully, she'd read it and get back to me soon.

Working eight-hour shifts at Holt's, lifting all those boxes and all that merchandise—not to mention pounding the pavement in search of a Delicious handbag and all the accompanying shopping—had worn me out. I changed into my pajamas and got into bed. I fell asleep right away.

I awoke shortly after three. Voices came from the hallway. My neighbors, keeping late hours again. A door slammed and everything got quiet. I fell back to sleep.

It was a Louis Vuitton day. Definitely a Louis Vuitton day.

I dressed in jeans and T-shirt—the uniform of the day at Holt's—and went down for the breakfast buffet.

Yeah, okay, I knew a Louis Vuitton bag was a bit of overkill for jeans and a T-shirt, but I wanted Maya to see it. It was a fabulous purse and I knew she'd love it as much as I did.

She spotted it right away—before she spotted me, I think—and rushed over.

"This is positively the most awesome handbag I've ever seen," Maya declared as I held it up.

Around us, motel guests served themselves from the buffet, poured coffee, and read the morning newspaper at their tables.

"I have a matching organizer," I told her.

I knew she wouldn't think I'd said it just to be bitchy or anything. She'd be happy for me.

And she was. Her eyes got big and a huge I-love-purses smile appeared.

"My boyfriend gave it to me," I said. "Ty."

"He must be one heck of a guy," Maya said.

I suppose he is. I didn't know, since he hadn't called me lately.

But no need to get into that now and spoil our fabulous-purse-and-accessories moment.

I gestured toward the registration desk across the lobby.

"Amber isn't here again this morning. Is she on vacation or something?" I asked. "I wanted to thank her for giving me a room."

Maya's smile vanished. "Amber got fired."

"What?"

She nodded. "That awful Bradley fired her because she—"

Silence hung between us for a few seconds before I realized what she was about to say.

"Because she gave me that room?" I asked.

"I feel bad, too," Maya said. "I was the one who pushed her into doing it."

"And he fired her for that?" I asked.

"He's a major pain," Maya said. "It's his way or the highway."

On rare occasions, I'm glad my mother was a founding member of the Beverly Hills I'm-better-than-you club. Immediately, I morphed into her outraged-indignant-mode, the one she used if a sales clerk showed her a dress from the clearance rack.

"Where does he get off firing somebody for giving a room to a deserving guest?" I demanded. "Who is his supervisor?"

"His family owns the Culver Inn chain. The Pennington family, remember? They own half of Nevada, I think," Maya said. "There's not much you can do."

That only made me madder.

"It's not right," I said. "Mine isn't the only room on that wing that's being used."

That got Maya's attention. She looked a little mad herself.

"Let's go talk to the new girl," she said.

The new girl—Whitley, according to her name tag—didn't seem all that happy to see us when we approached the registration desk. She looked tense and rigid, like being a bitch was a lifestyle choice.

No way would she out-bitch me. My mom was a pageant queen. It was in my DNA.

Or maybe it was that hideous green-brown-orange uniform that made her so cranky. It made me out of sorts just looking at it.

"I'm Haley Randolph, room three-thirty-four," I told her. "I just found out that—"

"Look," Whitley said, her gaze darting from me to Maya, and back to me again. "I don't want any trouble."

It was apparent that staying in room 334 was the equivalent of wearing a scarlet "A" on my chest.

"Okay, fine," I said. "Get Bradley on the phone. Let me talk to him."

"No."

I was so stunned, I couldn't speak for a moment.

Maybe I need to work on my I'm-better-than-you demeanor.

"Bradley expects me to handle this desk," Whitley said, pushing her chin up a little. "That's what I intend to do."

"We're not trying to go over your head," Maya said, sounding considerably more reasonable than I felt. "We're just saying that it's not fair Amber got fired for booking Haley into a room in that wing, when other guests are being booked there."

"They most certainly are not," Whitley told us.

"Yes, they are," I said.

"No, they aren't," she insisted.

"I heard them," I said. "Voices in the hallway, in the middle of the night."

She dismissed my claim with a wave of her hand. "You're mistaken. No guests are up there. Housekeeping and maintenance don't work after nine. If you heard anything at all, it must have been a guest who'd gotten off on the wrong floor."

"I heard a door slam," I told her. "Somebody went into a room."

"Impossible," Whitley declared.

She picked up the telephone and turned her back on us.

I just stood there.

Oh my God. If no guests were booked on that floor, in that wing, and housekeeping and maintenance weren't on duty, who had been outside my room in the middle of the night?

CHAPTER 10

Housewares—my assigned square footage of purgatory today—was an okay department. Lifting the heavy boxes of tableware wasn't easy, but I liked it better than children's. When I'd checked the assignment easel at the front of the store this morning, I felt a little wave of satisfaction that Fay hadn't put me there again. After yelling at her yesterday, I couldn't be sure which way she'd go.

I try to project an assertive demeanor without being perceived as a hard-ass. I shoot for something between I-won't-be-pushed-around-like-a-shopping-cart and cross-me-and-I'll-cut-you. Evidently, Fay got the message.

As I sliced open what felt like my thousandth box of plates, Preston appeared next to me.

"Good morning, Haley," he said, sounding a little more chipper than yesterday. Guess he was getting used to managing the whole somebody-died-in-my-store situation.

"How are you coming on that little project?" he asked.

Project? There was a project?

"The one we discussed in my office yesterday," he said. "Remember?"

I had no clue, so what could I say but, "Sure."

"Excellent." Preston rubbed his palms together. "What have you found out?"

I was supposed to find out something?

"I'll bet the employees are teeming with suggestions for their reward," he said.

A vague recollection surfaced in my brain. Something about Preston wanting to do something nice for the employees, asking me for my input.

Jeez, had he really expected me to do that?

"They are," I said, hoping he wouldn't ask me for an example.

"Like what?"

Crap.

"Preliminary thoughts, at this point. Nothing I'm ready to go forward with," I said and, thankfully, it sounded like I actually had some preliminary thoughts.

"Good, then. Good," Preston said. "Keep me advised."

As he walked away, a flash of brilliance struck me.

"Preston?" I called. When he turned around, I said, "Some of the employees said they'd like to take a half-hour lunch, instead of an hour, so they can get off sooner."

"Really?"

I nodded. "It's a big deal to them."

He squinted, tilted his head right, then left, and said, "I don't see any reason why we can't do that. Thank you, Haley. Keep up the good work."

I love this project.

"Hey, Dana." Cliff ambled over.

"It's Haley," I said.

"Yeah, okay, so how's it going?" he asked.

Cliff didn't seem like a bad guy, really. Maybe a little weird, but aren't we all, in our own way?

Everyone except for me, of course.

"The Sci-Fi Channel's running an *X-Files* marathon," Cliff said. "Did you catch it last night?"

"Missed it," I said as I heaved another box of plates off the U-boat.

"Oh, man, I saw the episode where Fox and Dana get drugged or something, and they think they're somewhere else, like, someplace different or something," he said. "It's my all-time favorite."

"Sounds like a dream come true to me, too," I said.

"So, like, I'm working over in men's wear," he said, nodding toward the other side of the store. "It's almost lunch time."

No need to look at my watch. Since I'd been checking it every two minutes, I knew my lunch hour was eight minutes away.

"You want to go get something to eat?" he asked. "I know this really great place."

I didn't figure Cliff as the kind of guy who'd know a really great place to do anything—except maybe score some dope—but maybe I was wrong.

I decided not to chance it.

"Some other time," I told him.

"Yeah, okay, sure, Dana," he said.

"It's Haley."

He waved and strolled away.

I knelt down to get another box from the bottom shelf of the U-boat when I heard Preston's voice. Since I'd already spoken with him a few minutes ago, I didn't see why I should subject myself to another conversation with him. He might want me to take on another project or something.

I eased backward, keeping low, and slipped around the back of the display table. I heard another voice, and realized he was talking to someone. Another man who sounded familiar.

In big-time stealth mode, I crouched lower and leaned forward ever so slightly.

Oh my God. Detective Dailey.

I jumped back.

What was he doing here again? Why was Preston bringing him to this end of the store? Nothing here had anything to do with the murder—except maybe for me.

I spun around and duck-walked at high speed—a technique I taught myself to enhance my own personal brand of customer service—and slipped through the double doors into the stock room.

No way—no possible way—was I going to talk to Detective Dailey again. He and his dog-breath partner had nearly ruined my day yesterday, and I wasn't going through that again.

Of course, I could lawyer up. I could flat-out refuse to talk to him. But that would only make me look guilty and possibly cause him to pursue me as a suspect more intensely. Better to dodge him—at least until he showed up with an arrest warrant.

I dashed through the stock room to the doors that opened near the customer service booth on the other side of the store, then slipped into the employee breakroom, grabbed my purse, and clocked out.

Cliff walked in.

"Hey, Dana," he said. "How's it going?"

"I've got to go," I said, stepping around him.

"You want to go get something to eat?" he asked.

Hadn't I already covered this with him?

"I know this really great place," he said.

Yeah, we'd covered this. And he was wasting my time. Preston and Detective Dailey could walk through the door any second—or worse, Detective Webster.

Cliff pointed. "It's kind of a long way from here, but the food is, well, you know, it's pretty good."

He had me at *a long way from here.*

"Okay, fine, let's go," I said.

I hooked his arm and pulled him through the stock room, out the back, and around the building to the front parking lot.

"You drive," I said, thinking it better to leave my car here so the detectives would think I was in the store or somewhere nearby.

"Sure, Dana," Cliff said. "I've got a sweet ride."

Cliff walked slow, really slow. Annoyingly slow. But I was afraid being seen dragging him through the parking lot like a dog on a leash might attract undue attention.

His sweet ride turned out to be a dinged-up, white Ford Taurus that had probably been new back before I got a driver's license.

"Get in," Cliff called from the driver's side. "It's not locked."

Probably just as well.

I got in. The car's interior was worn and battered. Fast-food bags and wrappers littered the back seat, and the distinctive scent that had permeated the cloth seats made me think that Cliff smoked his way to and from work—and not the kind of smokes you can buy in a grocery or convenience store.

"I got a great deal on it," he said, patting the steering wheel. "It was, like, wrecked or something, near L.A."

Cliff started the car and we headed out. I bounced in my seat, anxious to put a great distance between me and the homicide detectives.

Just what would happen when my lunch break ended and I had to go back to the store, I didn't know. I'd worry about that in an hour.

We crossed the parking lot. Cliff steered into a slot outside a Pizza Hut and killed the engine.

"This is *it?*" I'm pretty sure I screamed that. "This is the restaurant that's *a long way* from the store?"

"Well, sometimes I walk," Cliff said. "It's farther if you walk."

There was probably a good argument against that statement, but I was too flustered to think of it.

I needed a Plan B.

I couldn't count on Cliff to formulate a Plan B—we'd probably end up back in the Holt's breakroom—so I came up with one myself.

"Look," I said. "I need to get my tire fixed. Do you know a tire store that's *a long way* from here?"

"Sure."

"Listen carefully, Cliff. Focus. When I say *a long way* from here, I mean it's *not* in this shopping center. Got it?"

He nodded. "Yeah, sure. I've got it."

"Okay, where is it?"

"Well, I'm not sure."

"Crap . . ."

I pulled out my phone and found a tire store on Warm Springs Road.

"Look, Cliff," I said. "I want you to drive me to my car, then follow me to the tire store. Okay?"

"Sure," he said.

He made no move to start the car. I was tempted to reach across him, open his door, and push him out. I restrained myself.

"We need to go now," I said.

"You want to go get something to eat?" he asked. "I know this really great place."

I hate my life.

"We need to go now, Cliff. You know, as in, right this very minute," I said, and managed not to scream. "As in, start the car now."

"Okay, Dana, sure, whatever you say."

Cliff drove to the other side of the parking lot and, under my direction, pulled up near my car. I looked around and, thankfully, didn't see Detectives Dailey or Webster.

I reminded Cliff—twice—to follow me, then backed out of the space and headed for the tire store.

I liked Plan B better, anyway, I had decided as I'd entered the address into my GPS. If the detectives didn't see my car in the parking lot—I was sure they'd accessed my DMV file in California and knew the make, model, and plate number for my Honda—maybe they'd think I'd left for the day.

Of course, that only postponed my problem rather than solving it, but I'd take it.

The guy at the tire store said my tire would be repaired and mounted on my car by the end of the day. I reported this to Cliff as I climbed into his Taurus again.

"Cool," he said. "So, listen, do you want to get some lunch? I know this great place."

Sure I'd end up at the Pizza Hut again, I said no.

"There's bound to be a restaurant around here somewhere," I said.

Warm Springs Road was crowded with businesses of all sorts. We found a sandwich shop within a couple of blocks and went inside. Since I was dining with Cliff—rather than with a girl who was skinnier than me and would make me feel like a recovered anorexic at a Thanksgiving buffet if I ordered what I really wanted—I got chili cheese fries, a hot dog, and a banana split.

Cliff got a salad.

I didn't care.

"You know, Dana, working at Holt's is just something I'm doing for right now," Cliff said as we sat down at a table with our food. "I'm trying to get on the highway patrol."

"Good luck with that."

It came out sounding kind of sarcastic.

Cliff didn't notice.

"But, what I'm *really* doing is ufology," he said.

I paused, a chili-drenched French fry halfway to my lips. "U—what?"

"Ufology. You know, the study of UFOs."

Why didn't that surprise me?

"I'm training to be an investigator. I've got a field kit and everything. You know, for investigating," he said.

I don't know why—which just shows you how rattled I still was—but for some reason, I asked, "What exactly are you investigating?"

"Sightings, landings, encounters, stuff like that," he said. "We research them and analyze the information."

"We?"

"There's a club."

What has become of my life?

Under normal circumstances, I might have gotten up and insisted we leave, but I didn't want to go back to work early, nor did I want to leave my banana split uneaten.

I decided to roll with it.

"Who's in the club?" I asked.

"Me," he said. "And my friend Eric and my friend Dwayne, and . . . well, I guess that's about it. But that's just the Nevada chapter. It's a worldwide organization."

"Have you seen a UFO?" I asked. "Other than on *X-Files*."

"Well, not yet, I don't think so. Maybe I did. I'm not sure. Dwayne had a close encounter with a UFO. It really freaked him out," Cliff said. "All kind of weird stuff is happening out in the desert around Vegas."

"Alien encounters?"

"There're different kinds of encounters, you know. The first kind is when a UFO comes really close to you."

"That would be freaky," I agreed, and dug into my banana split.

"The second kind is when a UFO interacts with the environment, and physical changes happen. You know, like the ground gets scorched and animals and people get hurt or scared or something."

"Like Dwayne?" I asked. The guy who, I figured, had smoked a joint immediately before this alleged encounter occurred.

"The third kind of close encounter is when they make a movie out of it," Cliff said.

Guess I should have expected that.

"That's what ufology is all about," Cliff said. "Visiting hotspots, analyzing stuff. We have a form to fill out and everything."

Cliff hadn't touched his salad—I think he'd forgotten it was in front of him—and I was working on my banana split when he leaned sideways and waved to someone behind me.

"It's that guy from the store," he said, then called, "Hey, man, come on over."

Relieved it was a coworker and not Dwayne or Eric, I looked up and saw Detective Dailey walking toward us.

Oh my God. What was he doing here?

"Hey, man, sit down," Cliff said, when Dailey stopped at our table. "I saw you working in the security office. Cool."

That explained it. The security cameras were up and running now and the detective had seen my escape on the monitors in the security office and followed us here.

"Yeah, man, I'm into that security and investigation stuff. I'm going to work for the highway patrol," Cliff said. He pointed to me. "This is Dana. She works at the store, too."

"*Dana?*" Detective Dailey asked, looking down at me.

No way was I getting into the whole close-encounters-alien-investigation-*X-Files* thing with him.

"You're using an alias?" Dailey asked.

I ignored his question.

"I don't suppose you're here for lunch?" I asked.

"I'm here to talk to you," he said.

"Look, I already told you everything about me and Robbie Freedman," I said.

Detective Dailey leaned down a little.

"I'm here to talk to you about Tony Hubbard," he said.

Oh, crap.

CHAPTER 11

"How do you know Tony Hubbard?" Detective Dailey asked.

We'd moved outside the restaurant. The place had filled up with diners and gotten noisy. I didn't want to shout my innocence over the din.

Cliff still sat inside at our table. I hoped he wouldn't forget I'd ridden with him and leave without me.

It was hot, even though we stood in the shade of the building, but it was far better than sitting in Detective Dailey's homicide mobile. No sign of Webster.

"What makes you think I know Tony Hubbard?" I tried to sound indignant but didn't quite pull it off.

"I'm a detective. I detect things," Dailey said. "For instance, your name and phone number written on a piece of paper in Hubbard's kitchen."

Crap. I'd forgotten I'd left my contact info with Tony.

Well, no way to dodge Dailey's questions now.

"I went to pay my respects and Tony was there," I said. "He's a convicted felon, you know. Maybe you should talk to him—not me."

"I've done that," Dailey said. "We're checking out Hubbard's alibi. You, on the other hand, don't have one."

"What about Mike Ivan?" I asked.

I hated to throw somebody under the bus—somebody

who might very well be innocent—but I had to do something.

Detective Dailey flinched. I'm sure he practiced showing no reaction in front of a suspect, but I saw his left cheek twitch. I didn't know if that meant he hadn't heard of Mike Ivan, or if he was surprised that I had. Maybe both.

"He'd been stalking Courtney, sort of," I said. "Tony knew about him. Didn't he mention him?"

"Hubbard was less than forthcoming during our interview," Dailey said.

Guess I should have figured that.

"Mike lives in L.A.," I told him.

"Don't you live in L.A., too?"

Like that made me guilty by association.

I suppose I should have gotten angry, but I didn't. More than anything, I felt tired—and, yeah, a little annoyed.

Detective Dailey kept eyeing me, waiting for my response. I glared back. His face softened a bit. I realized I wasn't the only one who was annoyed—or tired.

"Where's your partner?" I asked.

He paused for a moment, then said, "Taking a personal day."

"So at least one good thing happened to you today, huh?"

Detective Dailey grinned. That little grin transformed him, made him look less like a hard-ass detective and more like the nice guy he probably was—off duty.

He didn't say anything—I didn't expect he'd diss his partner—but I could tell he wanted to agree.

"Look, I had nothing to do with Courtney's death," I said. "I don't even know how she died."

"Slashed." Dailey touched his neck. "Sliced the artery. Probably a box cutter."

I'd seen bowls of those things placed all over the store like candy dishes.

It creeped me out to think how I—and everyone else in

the store—had used them, made them a routine part of our day, when all along, one of them had been used as a murder weapon.

Dailey could have been trying another interview tactic, being nice, figuring that if he gave up some info, I'd do the same. If I'd known anything, I would have shared it with him—maybe. All I could do was speculate.

"Somebody followed her to the store—"

"Or was waiting there for her," Dailey said.

Translation: I was still a suspect.

I ignored him.

"Whoever it was grabbed a box cutter, slashed Courtney's throat, pushed her into the women's dressing room, and left her there to die," he said.

The image filled my head. I didn't like it.

"Why would somebody do that?" I said, mostly to myself. "Courtney wasn't the kind of girl who stirred a lot of passion in anyone. At least, not back in high school."

The restaurant door swung open and Cliff moseyed out.

"Hey, you guys heading back to the store?" he asked.

"Sure," I called.

I stepped around Detective Dailey. He blocked my path.

"I'll check into Mike Ivan," he said.

We stared at each other for a few seconds, then he stepped off.

I skirted around him. Cliff was in his car. I jumped in and we drove away. When I looked back, Dailey was watching.

The detective had lightened up a bit, given me some info about Courtney's death, but I didn't expect he'd continue to show me "his" even if I showed him "mine."

I decided I'd check out Mike Ivan myself.

"TTYL!" Taylor called, as she waved and pulled away from the tire store.

"Talk to you later," I echoed, as I got into my Honda.

I'd asked Taylor to give me a ride to the tire store after work, and she'd readily SY—said yes. When we arrived, my car had been parked under a web of plastic, multi-colored fluttering flags which, luckily, meant the work was finished. I'd paid the guy inside and, even though it maxed out my credit card, luckily the bill wasn't more than he'd quoted me when I'd brought my car in.

Maybe things had turned around, I thought, as I pulled out onto Warm Springs Road. Maybe the curse—which I'd never believed in, of course—had gone away.

This made me think that I should immediately head to yet another mall and make yet another attempt to find a Delicious handbag. I was on a roll now, luck-wise, and I shouldn't lose momentum.

My phone rang. The caller I.D. screen showed Marcie's name.

Yes! This proved it. Another good thing had happened. I hadn't heard from Marcie last night, but now she was calling.

I had to find a mall right away.

But, of course, I had to talk to Marcie first. A best friend always—mostly always—came before a handbag.

"Something happened yesterday," Marcie said when I answered.

A knot as big as a Betsey Johnson tote jerked in my stomach.

Marcie was using her something-seriously-bad-happened voice. I needed to brace myself, be prepared for whatever she was about to say.

I looked around. Where was a Starbucks when I needed one?

"Are you okay?" I asked.

"Not really," Marcie said.

I ran a yellow light. Surely a Starbucks was on the next block.

"After work, I went to that club that's just down the

street from my office building," Marcie said. "You know, that one we went to together when that girl you don't like was getting that new job she slept her way into. You wore that black dress with the pink scarf, and I had on that red blouse."

Immediately, I knew exactly which club she was talking about.

"What happened?" I asked.

"I saw Ty outside the club," Marcie said.

Oh my God. If Marcie thought it was bad, it must be mega-bad. My imagination ran wild, concocting all sorts of horrible scenarios.

Had he been in a car accident? Had he been injured? Crippled? Killed? Had he run someone over? An old lady? A child? Three kids? Three kids and an old lady carrying a kitten?

I sped up and whipped around three cars. I desperately needed a Starbucks.

A worse thought flashed in my head.

Had Ty been on a date with someone else?

Oh my God. *Oh my God.*

I cut across two lanes of traffic, whipped into the parking lot outside a convenience store, and skidded to a stop.

If that were true, if Marcie had seen Ty out with someone else, not even a Starbucks could help me now.

"Was he on a . . . date?" I asked.

"No, Haley, he was by himself," she said. "I'd have driven straight through the night to tell you in person, if I'd seen him with someone."

Yes, she would have.

I calmed down. A little.

"So what happened?"

"You know I don't stick my nose into anybody else's personal relationships," Marcie said. "I'd never go up to some guy and bitch him out, unless a friend wanted me to."

That was true. Sure, we'd talk about the most intimate details of our lives, but we'd never cross that line.

"Well, last night I did," Marcie said. "I saw Ty, and it made me so mad that he didn't pay attention to you, so I told him."

"You did?"

This did not sound like Marcie at all.

"I told him that you were struggling to pay for your classes, books, fees, your rent, car payment, everything," Marcie said. "And I told him that he was the one bright spot in your life, but he didn't appreciate you or even seem to care."

"You really said that?"

"Well, honestly, I'd been drinking."

Okay, that explained it.

"What did Ty say?" I asked.

"I don't know," Marcie said. "I fell off the curb and sprained my ankle."

"*What?*"

"Ty picked me up and carried me to his car. Actually picked me up in his arms, Haley, and carried me. Three whole blocks," Marcie said. "He's very strong."

I knew that. It was really hot.

"Then he took me to the emergency room and stayed with me until Mom got there," Marcie said. "In the exam room. Not the waiting room. And he even turned off his phone."

"Wow . . ."

"He's such a nice guy," Marcie said.

I knew that, too. It was way hot.

"So, of course, I felt like a complete idiot for telling him what an awful boyfriend he was," Marcie said.

I understood completely, having had a number of complete-idiot moments in my life.

"How's your ankle?" I asked. "Are you okay?"

"They x-rayed it. Nothing's broken," she said. "I'm wearing this ridiculous boot thing that weighs a ton. It's not very comfortable, but at least I can walk."

I should have been there with Marcie when it happened. I should be there now to go by her place, bring her the multipack of chocolate coated, double stuffed Oreo cookies—nothing less would do in a dire situation like this.

At that second, the idea of leaving Vegas behind and going home sounded really great—until I realized what would happen if my mom found out I was in town and had deliberately ditched her and beauty-queen-spa-week.

Still, Marcie was my best friend.

"I'll come back," I said.

"No, don't. I'm okay. It's not a big deal," she told me. "And it's not your fault. Not really."

"My fault?"

"You know, because of the curse."

Oh, crap. That damn curse.

"So, anyway," Marcie said, "I just wanted to let you know what's going on. Sorry I stuck my nose into your problems with Ty."

"Your heart was in the right place," I said. "Even if you were drinking."

She laughed and I did, too; then we hung up.

I pulled back onto Warm Springs Road, more desperate than ever to find a Starbucks. I drove for a couple of miles before I spotted one. I parked and rushed inside. The line was long—Starbucks needs an express line for emergencies such as this—but I eventually got my mocha frappuccino and found a quiet table in the corner.

This curse thing was getting on my nerves big time. I didn't believe in it, yet it wouldn't seem to leave me alone.

How deep would it go? How far could it reach? Was nobody I knew safe from it?

I sipped my frappuccino and decided not to dwell on it. I had bigger problems.

After talking to Detective Dailey this afternoon, I'd been

glad to hear him say he intended to find Mike Ivan. I wasn't sure how long that might take, given that he was in Los Angeles. Would Vegas detectives make that sort of trip? Did they consider Mike Ivan a suspect that warranted it?

I didn't know.

Either way, I couldn't rely on Detective Dailey to follow through. I had to do that myself. Or rather, I had to turn to someone who would do it for me.

I pulled out my cell phone and hit the speed dial number for Jack Bishop, the sexiest, hottest—and only—private detective I knew.

CHAPTER 12

Jack is hot. Really hot. Tall, dark hair, gorgeous eyes, great build. He's got a way-hot job as a private detective, and he's hooked into most everything that's happening in L.A.

I met Jack back in the day when I worked for the mega-high-power law firm, Pike Warner. I toiled away in the accounts payable unit and he investigated cases for the attorneys handling rich and famous—and infamous—clients.

Jack also did side work. I've helped him out at times, and he's done the same for me. Strictly professional, of course, though I admit at times I've been tempted by his good looks and toe-curling voice.

Jack's been tempted, too—that's what I'm telling myself, anyway—but he knew I was with Ty Cameron. Plus, Ty's family had been represented by Pike Warner for decades. Jack was too smart to create a conflict of interest that would call his integrity into question.

Jack answered on the third ring.

"What's up?" he asked.

Sitting in Starbucks, staring out the window at the traffic passing by, it hit me that involving Jack in this might not be my best move—for Jack, anyway. A lot of bad stuff had happened. I didn't want to bring anything down on him.

But I couldn't see Jack believing in a curse, or shying away from something because of one. That's not how hot L.A. private detectives roll.

"I'm in Vegas," I said.

"Behaving yourself?" he asked.

I smiled. "You know the old saying: what happens in Vegas stays in Vegas."

"If you're trying to get me to come up there, it's working," Jack said.

He used his Barry White voice.

My toes curled.

"I just want you for your mind," I told him. It came out sounding sort of breathless but, jeez, I couldn't help myself. I'm defenseless against the Barry White voice.

"My mind, huh? Not my best asset, you know," he said.

I'd figured that, but I decided to ignore it.

"I need info on a guy named Mike Ivan," I said. "Have you heard of him?"

"What's the deal?" Jack asked.

His normal voice was back now, which was good. I guess.

"He's in L.A. somewhere," I said. "A friend of mine, Courtney Collins, was involved with him somehow."

"Somewhere? Somehow?" Jack asked. "That's all you've got for me?"

I could have given him all the info I had but decided not to. I wanted Jack's take on him, untainted by Courtney's murder.

"You'll figure it out," I said. "I owe you."

"Damn right you do. I'll let you know what I want, when I want it," he said, and hung up.

Jack had given me that line before, but he'd never followed through. It made my toes curl again, like always.

I finished my mocha frappuccino and went to my car. As soon as I got in, my cell phone rang. I figured it was Jack calling back, but my caller I.D. screen said Ty.

Ty? Ty was calling? *Finally?*

My heart took off, working faster than a cash register at a sample sale.

Oh my God. What did he want? What would he say? Was he about to tell me to forget the whole we're-moving-in-together thing? Or would he profess his undying love and insist we go curtain shopping for our new place?

Where was Marcie at a time like this?

"We need to talk," Ty said when I answered.

I couldn't tell from his tone if he wanted a we-need-to-talk-because-I'm-breaking-up-with-you kind of talk, or a we-need-to-talk-because-it's-too-important-to-say-over-the-phone kind of talk.

I played it safe and said, "Okay."

"Good." He sounded relieved. "I'll swing by your place and pick you up in about an hour."

Okay, this was weird.

"Where are you?" I asked.

"My office."

His office is in downtown Los Angeles.

My heart rate slowed down.

"Didn't you listen to the message I left you?" I asked.

He paused. "Well . . . uh . . ."

"I'm in *Vegas*," I told him. I said it kind of loud.

He didn't respond.

"I've been here for *three days*." I shouted that.

Still nothing.

"You are the *worst* boyfriend in the history of boy-friends!" I screamed that. "Don't ever, ever, *ever* call me again!"

I hung up and started driving.

There was nothing to do but go shopping. I headed for the Galleria Mall.

This was my second trip to the Galleria—I really hadn't done it justice the first time, concentrating as I was on finding a Delicious handbag—and I needed to give all the stores my undivided attention.

Maybe that would help me get over that awful conversation with Ty.

Hot weather called for beach attire and I found plenty of it at the stores in the Galleria. In Macy's I bought three bathing suits. New bathing suits were useless, of course, without accessories, so I also got myself matching cover-ups, sandals, and totes.

Standing in the dressing room, looking at myself in the mirror, I'd decided more emphasis on exercise would be good—not that I looked bad in my bathing suits, of course—but a workout more enjoyable than the monotonous grind of exercise machines at the gym would be fun.

In-line skating came to mind. It seemed perfect. Firming my thighs as I glided along the bike path at the beach, the wind in my hair, the sparkling Pacific at my fingertips.

I needed the right type of clothing, of course.

I rushed onto the sales floor and picked up shorts, tank tops, and T-shirts in a beach-worthy pallet of colors. While ringing up my sale, the clerk and I spent several minutes discussing necklines—scoop, V, crew, turtle, boat—and which sleeve length looked best with each—long, three-quarter, short, cap—and I realized I didn't have nearly enough of each. I hit the racks again.

I left the mall feeling good about my new and improved exercise program. I vowed to get right on it as soon as I got back to L.A.—and as soon as I got some in-line skates. In the meantime, I figured it was okay to go ahead and wear the shorts and T-shirts.

After hours at the Galleria Mall, I returned to the Culver Inn. I'd set a quick pace for myself in an effort to burn off my anger at Ty, and kept my energy up with a stop at Ben and Jerry's for ice cream and a couple of mocha frappuccinos from Starbucks.

Without Marcie here to talk me down, I could have done a lot worse.

Yeah, okay, another credit card was now maxed out, but sometimes that's what it takes to put things in perspective. Not that I'd come to terms with the whole Ty-didn't-know-I-was-gone, what-am-I-going-to-do thing, but regardless, I was keeping the clothes.

I gathered my shopping bags out of the trunk and made my way into the lobby of the Culver Inn. The desk clerk called to me—guess everyone here knew me on sight thanks to that whole I-got-Amber-fired thing.

She pointed to a huge arrangement of flowers sitting on the desk.

"These came for you," she said.

I put down my bags and opened the envelope almost hidden in the greenery. The card read: *I'm sorry.*

No name. But I knew who they were from.

Ty.

A lot of women would probably be flattered to receive a gorgeous bouquet of flowers from a good-looking, well off, really hot man.

Not me. Not if they were from Ty.

I grabbed the arrangement and stuffed it into the trash can, then picked up my shopping bags and stomped over to the elevator. I jabbed the call button six times. While I waited, I fumed and stared at the ruined flowers.

The elevator dinged. I rushed back to the trash can, pulled out the card, then got into the elevator.

A noise distracted me from my laptop.

I'd been thoroughly engrossed in plotting a search pattern for the Delicious handbag. Vegas teemed with shopping opportunities and I'd hit a few, but the mother lode lay on The Strip.

The Fashion Show Mall, City Center, Caesars Palace Forum Shops, Planet Hollywood's shops plus many more abounded with high-end merchandise. But these places weren't for the casual shopper, or the faint of heart—or someone wearing uncomfortable shoes.

I glanced at the clock on my night table. A little after one in the morning. Yeah, okay, I knew it was too late to be up when I had to go to work in the morning, but I couldn't sleep.

The noise sounded again. I realized it came from the hallway outside my room.

I put my laptop aside and sat up.

Ty flew into my head—which didn't suit me. I'd spent the last seven hours—and maxed out a credit card—trying to forget about him.

Was he outside? Had he dropped everything and rushed here to beg my forgiveness?

Somehow, I doubted it.

Another thought hit me: maybe motel guests were outside, the ones the oh-so-delightful desk clerk Whitley had claimed weren't booked into a room up here. Well, I'd show her. I'd prove they were here and get Amber's job back.

I jumped off the bed and jerked my door open.

A man stood in my doorway—tall, square shoulders, looming over me.

Yikes!

I hopped back to slam the door. He caught it before it latched and threw it open.

"Not exactly the reception I'd hoped for," he said.

I gasped as I realized it was Jack Bishop.

"What are you doing here?" I demanded. "You scared the crap out of me."

"You shouldn't open your door without knowing who's out there," Jack said.

"Thanks, that's so helpful," I told him.

He stepped in and closed the door. "Is that any way to treat an invited guest?"

"I don't recall inviting you," I said, though, honestly, I wasn't sorry to see him—which is awful, I know, but there it was.

"I've got the info you asked for."

"On Mike Ivan?" I asked, my heart rate finally slowing. "Already?"

"When called upon, I can deliver," Jack said, and his gaze dipped.

I had on sweatpants.

Jack didn't seem to notice.

I also had on a T-shirt and no bra.

Jack definitely noticed.

I yanked a sweatshirt out of my suitcase and pulled it on.

He walked to the window and peeked out, then turned to me again.

"Nice place," Jack said, not bothering to hide his sarcasm. "Is this the best your boyfriend could do for his employees?"

Just how Jack had found out I was in Vegas to help open a new Holt's store and was staying at this particular Culver Inn, I didn't know. Nor did I waste my breath to ask. Jack never gave away his sources.

"I doubt Ty checked out the motel personally," I said, then was annoyed with myself for defending him.

"You could move to a better place," Jack pointed out.

I'd thought of that. But since Holt's was picking up the tab and my funds were limited, I was stuck here.

"Want something to drink?" I asked, opening the little refrigerator wedged under the TV. "I have soda and bottled water."

When Jack shook his head, I said, "We could go out and get something."

"I like it here," he replied.

So did I—which was really awful of me, I know. Ty was my boyfriend—my official boyfriend. We'd done the bedroom bop on two continents, numerous times, numerous ways. We were a couple.

But Jack was *here*. I'd called, he'd dropped everything, and here he was. No ignored voicemail, no floral arrangement stand-in. Just him, here when I needed him. And Ty wasn't.

Still, Ty and I were officially a couple. I'm a stickler for things like that.

It's how I roll.

Jack must have read my reluctance because he pulled out the desk chair and sat down.

"So you're a murder suspect again, huh?" he asked.

How did he know these things? It's so cool being a private detective.

I hate my life.

It wasn't difficult to figure out how he knew most of it. I'd given him Courtney's name; the Internet had done the rest. And, of course, he'd probably made a couple of logical assumptions—I am, after all, *me*.

"What's the story on Mike Ivan?" I asked, and sat down in a chair across the desk from him.

"You first," Jack said.

"I knew Courtney in high school. She moved to Henderson and got hooked up with a guy named Tony Hubbard who'd been in prison," I said.

Jack made a little spinning motion with his hand. "Tell me something I don't already know."

"Tony told me—"

He sat forward. "You talked to Tony?"

"I went to their apartment to—"

"Alone?" He sounded kind of mad now.

"I expected Courtney's parents or friends would be there," I said.

"Stay away from Hubbard," Jack said.

"He left town, I think. He stole her TV and stereo, and disappeared," I said. "Anyway, Tony told me this guy

Mike Ivan had been looking for Courtney—but not in a good way. He'd come to Vegas trying to find her. Some problem from when she lived in L.A."

Jack just looked at me for a few minutes, like he was taking it all in, piecing it together.

"Mike Ivan runs a number of businesses in Los Angeles," he said.

"Courtney, supposedly, ran a fashion accessory line," I said. "Maybe that's how they knew each other."

"Could be," Jack agreed. "Ivan has money. He spreads it around."

"From what Tony said, I gather Courtney left L.A. rather suddenly. I wonder if there was bad blood between Mike and Courtney over money?" I asked. "Enough for him to murder her?"

We were quiet for a moment, then I said, "It doesn't make sense. If he murdered her, he'd never get his money back."

"Maybe he wanted to set an example," Jack said.

I got a weird feeling.

"Everything I hear about Mike Ivan says that he's clean. A legitimate businessman," Jack said. "You know what 'Ivan' is short for?"

My weird feeling got weirder.

"Ivanov," Jack said.

"Is that Russian?" I asked. "As in the . . ."

"The Russian mob."

Oh, crap.

CHAPTER 13

"He's really hot looking," Maya said. "Is he your boyfriend?"

The breakfast buffet at the Culver Inn was in full swing as Maya and I stood in the corner admiring Jack Bishop as he sat at a table across the room. Somehow he made drinking coffee and eating breakfast look sexy.

"Just a friend," I told her.

"Really?" She sounded as if she couldn't believe it.

I couldn't blame her.

Jack and I had shared a tense moment in my room last night when he'd gotten up to leave. He hesitated beside the bed. I did, too. Both of us were thinking the same thing—at least, that's my take on it.

But Ty may as well have been in the room, standing between us, because Jack left.

That's how he rolls.

Even that's hot.

I hadn't expected to see Jack here this morning. I didn't know where he spent the night.

Maybe it's just as well.

"Is he the guy who bought you the Louie Vuitton organizer?" Maya asked.

"Ty bought it for me. He's my official boyfriend," I explained. "Ty's a business executive. He looks so hot in his suits."

"Personally, I'm looking for something a little different in a boyfriend. I want to see him sweat, and I want to see him fix something," Maya said. She nodded toward Jack. "Who's this guy?"

"Jack Bishop. He's a private investigator," I said. "He drove up from Los Angeles last night."

Maya cut her eyes to me. I knew what she was thinking—not that I blamed her, of course—and she asked, "Where's Ty?"

"In L.A. He's very busy. Major responsibilities," I said, and found myself defending him—again.

"So Ty's in L.A. and Jack is here," Maya said. She shook her head. "Why aren't you dating Jack?"

Good question.

I had no good answer.

"Come over and meet him," I said.

Maya smoothed back her bangs and straightened her apron as Jack came to his feet and I introduced them.

"Maya made the muffins," I said. "Her own recipe. She's a fabulous cook."

"I imagine you do a lot of things well," Jack said.

Maya blushed.

"I've got to get to work," I said.

"Catch you later," Jack said.

Crossing the lobby, I glanced at the trash can. Ty's flowers were gone, which made me mad, sad, disappointed, hurt—something, I don't know what. Maybe all of those things.

I got in my car and drove to Holt's.

If I was late, I wondered if Fay might have the security guard at the door lock me out. Not that it would be so bad to miss work, especially with Jack in town—which was awful of me, I know—but I needed the day's pay.

I joined the crowd of employees who'd gathered around

the assignment flip chart on the easel at the front of the store.

"Check your assignment, okay, then clock in, then go to the training room, okay?" Fay said, her nasal voice grating on my nerves a little more than usual this morning. "After the meeting, go to your assigned department, okay? Everybody got that?"

Nobody said they didn't get it, but Fay started over anyway.

I hate my life.

But maybe a meeting wouldn't be so bad this morning, I decided as I worked my way to the assignment easel. I had a lot to think about.

"OMG!" Taylor exclaimed as she bounced on her toes beside me. "We're both in housewares! That's SC!"

"Yeah, so cool," I said, but with none of the excitement she displayed.

I don't think she noticed.

I clocked in, then found a seat in the last row—my customary spot for any type of meeting—in the training room. Employees filled the chairs, forming a wall of bodies in front of me, cutting off my view of the front of the room. Perfect. I could get a lot of thinking done—or take a nap—whichever came first.

Preston stepped up and addressed the employees, expressing concern over the unfortunate situation that had occurred—I'm pretty sure he meant Courtney's murder—thanking them for their understanding, their patience, their continued employment under difficult circumstances. His words turned to *blah, blah, blah*, and I drifted off.

The more I learned about Courtney's murder, the less sense any of it made. How could quiet, unassuming, not-so-bright Courtney have gotten hooked up with so many bad people? Tony Hubbard, a convicted felon, was bad enough, but the Russian mob?

Jack had told me that from everything he'd learned, this

Mike Ivan guy ran legitimate businesses. Maybe he was trying to distance himself from his roots—if my family was in the Russian mob and I wanted to go legit, I'd change my name, too.

But maybe he'd changed it to evade law enforcement and cover his tracks to some degree. That made sense.

Yet it didn't explain why the Russian mob, operating on a global scale, would be interested in a small, poorly run fashion accessory business like Courtney's.

Danielle floated into my mind. She'd probably know what the deal was between Courtney and Mike. I'd call her tonight and see—

"Haley? Haley?"

Preston's voice interrupted my thoughts, jarring me back to reality.

"Where are you, Haley?" he called.

I leaned sideways and saw him at the front of the room, squinting his eyes, scanning the crowd. I gave him a little wave.

"There she is," he announced, as if he'd just discovered life on Mars. "Stand up, Haley, stand up."

Reluctantly, I rose from my chair.

"Let's all give her a round of applause," Preston declared. He clapped his hands together. The employees turned to me and joined in.

Okay, this was kind of nice. I'd discovered a few dead bodies before—long story—but I'd never been recognized for my quick actions and on-the-scene leadership.

Effortlessly I channeled my mother's I-know-I'm-better-than-you-but-I-can-appear-humble smile along with her I'm-being-nice-because-it's-expected beauty queen wave.

"Haley has assured me you can all count on her," Preston said.

I guess that meant everyone in the store would know who to turn to if another dead body showed up. Not the best way to end a motivational meeting, to my way of thinking, but this was Preston's show.

"Okay, that's it. Thanks for your hard work," he said, which was our cue to get to work.

We filed out of the training room and, as I took the long way to the housewares department, Cliff wandered over.

"Hey, Dana, how's it going?" he asked.

I'd given up on correcting him. If he ever introduced me to his friends, I figured it would be better if they didn't know my real name anyway.

"Did you catch the *X-Files* marathon on the Sci-Fi Channel last night?" he asked.

"They're still showing the marathon?" I asked.

This seemed odd to me. Television channels never ran a marathon for days on end. But maybe they'd made an exception for the *X-Files*—either that or Cliff was watching a DVD.

"Later, Dana," he said, and ambled away.

Taylor was already in housewares cutting open the boxes stacked high on a U-boat.

"OMG!" she said, pulling out bundles of plastic wrapped place mats. "I can't believe I'm working in this department today!"

"I can hardly believe it, either," I said, with considerably less enthusiasm.

"It's like the RW," Taylor declared, her eyes wide.

RW . . . RW . . . I could think of no text translation.

So far, this was the most interesting thing about my workday, which is kind of sad, but there it was.

I hate my life.

"RW?" I asked.

"The reverse world," she told me. "You know, opposites."

"Oh, yeah," I said, as if I understood. I didn't, but this was easier.

"Yesterday I worked in women's clothing on the other side of the store," she said, gesturing like a flight attendant pointing out the emergency exits. "Now, today, I'm working here on the opposite side of the store. Get it? The reverse. The reverse world."

Yeah, I got it, but I was sorry that I had.

"Did you make this up yourself?" I asked.

"OMG! NW!"

No way? I could have sworn she had.

"Life is all about opposites. You have to respect the reverse world," Taylor told me. "You don't like your hair blond, you color it brown. You don't want to be fat, you get thin. You don't want to live in America, you move to China. Understand? It's SC!"

Taylor kept talking, but I drifted off, mindlessly stocking tablecloths and napkins on their designated shelf on the display unit. These boxes were lighter than the plates, but no more interesting.

Ty appeared in my thoughts, bringing all sorts of emotions with him. I didn't know what to think or feel anymore. And, of course, there was no way to figure it out, since he hadn't called.

I'd put my cell phone in my pocket but hadn't felt it vibrate all morning. I checked it. Nothing.

Just because I'd told him not to ever, ever, *ever* call me didn't actually mean I didn't want him to call. He should have known that. He was my official boyfriend. Honestly, what sort of relationship was this?

I centered my thoughts on my upcoming trip to the upscale stores along The Strip and my hunt for the Delicious handbag, and my spirits lifted a little. I planned to attend a meeting of the handbag club Maya had told me about, so that made me feel a little better, too.

"Excuse me?" someone called.

Lost in thought, I reverted to sales clerk mode and immediately ducked down, then remembered where I was and stood up again.

A guy pushing a Z-rail of blouses smiled at me.

"The food is terrific at Bally's Steakhouse Restaurant," he said.

I just looked at him. He looked back.

"Okay," I said.

He smiled, and went on his way.

Jeez, that was kind of nice. None of the employees had seemed all that friendly before—that whole dead-body-in-the-store thing had soured the mood, I suppose—but maybe that was changing. Preston must have mentioned I was from out of town this morning—maybe I should stop drifting off during meetings—and the employees who lived in Henderson were taking it to heart.

Evidence of Taylor's RW—reverse world?

Weirder things had happened.

Another day of my life slipped away. I clocked out and headed for the front of the store.

"The Red Rock Resort is awesome," a guy next to me said. "I think they have fireworks out there."

"Fireworks are great," I agreed.

He smiled and walked away.

"Dana, guess what happened," Cliff said, falling into step beside me. "My car got stolen."

I expected him to tell me it had been beamed up, but he didn't.

"That's too bad," I said. "A car like that won't easily be replaced."

"Yeah, I know," he said. "I needed to get something out of it for my afternoon break and, like, wow, man, it wasn't in the parking lot."

"Did you report it to the police?" I asked.

"Yeah, sure. I think. Well, I'm pretty sure . . . kind of."

I felt bad that his car—such as it was—had been stolen. He'd taken me to get my tire fixed—though I wasn't sure he remembered it—so I figured I owed him one.

Besides, I had nothing going tonight. Jack hadn't told me his plans this morning and I hadn't heard from him all day, so I figured I was on my own.

"Do you need a ride home?" I asked.

"Eric and Dwayne are picking me up," Cliff said. "We're investigating a sighting tonight."

"A UFO sighting?"

"Aliens," he said.

I imagined Eric and Dwayne rolling up in a lead-lined, early '80s Winnebago with a green Martian painted on the back under the caption HONK IF YOU BELIEVE THE TRUTH IS OUT THERE.

"Eric saw them last night," Cliff said.

"Aliens?" I asked. "Where?"

"The Rio."

"The Rio Hotel and Casino in Vegas?" I asked.

"Everybody loves the buffet there," Cliff said.

I couldn't argue with that.

"Do you think the aliens stole your car?" I asked.

"Oh, man, I hadn't thought of that." Cliff slapped himself on the forehead. "Well, at least they didn't get my field investigation kit. I had it at home. Or . . . I think it's at home. Maybe."

"I'm sure Eric or Dwayne will let you borrow theirs," I said.

"Yeah, we're tight like that," Cliff said. "See you later, Dana."

I held back a little and let him leave the store ahead of me—just in case Eric and Dwayne were waiting—then went outside. The parking lot in front of the store was emptying out. I stood by the door digging in my purse—a fabulous Gucci—for my keys, when a car whipped to the curb and hit the brakes.

My heart jumped. It was a gorgeous blue, BMW Z4 Roadster convertible. The top was down. Jack sat behind the wheel. I knew he owned a Land Rover. I'd never seen this car before.

"Must have been a cool ride here from L.A. in this," I said and walked over.

He gave me his sexiest grin. "Want to go for a ride?"

"Go for a ride? No way. I want to *drive it*."

His grin got sexier. He stepped from the car and eased close. I felt the heat from his body and smelled his cologne.

"You know what they say," he whispered. "What happens in Vegas stays in Vegas."

Oh, wow. This was way hot.

Another car rolled to a stop, nosed up against Jack's BMW. A black Lincoln Town Car. The driver's side door opened. A uniformed chauffeur jumped out and opened the back door.

Ty got out.

CHAPTER 14

Ty and Jack spent a few minutes doing some male whose-is-bigger posturing, puffing out their chests, squaring their shoulders, stretching up to see who's tallest—which was all really hot—while shaking hands and pretending to like each other. Jack left. The chauffeur drove the Town Car a few yards away and waited.

I wondered if I was looking at my future ex-boyfriend. Had he flown all this way to break up with me? Would he have sent me flowers if that were his intention?

Yes, he would. Aside from being a sometimes crappy boyfriend, Ty was still a nice guy.

My heart thudded in my chest, waiting for him to say something.

"I'm sorry," he said.

His suit jacket hung open, his tie was pulled down, and he'd popped the top button on his shirt. A few strands of hair were out of place. This was the closest to disheveled Ty ever came.

He looked tired, too. Something more than just lack of sleep.

I should have been angry with him and, deep down, I was. But that warm gooey feeling in my stomach I always get when he's around told me I still cared for him.

"I know I haven't been the best boyfriend in the world. I know I haven't treated you the way you deserve to be treated. I get that, and I'm sorry," Ty said. "But I've always been up front with you about it. I told you from the start that I can't be a twenty-four-seven guy."

It was true. He'd said it the first night we'd been alone in his apartment and were about to make love, only to be interrupted by some problem involving Holt's. We'd had this conversation before.

A wave of here-comes-the-breakup-speech swamped me. Not a great feeling.

"That's why we should move in together," Ty said.

I just looked at him. Had I heard him right? I hadn't drifted off or anything—at least, I didn't think I had.

"If you move in with me, we'll be together every night," Ty said. "We'll wake up together every morning."

He wanted us to move in together? For real?

"I can't be the guy who's always there, Haley. But I can give you a comfortable life." He shook his head, looking troubled. "I didn't know you were struggling with your school expenses. I thought you had it covered."

Guess I shouldn't have been surprised to hear him say that. Last thing Ty knew, I'd come into a whopping big sum of money—long story—and he probably figured I still had it. I'd never gotten around to telling him that the money was long gone.

He grinned a little. "I know you well enough that you didn't ask your parents for it."

I grinned back. He knew me pretty well, for sure.

"I can pay your college tuition. Books, fees, everything," Ty said. "You're just about to graduate by now, aren't you?"

No way was I answering that one.

"I'll cover everything," he said. "Rent, your car payment. You can go to school full time. You can quit work."

My heart leaped. Quit my job at Holt's? Could my dreams really come true?

Ty eased a little closer. "I wouldn't care how much money you spent, Haley. You can buy whatever you want."

Now I was speechless.

"I don't want to lose you, Haley. You're the magic in my life. Please say you'll move in with me."

I guess he mistook my stunned silence as reluctance.

He nodded. "Think it over."

I opened my mouth, but nothing came out.

"Just promise me you'll think about it," Ty said.

He touched his palm to my cheek. My knees wobbled.

"I'll take care of you, Haley. You'll never want for anything. I swear."

He leaned down and kissed me. Not a hot we're-about-to-make-love kiss. This one was tender, caring, loving.

"I have to go," Ty said.

That snapped me out of my move-in-together stupor.

"Already?" I asked. "You just got here."

"I have a meeting."

Oh my God. Ty had flown all the way here from Los Angeles just to tell me these things in person? Wow.

"I'll give you a ride to McCarran," I said. The airport was only a few miles away, but it would be great to spend the time together.

"The jet is waiting for me," Ty said, and gestured for the Town Car.

I'd seen a sign for the Henderson Executive Airport on St. Rose Parkway.

"The jet?" I asked. "You own a jet?"

"Holt's owns it, technically," Ty said.

The Town Car rolled up. The chauffer hopped out and opened the rear door.

"Come to L.A. with me," Ty said.

"What—now?"

I was as spontaneous as the next gal—and I'd always wanted to join the Mile High Club—but I wasn't ready to go along with Ty's plan just yet. And, of course, I was a murder suspect and had been told not to leave town.

No reason to mention that to Ty.

"I've got a lot of thinking to do," I said.

He nodded. "Think about where you'd like to live. We can buy a new place, wherever you want. Do you like the beach?"

"Of course."

"I'll call you," Ty said. He gave me another kiss—a quick one—got into the Town Car and pulled away. I watched him disappear onto Valle Verde.

What the hell had just happened?

Something stronger was definitely called for after the conversation I'd just had with Ty, but I settled for a mocha frappuccino. I went through the Starbucks drive-through and headed for the Culver Inn.

Honestly, I could barely stomach the thought of going in that place right now. It wasn't particularly pleasant under the best of circumstances, and at the moment it seemed especially dismal.

Jack had been in my room last night, and I knew he wouldn't come back tonight. Yes, I knew it was for the best, and that he was taking the high road—even though he'd showed up at Holt's wanting to take me for a ride in a hot sports car. But the point was that we were both respecting my relationship with Ty. Jack would expect that Ty would be with me at the Culver Inn tonight or, more likely, that he'd take me to someplace really fabulous.

Only Ty wouldn't be here, either.

Just moments ago I'd had two—count them, two—

really hot guys orbiting me like smoldering fireballs, and now both of them were gone. So here I was, alone, self-medicating with a mocha frappuccino, trying to find a way to fill my evening.

What's up with my life, anyway?

A chill swept over me—and it wasn't from the frappuccino. That curse. That stupid curse. Could it really have caused all this?

I pulled into the Culver Inn parking lot, left my car in the check-in lane, dashed up to my room, and retrieved my laptop. On the way back through the lobby, I picked up a map of Vegas from the display of brochures by the elevator, got into my car again, and took off.

Last night the search pattern for the Delicious handbag I'd been formulating had been interrupted when Jack had shown up at my door, so I now intended to finish it.

Yeah, okay, I knew it wasn't the most exciting way to spend my evening, but I didn't have lots of choices here. It beat investigating an alien sighting with Cliff, Eric, and Dwayne, I guess.

Although the Rio buffet would be good.

If Marcie had been in town, we'd have gotten together with beer and snacks—heavy on the chocolate—and discussed this new chapter in my moving-in-with-Ty saga in depth. I hadn't heard from her today, so I figured that meant her sprained ankle hurt too much and she was probably floating someplace above reality on prescription painkillers.

Lucky her.

I thought about calling Maya. She was my Henderson BFF, but I didn't know her well enough to discuss the whole should-I-move-in-with-Ty situation. Besides, explaining our history would take forever.

Maybe it was for the best, I decided, as I sucked down

the last of my frappuccino. I didn't really know how I felt about moving in with Ty—or the things he'd offered to do for me. I needed time to process it.

I pulled into another—yes, another—Starbucks. Inside, I bought another mocha frappuccino—only because it was rude to take up space and not drink something, of course. Luckily, I had my pageant queen mother's metabolism and could burn off calories quicker than a supermodel could make the turn at the end of a Paris catwalk.

I set up my laptop at a table by the window and got down to business.

The search for the Delicious handbag had proved more difficult and complex than I'd experienced before—which was saying a lot. Truthfully, I've got mad skills when it comes to hunting down something important like a fabulous handbag.

Yet, oddly enough, I didn't like looking for something that was lost—like keys, or a wallet, or a cell phone. The whole process irritates me worse than finding an expired 50-percent-off coupon at the bottom of my purse.

Probably just as well I didn't work for the FBI's missing persons bureau. My what-the-hell-they'll-turn-up-sooner-or-later attitude probably wouldn't go over very well.

Since I'd exhausted my usual search methods, I decided to kick up my pursuit of the Delicious to the next level—color coding. I broke out my marking pens and the map of The Strip.

Of course, before I started any project on my laptop—yeah, okay, mostly it was homework—I first checked my e-mail and my Facebook page. I saw that Stephanie Holden, Courtney's Vegas friend, had contacted me.

Wow. That surprised me a little. Guess she and Courtney had been close if she was willing to talk to a stranger. I dialed the number she'd given me.

"Oh, yes, Haley, of course," Stephanie said, when I introduced myself. She sounded tense and rushed. "I'm glad you—hang on."

She covered the phone, then came back on the line.

"Look, I'll talk to you," she said, "but—wait a minute."

Stephanie shielded the phone again. I heard muffled shouts in the background. She came back and said, "I don't want any trouble. Is that clear?"

Less than a minute into the conversation and already I was lost.

"It's clear," I said, which wasn't true, of course, but, oh well.

"I liked Courtney," she said. "But friendships only go so far."

I got a weird feeling.

"I did what I had to do. Can you understand that?" Stephanie asked. She sounded upset, a little desperate maybe.

Oh my God. Was she telling me she'd somehow been involved with Courtney's murder?

I had no clue what the heck she was getting at so what could I say but, "Sure."

"All right, then. Come over," Stephanie said, sounding relieved. "I'll explain everything that happened."

She gave me her address. I wrote it on the map of Vegas in bright blue marker.

"After seven. Not before—not a minute before," Stephanie said.

"Okay. After seven."

"My husband isn't here," she said, as if that explained something, and hung up.

I closed my phone, not sure what had just happened—I was getting a lot of that tonight.

One thing for certain, I didn't feel so great about showing up at her house at a designated hour—one she'd absolutely insisted on. I mean, I didn't know her or anything, and from the things she said, Stephanie might very well have been involved in Courtney's murder.

Was she taking the time between our phone conversation and my arrival at her house to load a gun? Did she intend to confess, clear her conscience, then blow me away?

Not a great feeling.

Maybe I should call Jack.

I stared out the window at the Starbucks parking lot, thinking over my options.

Jack would know how to handle the situation, plus I was sure he was always packing heat. What's the point of having a private detective for a friend if you couldn't call on him at a time like this? Jack had always been there for me before. I knew he wouldn't let me down.

Of course, Jack would ask why I wasn't with Ty tonight. I didn't want to tell him that Ty had flown in just for a few minutes, then left again. It would make Ty look like a jerk and no way would I do that. Plus, it might make me look like a complete idiot for putting up with it, and I wasn't anxious to have Jack think of me that way.

For a split second, I considered calling Detective Dailey just so someone would know where to start searching for my body if I didn't show up for work tomorrow morning. Just as quickly, I disregarded the idea. The farther I stayed from the homicide detectives, the better.

If something went down at Stephanie's house tonight, the detectives would eventually look at my Facebook page and see that she'd contacted me. It wasn't much comfort, but it was all I could get at the moment.

On the brighter side, Stephanie might very well confess to the murder and stand by quietly while I called Detective Dailey with the news that I'd solved the case for him, and

let him know where he could come to pick up his murderer.

I'd insist he bring Detective Webster, of course.

I gathered my things, the way-cool scene playing in my
mind, and left Starbucks.

CHAPTER 15

The GPS unit in my car routed me to the 215. Traffic was kind of heavy, but since I routinely drove the L.A. freeways, it didn't bother me. In fact, I kind of enjoyed it. Driving was a perfect opportunity to think over major problems. I did it with ease.

It's a gift, really.

Ty swept into my mind, his image bringing with it his offer to pay my college tuition. No way had I expected that. I figured I'd be doing well if he just didn't break up with me.

But Ty being Ty—he's incredibly generous—hadn't just left it at paying for everything so I could finish school without worry about money; he'd offered to pay my living expenses as well. Plus he'd be okay with it if I quit my job.

I merged onto the northbound 15 toward North Las Vegas.

It all sounded great. Really. And, better still, did it mean that the ridiculous curse—which I still didn't believe in— had finally vanished, or floated away, or worn off, or whatever curses did when they were done?

Really, I'd like to get in some gambling while I was here.

Then another thought hit me: did it mean something that I hadn't jumped at his offer when he'd made it in the

Holt's parking lot? Did *I* not want to move in with *him*? Or was something else going on?

Yeah, okay, enough thinking about that.

I exited the freeway and wound through a residential neighborhood of middle class homes with front yards filled with rocks instead of grass—translation: desert landscaping—and SUVs parked out front.

Stephanie Holden—and her husband, presumably, though she'd made a point of saying he wouldn't be home—lived on the corner in a house that, by design, looked a lot like every other place in the neighborhood.

I left my Honda at the curb. The sun was going down. Long shadows stretched across cactus plants lining the sidewalk. I rang the doorbell.

Stephanie answered the door and, luckily, didn't cut lose with an AK-47 or anything. She looked like, if she had an AK-47, she'd turn it on herself.

I would, if I looked like her.

I figured her for around my age, probably, tall, with easily a hundred pounds on me. Regrowth from hell left her hair brown on top and blond from the ears down. No makeup. A T-shirt with stains on the front. Stretch pants that had reached their limit. Chipped toenail polish that screamed for a fresh pedi.

She stood in the doorway looking at me in the fading light and said, "You look fabulous."

"Thanks," I said, though it wasn't a compliment. It was more an I-hate-you-for-looking-fabulous-when-I-look-like-crap kind of thing.

Stephanie sighed heavily. "You don't remember me, do you."

It wasn't a question, more an accusation.

I got a weird feeling.

"Monroe High School?" she asked.

My weird feeling turned really weird.

"Senior year? Mrs. Moore's English class? Mrs. Winn's history class?" she said. "I was Stephanie Patterson back then."

Oh my God. I hadn't recognized her at all. But I'd gone to high school with her. She was my age. She was my age and she *looked this bad.* How was that possible?

"I had kids," Stephanie said, as if she'd read my mind.

She stepped back and let me into the house.

The living room and dining room combo area was huge, made to look bigger by the vaulted ceiling. The place was mostly empty space. A couch, rocker, coffee and end tables, flat panel TV. No pictures on the walls, no artificial flowers, no fake ficus tree in the corner. The fireplace mantel was lined with photos of babies, some in their own frames, others stuck into the corners of frames.

Toys were scattered across the floor and atop the couch and rocking chair. A laundry basket running over with clothes sat by the fireplace. Another pile of laundry lay in the rocker. I glimpsed the adjoining kitchen. Two high chairs, overturned cups on the table, and dirty dishes overflowing in the sink. The place smelled vaguely of pee.

"How many children do you have?" I asked. I tried to sound interested but I don't think I pulled it off.

"Four."

Yikes!

"Sorry I didn't recognize you," I said.

Stephanie raked the toys off the couch and onto the floor, and gestured for me to sit. She did the same for the rocker.

"Four kids in five years," she said. "The last were twins."

"Wow," I managed to say. It was the nicest thing I could think of.

"They're all in bed now," Stephanie said. "They go down at seven—and not a minute after."

"Where's your husband?" I asked.

"Business trip."

Lucky him.

"How about some wine?" Stephanie asked.

She looked so exhausted I didn't want to take her up on her offer—plus, I'd seen her kitchen.

Before I could answer, she disappeared into the kitchen. At my elbow was an end table cluttered with Legos, Matchbox cars, and an assortment of baby bottles and juice cups. A photo of the kids showed the four of them dressed in red, standing beside a fake Christmas tree. Their names were engraved in the frame.

The oldest was a boy named Avian—jeez, why didn't she just name him beat-me-up—standing next to a girl named Shannon. The twins, looking none too happy, were named Jim and Joe. Apparently, Stephanie's enthusiasm for names had waned as the kids popped out.

She came back from the kitchen with two glasses of red wine, drinking hers as she crossed the room.

"Thanks," I said, as she passed me the glass. I took a sip, then placed it on the end table.

I wasn't all that anxious to stroll down high school memory lane—nor be in this house any longer than I had to—so I got down to business.

"I guess you and Courtney stayed in touch after high school?" I asked.

"Not really," Stephanie said.

She plopped down in the rocking chair and started sorting the clothing on the floor into piles, wine glass in hand. Tiny socks here—*sip*—tiny pants there—*sip*—tiny shirts over there—*sip*.

"I don't—can't—get out much, so I'm on the Internet a lot," Stephanie said. She cut her gaze to me. "I see you're working undercover. Something about national security?"

Jeez, I'd forgotten all about posting that on the Monroe High School alumni site. Nothing to do now but run with it.

"I can't really discuss it," I told her.

Stephanie nodded as if that were just another reason to hate me, drank more wine, and went back to sorting clothes.

"I saw Courtney's info on the school site back last year sometime, when she was still living in California," Stephanie said. "That fashion business she ran. It looked like—well, it looked like typical Courtney."

I'd visited the Monroe High School site just a few days ago, but Courtney's page had stated nothing more than that she lived in Henderson. She must have taken down the info about the business she was involved in. I figured she didn't want her old classmates to know how bad it was doing—not that I blamed her, of course.

"I contacted Courtney on Facebook," Stephanie said. "When she moved to Henderson, we got together a few times. You know, for old times' sake."

"Did she talk about her business?" I asked.

"Oh, yes, she was thrilled with it. All sorts of big plans. Upscale this, and ultra that. Artisans and exclusive clientele," Stephanie said, sipping and sorting more quickly now. "A partner who knew everything about everything, of course."

"Danielle?" I asked.

Stephanie waved a sock around, as if to dismiss my question.

"I guess that was her name. She convinced Courtney to come to Vegas." Stephanie gave a disgusted grunt. "Seems to me L.A. would be the place to run a fashion business—or New York, maybe. But what do I know? I'm just a mom with four kids."

It seemed odd to me, too. The Los Angeles Garment District was home to all sorts of textile manufacturers, so it followed that Courtney would want to live near there.

Unless she was hiding from Mike Ivan.

"Anyway, our attempt at rekindling our high school friendship didn't amount to much. Our lives were too different," Stephanie said, and tipped back her wine glass again. "Courtney had a boyfriend keeping her busy. He called her every time we were out somewhere."

"Tony Hubbard," I said.

Stephanie pushed the piles of clothes toward me with her foot. "No, his name wasn't Tony. I'd have remembered that. My husband's name is Tony."

Okay, this was odd. I had no idea Courtney had a boyfriend besides Tony Hubbard.

"Was his name Mike?" I asked. I doubted it, but it was worth a try.

"How the hell could I possibly remember?"

Stephanie got to her feet, one hand on her hip, the other clutching the wine glass. She glared down at me like she'd suddenly morphed into some kind of angry, crazy-ass Decepticon and wanted to crush me and the entire world.

"Look, Haley, I did what I did, and that's it. I don't know how you found out, but you did," Stephanie told me. "So now we're just going to have to deal with it."

Oh, crap. What was happening?

My senses rocketed to high alert—like when you go into the mall and somehow you just *know* there's a sale at Nordstrom.

Was she about to tell me she'd murdered Courtney? Was she really a complete psycho masquerading as a suburban mom?

She'd lulled me into a false sense of security, plied me with wine. She'd piled a mountain of toys and clothes at my feet. I'd never make it to the front door through this obstacle course.

I glanced around the room. She could have hidden a pistol, a rifle—a bazooka—anywhere in this mess.

Was her husband really away on business, or had she shot him and buried him beneath the desert landscaping in the back yard? Not that I blamed her, really. If my husband had gotten me pregnant with four kids in five years, I might be tempted as well.

"It was me," Stephanie said. "I'm the one who told the detectives how you hated Courtney in high school because she stole Robbie Freedman from you."

I just looked at her, relieved that she wasn't about to kill me, but disappointed that she hadn't confessed to killing Courtney.

"But I guess you already figured that out, Haley, with your undercover work and your national security job," Stephanie said. She gulped down her wine. "Courtney and I were friends. I always liked her. I told those detectives what had happened back in high school because it was my civic duty. And, besides, I didn't want to get into trouble for being an accessory to murder after the fact, or whatever they call it—certainly not to protect *you*."

I'd had enough of Stephanie's my-life-sucks-and-I-hate-you-because-yours-doesn't attitude. I got to my feet and left. I didn't even say good-bye, just walked out the door, got into my car, and drove away.

I made a mental note to call Fay and tell her I'd be late coming to work in the morning. I intended to stop and have my tubes tied on the way in.

My room at the Culver Inn didn't seem quite so bad when I crawled into the bed. Anyplace would be better than Stephanie's house. I switched off the light, hoping I could fall asleep right away, but too many things kept popping up in my mind.

The list of reasons for me to dislike being at Stephanie's house tonight was understandably long and justified. But I couldn't help thinking maybe there was more to it than the obvious.

Had I seen my future with Ty in Stephanie's living room? If I moved in with Ty, would he expect me to cook and clean? Wash his underwear?

Oh my God. What if I got pregnant? Ty was hardly around now. What would it be like if we had kids? Would I turn into kind-of-psycho Stephanie?

Not a great feeling.

I rolled over and stared at the ceiling. Dim light filtered in around the curtains, casting thin shadows across the hopelessly out of style popcorn ceiling.

Maybe tonight I'd seen my could-have-been past.

Robbie Freedman. What if he'd dated me instead of Courtney? I'd never learned why the two of them had broken up after high school, but what if Robbie and I had dated and stayed together? What if we'd gotten married?

Would I *already* be kind-of-psycho Stephanie?

Maybe she and I would have been best friends, somehow, filling our days changing diapers and organizing play groups, and our nights trying to forget it all with bottles of red wine.

Yeah, okay, enough of that scenario, I decided, and sat up.

The image of Jack bloomed in my mind.

Where was he tonight, I wondered? Had he gone back to Los Angeles? Was he still here in Vegas? I imagined him at a hot club on The Strip, looking hot, acting hot, hanging out with hot people.

I wondered, too, if he was thinking about me—which

was really bad, I know. Was he wondering if I was having hot sex with Ty right now? Would he care?

My cell phone rang. Ty, according to the caller I.D. I glanced at the clock on my bedside table and saw that it was after two.

Okay, that was weird. Ty almost never stayed up past ten o'clock.

"What's wrong?" I asked.

"I figured your voicemail would pick up." His voice sounded deep and mellow. "I couldn't sleep. I was lying here missing you."

Jeez, what kind of crappy girlfriend was I, thinking about Jack and hot sex, when my official boyfriend was calling just to tell me he missed me?

"Want to have phone sex?" I asked.

Yeah, okay, maybe that was overcompensating a little.

"That doesn't really work for me," Ty said, and chuckled. "I'm more of a hands-on kind of guy, as you know."

Oh, yeah, I knew that all right.

"Have you thought about our earlier conversation?" he asked.

Our conversation about moving in together.

This probably wasn't a good time to mention that I'd also been thinking about Jack Bishop and Robbie Freedman.

"Of course," I said.

"Good," Ty said. "As long as you're thinking about it."

I appreciated that he wasn't pushing me.

"Have you checked your e-mail?" Ty asked.

"Not in a while," I said.

"I sent you something," he said.

"Go to sleep," I said. "You have a meeting in the morning."

"How do you know?"

"You *always* have a meeting in the morning," I said.

He laughed softly, sending a warm shiver over me.

"Good night," he said.

Luckily, we didn't go through that whole who's-going-to-hang-up-first thing. I said good night and we hung up.

No way could I go to sleep now. I got my laptop into the bed and opened the e-mail he'd sent. His message simply read, Do you like this one?

Attached were photos of a beachfront house in Malibu, waves crashing only yards from the deck, and interior shots of the gorgeous living room, kitchen, and bedrooms.

My jaw sagged open and I just stared.

Wow, he'd remembered. Ty had actually remembered that I'd said I liked beach homes. He'd even looked them up, found one, and e-mailed it to me.

Jeez, he really was serious about us moving in together.

A noise sounded in the hallway and a door slammed, jarring me back to the Culver Inn. Then I remembered Amber losing her job and the oh-so-lovely Whitley insisting no one but me was booked into this wing. I launched myself out of bed, yanked open the door, and leaped into the hallway.

Empty.

I ran to the end of the hallway and looked down the corridor toward the elevator.

Nobody.

I ran back, threw open the door to the stairwell at the end of the hall.

Silence.

I walked back into the hallway, stopped still, and listened.

Not a sound.

I figured that whoever had been booked into a room had to be staying in one of the two across the hall from mine. Otherwise, I'd have heard them through our shared, common wall.

But who were they? And why did they keep such late hours?

Night prowlers were the norm at the casinos on The Strip. Hardcore gamblers stayed up all night, feeding the slots, obsessing over the turn of a card, the spin of a wheel. You'd see them at breakfast, sometimes, with a bleary-eyed what-have-I-done look on their faces.

Serious gamblers didn't usually stay in Henderson, in places like the Culver Inn.

So who was staying in one of the rooms across the hall from me?

CHAPTER 16

"He's here," Maya said, and immediately smoothed her hair back and straightened her apron.

I didn't need to turn around to know that it was Jack Bishop who'd gotten her all excited this early in the morning, in the middle of the Culver Inn breakfast buffet service. I did turn around, though, because Jack was always great to look at.

He didn't disappoint. Freshly showered, shaved, hair damp, dressed in jeans and a white Henley shirt just snug enough to show off his chest.

Oh, yeah, Maya's day—and mine—was off to a great start.

"Morning," Jack said, joining us near the kitchen door. He grinned. "Did I interrupt something?"

Maya and I had been making plans for this evening before we'd gotten distracted and flustered over Jack walking in. No way would we admit it, of course.

"We're going to Macy's tonight," I told him. "Want to come?"

"It's free giveaway week," Maya said.

Jack paused. "Free—what?"

Jeez, how was it men didn't know the simplest things? *Everybody* knew what free giveaway week was.

"At the cosmetics counter," I told him. "You buy makeup or something that costs thirty bucks or more and they give you free stuff."

"In a special bag," Maya added.

"So you two both need makeup?" Jack asked.

Maya and I glanced at each other like he'd lost his mind.

"No," I said. "Of course not."

"We're just buying something to get the free items," Maya explained.

"So these free items are cosmetics you need?" he asked.

"No," I said. What's up with him? Why didn't he *get it?*

Jack frowned. "So it's this special bag you want?"

"Not really," I said.

"I never use the free bag," Maya said.

"Me, either," I agreed.

"So let me get this straight," Jack said. "You buy something you don't want, to get something you don't need, and it comes with a bag you'll never use?"

Finally, he got it.

"Exactly," I told him.

Maya nodded, pleased too that he understood, then pulled her cell phone from her apron pocket.

"I've got to take this," she said, and disappeared into the kitchen.

Jack glanced around at the Culver Inn guests eating at tables.

"So where's Prince Charming?" he asked.

I took that to mean Ty.

"In L.A."

Jack raised his brows. "Already?"

No way was I answering that question.

"Want something to eat?" I asked.

He rolled with my abrupt change in topic.

"Maya told me yesterday about wanting to start her own bakery," Jack said.

Hum . . . so Jack had stayed yesterday morning after I'd left and he and Maya had talked. Interesting.

"She'd be further along if that jackass Bradley, who runs the place, would recommend her to the other motels in the chain," I said. "She needs the money to finish college and get her business going."

"Bradley, huh?" Jack mumbled the name with more than a little contempt.

"He's a real piece of work," I said. "But since his family owns the chain, there isn't much anybody can do. It's his way or the highway."

"Is that so?" Jack asked. He was quiet for a minute, then said, "I'm heading back to L.A. this morning."

A wave of disappointment hit me—which was really bad, I know—but I tried not to let it show.

I figured he'd been investigating Courtney's murder while he was in Vegas and he'd accomplished everything he could. Jack never told me anything until he was ready. Still, I wanted to know if he'd learned something—especially since I was a suspect.

"Courtney had another boyfriend," I said.

With Jack, I'd learned long ago that I had to give before I could expect to receive. This didn't suit me, of course, but since I wasn't the one who could hop into a way-cool BMW Z4 and leave town in style, I didn't have much choice.

"Before she got hooked up with Tony Hubbard," I added. "Any idea who it was?"

Jack didn't respond, just listened. "I'll check it out," he finally said.

When he didn't say anything more, I got a little annoyed.

"Did you learn anything new?" I asked. "From the cops or anybody?"

"Same story as before," Jack said. "You're their favorite suspect."

Oh, crap.

Jack opened the kitchen door and leaned in. I saw Maya still on the phone. She covered the mouthpiece and said something to him. He answered, then left the kitchen. I couldn't hear what either of them said—which wasn't my business in the first place, but still, I was curious.

"Catch you later," Jack said to me.

He didn't leave, though, just stood there looking at me. I wasn't sure if he wanted to say something—or wanted me to say something.

"Ty went back to L.A. after I talked to him at Holt's," I said.

"Is that so?" he asked.

"He wants me to move in with him," I said. "But I don't know."

"Big decision," he agreed.

We just looked at each other for another long minute.

"I've got to get to work," I said.

He nodded toward the exit to the parking lot. "And I've got to hit the road."

Still, he stood there. I stood there, too. It wasn't that goofy tenth-grade-can't-think-of-anything-to-say kind of thing. Something different. Something deeper.

I don't know what it was. Jack didn't seem to know, either. He left and I watched as he climbed into the Beemer he'd parked in the check-in lane and drove away.

Yeah, okay, I knew I shouldn't have told him that stuff about Ty and me. I didn't know what it was with Jack. He made me do the craziest things—without even doing anything.

"Haley! Haley!"

Maya barreled out of the kitchen and grabbed my arm. Her eyes were round, her mouth open—two indications that something absolutely *huge* had happened

"That was Arlene," she said, still clutching her cell phone as if it were Arlene herself. "She's the one who gets all the jobs for the convention centers. Remember I told you? I work for her sometimes handing out brochures at conventions, doing hospitality at banquets and things?"

"Yeah, I—"

She burst ahead—another indication that something absolutely *huge* had happened.

Oh my God. This was getting better and better—way better than free giveaway week at Macy's.

"She wants me to work for her at a convention." Maya took two deep breaths, trying to calm herself. "A *handbag* convention."

The earth stopped rotating—I swear. Time stood still. Really.

Oh my God. *Oh my God.* Had I heard her right?

I drew in two deep breaths, too, trying to calm myself, bracing myself just in case I hadn't heard her correctly.

"Did you say a *handbag* convention?" I asked. Actually, I think I whispered it.

"Yes."

"A handbag convention." I didn't ask. I just said it, a little louder this time.

"Yes."

"A handbag convention—for real?" I'm pretty sure I shouted that.

"Yes!" Maya shouted, too. "It's at the Mandalay Bay."

"When?"

"Next week."

"Next week?"

"Yes!"

"Oh my God!"

"All the designers will be there," Maya said.

"Oh my God!"

"Handbags everywhere. Fall lines will be previewed. New designers nobody's ever seen before."

"Oh my God!"

"Fashion shows. Displays. Accessories."

"Accessories?" I screamed.

Okay, now I felt dizzy. Maya grabbed my hand. She seemed kind of wobbly, too. We helped each other to an empty table and dropped into chairs.

We both just sat there for a few minutes, trying to recover, trying to take it all in.

Maya pulled herself together first. I had to hand it to her.

"Arlene says some of her usual people cancelled last minute," she said. "She asked me if I could do it and, of course, I said yes. I gave her your name, too. We can do it together."

I froze. What was this? Did she just say I was going to have to *work* at the handbag convention?

I guess Maya saw my hesitation.

"It will be great," she said. "We get to go in before the public. We get to see everything first. We can come and go to any of the displays or events, anytime we want, for as long as we want, because we'll have unlimited employee passes."

Okay, now she was talking. And, besides, as I'd learned long ago: just because you had a job didn't mean you had to actually work.

"Plus," Maya said, "we'll get paid."

I could see where that was a definite benefit for Maya—and me, too, really.

The biggest benefit for me was that if I saw a handbag I absolutely had to have—and I was certain I would—I could buy it on the spot before anyone else even saw it.

I jerked straight up in the chair.

Oh my God. They were bound to have a Delicious handbag there.

"So you'll do it?" Maya asked.

"Hell, yes," I vowed.

Really, what could possibly go wrong with my day now that I would be getting a sneak preview to a world-class handbag convention—and the first shot at a Delicious handbag?

Nothing. Not even at Holt's.

I breezed through my day unloading U-boats of boxes filled with table linens, flatware, plates, cookware, glasses, pots, and pans. My thoughts were consumed with the handbag convention, what I'd see there, what events might be scheduled, what gorgeous handbags I could buy.

Once or twice throughout the day, I may have actually put an item or two in its designated display location.

Fay walked up as I was forcing a dozen casserole dishes into a spot probably meant for place mats.

"I need you to stop that, okay?" she said.

Even her nasal tone didn't grate on my nerves as much as usual, and I actually stopped what I was doing.

"I need you to help with training, okay?" Fay asked.

She wanted *me* to help with *training*? Had I passed into another dimension somewhere between stocking the wine glasses and the steak knives?

"Preston says you're one of our most experienced employees, okay?" Fay said. "So I need you to help with training. Can you do that?"

I'd never trained anyone in my life.

"Sure," I said.

"Okay, good. Take this, okay?" Fay passed me a bright yellow bibbed apron with a neon blue H embroidered on the chest.

I'd worn an apron like this one when I'd handed out Bolt, Holt's energy drink, in the Santa Clarita store. Here, I'd seen management circulating through the store wearing the apron, asking questions about Holt's policies and procedures at random. An employee was rewarded with a Hershey's chocolate kiss for a correct answer.

"I need you to train on CBT, okay?" Fay said.

CBT . . . CBT . . . what was CBT?

"Can you do that?" Fay asked.

"Of course," I said.

I donned the apron as Fay walked away, found the kisses in the big front kangaroo pocket, unwrapped one, and popped it into my mouth.

So far, I liked being a trainer.

I walked to the next aisle where a woman who'd introduced herself earlier—and whose name I'd already forgotten—stocked vacuum cleaners.

"Got some training questions for me, huh?" she asked.

"Yes," I said, and stood a little straighter, giving myself what I hoped was an air of authority. "First question: what does CBT stand for?"

"Computer based training," she told me.

Really? That's what it stood for?

"Very good," I declared.

I gave her a chocolate kiss, took one for myself, and moved along.

I moseyed through the aisles thinking it better to take a lap through the store—just to get the lay of the place, of course—before I selected another employee to quiz. I ate two more kisses along the way.

Taylor jumped out from behind the cosmetics counter.

"OMG! You've got your own apron!" she exclaimed. "It's got your initial and everything!"

I looked down at the H on my chest.

"Is everybody getting one?" Taylor asked.

"Yes," I said. "And it will have your own initial on it."

"SC!"

Now I definitely needed another chocolate kiss—make that two.

A woman popped up from behind the jewelry counter.

"Haley," she called. "The Cirque du Soleil show at the Mirage is terrific."

"Good to know," I said.

Jeez, everybody was so friendly today.

I headed down the main aisle and spotted Cliff in men's wear. I shoved in two more kisses.

"Hey, Dana," he said, and ambled over. He leaned his head back and shook out his long wavy hair. "Listen, could you, you know, uh, like give me a ride home from work? The police haven't found my car yet."

"You're kidding."

Honestly, I figured that whoever had stolen the thing would have brought it back by now.

"No, man, like I don't know if they're even trying," Cliff said.

"Imagine that."

Maya had called earlier and cancelled our trip to Macy's—some problem at home—so I didn't have anything definite planned. I doubted Ty would fly in again, and Jack was long gone.

"Sure, Cliff," I said. "I'll meet you out front after work."

By the time I punched out, I'd finished off the entire bag of Hershey's kisses and asked a total of two training questions. Really, every trainer has their own style and that's mine.

Cliff waited outside the store. He got into my car and gave me directions to his house. We headed north on the 515, then exited on Charleston and turned onto Arden.

This was definitely not Stephanie Holden's neighborhood.

The houses here were older and in need of repair. Windows and doors were barred. Weeds sprung up among the rocks in front yards. Trash and old junkers cluttered the sides of the houses. The Stratosphere Tower loomed in the distance.

"Here's my place," Cliff said, pointing.

I pulled up to the curb in front of a house that hadn't seen a new coat of paint since it was new, apparently.

"You own a house?" I asked.

"Well, you know, technically it's my grandma's," he said. "But I help her take care of it."

I eyed the house, then Cliff.

"Really?"

"Oh, yeah," he said. "I've got my own room in the garage. Want to come inside?"

I had no desire to spend the evening on a threadbare futon, watching *X-Files* Season Five wearing a tinfoil hat.

"Some other time," I said.

Cliff made no move to get out of the car. For a minute, I worried that he'd forgotten where we were.

"Want to go see something cool?" he asked.

"No thanks."

"I'm not supposed to tell anybody, but hey, you being Dana and all, you can see it," Cliff said.

"No, really, that's okay."

"Eric and Dwayne—those dudes took somebody to see it," Cliff said. "Like, hey man, they said they didn't, but, hey man, I know they did."

"Does this have something to do with the aliens?" I asked.

"Wow, dude, you're one smart chick," he declared.

"Are they still at the Rio?" I asked.

"No way," Cliff said. "We staked out that place for hours. Eric sat in the buffet eating for, wow, like all night or something."

"You didn't get to eat?" I asked.

"Dwayne and me, we kept watch out back, you know, like where they bring in the food," he said. "We hid behind the Dumpsters. Like, wow, dude, they've got some huge Dumpsters at the casinos. But that's okay, because we've got ways of checking out everything."

I don't know why, but I asked, "What sort of ways?"

"Our field investigation kits," Cliff said.

"Oh, yes, your ufology field kits. How could I have forgotten those?"

"We've got cool stuff. Binoculars, night-vision goggles, flashlights. We've got, like, little cameras on wires that can look around corners. Real spy equipment and everything."

"That does sound cool," I said.

"Damn straight it's cool," Cliff said. He pointed to the house. "You want to come inside and see it?"

"Another day," I told him.

"Okay, sure," Cliff said. He gazed out the window for a minute, then turned to me again. "Hey, do you want to go see them?"

Hadn't we just been over this?

"I don't think so, Cliff. I don't want to catch alien cooties or anything," I said.

"We've got special spray."

Guess I should have figured that.

"I got this buddy, his name is Ronnie," Cliff said. He frowned. "No wait. His name is Donnie. Yeah, it's Donnie."

"Let me guess, he's a ufologist, too?"

"Donnie's the guy who broke the whole thing open, man," Cliff told me. "It was all Ronnie's doing."

"You mean Donnie?"

"Wow, dude, he drives a truck for a grocery warehouse."

Jeez, I really hoped they drug tested before they let Donnie—or Ronnie—on the highway with that big truck.

"That's how he found out," Cliff said. "He's like, you know, driving for a grocery place."

"Yes, I got that part," I said. "So the aliens are at the grocery warehouse where he works?"

"No way, man," Cliff said. "Want to see where they are?"

At this point, I was confused and completely worn down.

Where was my best friend at a time like this? Where was my hot private detective friend? And my official boyfriend?

Nobody was here. It was just Cliff and me.

"Sure," I said. "Let's go see the aliens."

"Cool, man," Cliff declared.

I started the car and he directed me onto the freeway again, then north onto Highway 95.

"They've been here a long time," Cliff said. "Like decades or something. They're the gray ones. Gray aliens. Eric says they probably got stranded here. They can't get home or something. Like, maybe, they're trying to make some fuel so they can get away."

"I'm pretty sure I saw this in a movie," I said.

"Yeah. Good cover, huh?" Cliff said.

We continued north. I'd never been to this part of Vegas before and expected to find nothing but a barren expanse of desert. I was wrong. Stores, shops, restaurants, apartments, and office buildings lined both sides of the freeway. Greenery was limited to palm trees and patches of sagebrush, which was typical. Rocky, windswept mountains rose in the distance.

Then, as if someone had drawn a line in the desert, all signs of civilization abruptly ended. I realized that, yes, someone had actually done that as we passed a sign indicating we were now on the Paiute Indian Reservation. Open desert dotted with Joshua trees and more sagebrush stretched for miles to the base of the mountains.

"Where are we going?" I asked.

"Creech Air Force Base," Cliff said.

"There's an air force base on an Indian reservation?" I asked.

"The base is on the other side of the reservation," Cliff said. "Nobody can get into that place. They've got guards with guns. If anybody tries to break in, look out. You're dead. There are sensors all over the desert and surveillance cameras that see everything."

"Then how do you know aliens are there?" I asked.

"Like I told you. Donnie drives a delivery truck for a grocery warehouse. He's been on the base. There's a man-camp about twenty miles in. Everything is like that, way back off of the road so nobody can see it. He brings food—crazy stuff."

"What, exactly, is crazy food?"

"Fish eyes, squid, octopus, frog—not the legs, the whole frog," Cliff said.

Yeah, okay, that was odd.

"There's a whole colony of aliens. The government keeps them there, takes care of them, gives them food, a place to live. And in exchange, we get their technology."

I could have been at Macy's free giveaway right now.

"They must not like staying there all the time," Cliff said, "because they come to Vegas."

Or even bitchy-beauty-queen-spa-week.

"They escape," Cliff said. "They come to Vegas and hang out in abandoned buildings."

Maybe hitting a hot club with a hotter-than-hot private detective.

"They like to eat at the buffets," Cliff said.

Or doing the mattress mambo with my official boyfriend.

"Wait a minute," I said. "You're telling me that aliens are walking the streets of Vegas?"

"Mostly at night," Cliff said. "Come on, you've seen some of the characters on The Strip at night. Do they all look human to you?"

I couldn't argue with that.

"So if you ever see anybody really odd looking, or see anything weird happening at night, it's probably aliens," Cliff said. "Call me. I'll come right over."

I'd fought it for days. I'd refused to believe. I'd convinced myself that it couldn't be true. But it was.

"If I see an alien, you'll be the first one I call," I assured him.

Yeah, I was cursed, all right.

Oh, crap.

CHAPTER 17

I spent a forgettable day at Holt's. I filled the mind-numbing hours unpacking and stocking enough bed sheets to drape the Eiffel Tower—in a multitude of colors and patterns sure to horrify the high-fashion French—and occupied my mind thinking about Courtney's boyfriend—the one before Tony—whom Stephanie had told me about.

Who was he? Why had nobody mentioned him before? Where did he fit into her life? And, of course, the biggest question of all—could he have murdered Courtney?

Danielle could give me some answers, if I could reach her. I only had her cell phone number and she hadn't returned my calls, so I figured I could get some contact info for her from the place where they made their accessory line.

I left the store on a mission

The Eastern Industrial Complex had been easy enough to find—thanks to a mocha frappuccino, the Internet, Tony Hubbard's general directions, and the facility owner's lack of imagination in naming the business—on Eastern Avenue, not far from Warm Springs Road.

I swung into the complex and drove slowly through the facility. It housed businesses such as stereo shops, custom car parts, print shops, most anything requiring a work space/office combo that didn't need a flashy storefront.

Each unit consisted of an office attached to a workroom with a rollup garage door.

I'd never gotten the name of Courtney and Danielle's fashion accessory line and, thanks to Courtney's nonexistent business sense, had not seen it on the Internet, so I drove the U-shaped complex hoping I'd spot it. I didn't.

I hadn't exactly expected to see Danielle there, either, but it would have been nice since this was the only place I knew to look for her.

If anyone could give me info on Courtney's other boyfriend, it would be Danielle. This was just the kind of thing the two of them would have discussed. They were business partners and, naturally, friends. Maybe best friends. I hadn't found anyone in Vegas or Henderson yet who qualified as Courtney's BFF, so that left Danielle.

Stephanie flashed into my head. I supposed she—and Courtney—had thought at one time they might be BFFs here. Their relationship had soured in no time, according to Stephanie.

The thought that Stephanie might have killed Courtney ran through my mind. If she hated Courtney even a fraction as much as she seemed to hate me, it was a possibility.

Stephanie never said how long it had been since they'd last spoken. Maybe it was the night Marcie messaged Courtney and told her I'd be at Holt's. Courtney could have called her, said she was going to the store to visit me, and asked Stephanie if she wanted to come along.

Maybe she'd snapped. Maybe she'd killed Courtney as she, apparently, wanted to kill every other girl on the planet whom she perceived had a better life than hers.

Yet I couldn't see Stephanie pulling it off. What would she do? Load up four kids in her mom-mobile, drive them to Holt's, leave them in the car while she ran in and killed Courtney? And then what? Hit the McDonald's drive-through for Happy Meals on the way home?

Not likely.

I'd called Danielle three times today, but I hadn't heard back from her, which seemed kind of odd. I mean, really, why wouldn't she answer her phone? Or return my messages? Best I could figure, she was busy with the funeral arrangements.

I pulled into a parking slot outside the rental office and got out. It was late, after five already, and not much was going on. Through the window of the office, I saw a woman seated at a desk, talking on a telephone. I let myself in. A little bell clanged.

The room was tiny, offering space for a desk, chair, small credenza, and a couple of book cases. Every flat surface was packed with teetering stacks of magazines, folders, and papers. A good dusting wouldn't have hurt anything.

The door to the adjoining workroom stood open a few inches. Inside, I glimpsed a corner of the room and a hodgepodge of ladders, paint cans, boards, desks, chairs, file cabinets.

The woman seated at the desk glanced up at me and covered the telephone receiver with her hand.

"We're closed," she whispered.

The nameplate on her desk read, ESTELLA BURNS, PROPERTY MANAGER. I figured her for mid-sixties, maybe. She had a helmet of gray hair, oversized glasses, and was dressed in enough polyester to make Carol Brady jealous.

I guess she thought I'd leave. I didn't, of course. Instead, I attempted to look interested in a brochure detailing the amenities and benefits of renting a unit at Eastern Industrial Complex—I wasn't—and pretended not to listen to her phone conversation—I was, of course.

Estella hung up the phone—personal call, dinner plans—and before she could ask me to leave, I introduced myself.

"I'm a friend of Courtney and Danielle's," I added.

Yeah, okay, it was a bit of a stretch, but I thought the sympathy angle would soften her up a little.

"Did you bring the money?" she asked.

So much for sympathy.

"The rent money," Estella said, none too pleasantly. "I told Danielle I needed it—yesterday. "

"The rent for their workroom?" I asked, just to be sure.

Estella pushed herself out of her chair. "Two months behind. Two months behind and coming up on three. And now that Courtney girl is dead. Tragedy. I told Danielle I was sorry. But *sorry* won't satisfy the property owners."

I didn't know what to say to that. Luckily, Estella didn't seem to notice.

"She promised to get me the money." Estella glared at me like I'd disappointed her, but not surprised her. "I guess you're not bringing it."

"No," I admitted.

Estella pursed her lips and picked up her handbag—a Coach knockoff I could have spotted from across the street.

"I waited on those girls to get me the rent money for way too long," Estella said. "Always behind. Always with the excuses. Always some big story about a big business deal in the works. Then there's no business deal, then the deal's on again. Always with a different story from those two."

Yeah, okay, I knew Courtney was dead and it wasn't right to think ill of her, but apparently she'd bungled their finances so badly they hadn't been able to pay their rent on time. And now Danielle was left to come up with the money somehow which, maybe, served her right for leaving the business in the hands of usually-kind-of-out-of-it Courtney.

"You tell Danielle she'd better get me that money. These owners, they don't fool around," Estella said, waving her hand as if said owners were lurking in all four corners of the office.

"I haven't heard from Danielle," I said, steering the conversation to the reason I'd come here in the first place. "Do you have a home address for her?"

"Courtney's apartment is at Bay Breeze. Warm Springs Road. That's all that's in the file," Estella said, pulling a massive set of keys from her purse.

She opened the door and walked outside. I think she might have actually locked me inside the place if I hadn't hurried out after her.

"Which unit is theirs?" I asked.

"Number six," she told me, locking the door. "Next time you talk to Danielle, tell her I need that money. She needs to borrow it, or get a loan. Tell her to pawn that big TV I saw in the back of her van. Tell her to do *something*."

Estella headed toward a Cadillac parked near my car. I decided to check out unit six. I took a few steps and stopped.

Hang on a minute. What did she just say?

I hurried over to the Caddie. Estella was already in her car, ready to back out. She buzzed down the window.

"Did you say you saw a TV inside Danielle's van?" I asked.

"Darn right I did. One of those big flat screens," she told me. "It's not right. If she can have one of those huge televisions, she can pay her rent. These girls . . . I swear."

The window rose, Estella backed out of the parking lot and left.

Okay, that was weird. Danielle had a TV in the back of her van? When I'd seen her at Courtney's apartment and mentioned that the TV and stereo were gone, she'd kind of blown me off.

Of course, I hadn't seen the television Estella had mentioned, and she'd said nothing about a stereo. There was no way of knowing if it was the one missing from Courtney's apartment.

But it was one heck of a coincidence.

Tony certainly couldn't have hauled them off on his motorcycle. But maybe he'd had a friend with a truck who'd helped him out.

Danielle had that huge van. Had she taken the TV and stereo from the apartment and loaded them up only minutes before I'd gotten there? Was that why she'd seemed so nervous that day?

Or was that just another coincidence?

Of course, those items could have belonged to Danielle all along and she was just taking back what belonged to her. But if that was true, why would she say Tony had stolen them?

Another unpleasant thought stuck me.

What else might Danielle have taken from the apartment—if she'd taken anything at all? Something more valuable? Something incriminating that the police should have seen?

Maybe Danielle was just trying to gather enough assets from Courtney to catch up on their bills. With Courtney dead, Danielle had no one to help clear their debts.

I headed deeper into the complex looking for unit number six. Shadows stretched across the driveway. The breeze picked up. Nobody was around.

I located unit six sandwiched between a print shop and a custom sign shop. The blinds on the office window were open. I cupped my hands against the glass and peered inside.

Nothing. Absolutely nothing. The place had been cleared out.

The door to the adjoining workroom stood open, allowing a full view inside. Nothing in there, either. Furniture-wise, at least.

Scattered across the floor, scraps and remnants of fabric in almost every color imaginable mingled with knots of thread and bits of thin pattern paper. I tried to get a feel for what Danielle's accessory line might have looked like if she'd had the financial resources to complete it, but seeing so many different colors, I wasn't sure Danielle herself knew what she'd wanted to do. Seemed she was experimenting with all kinds of pallets and hues.

Other than the debris left behind, absolutely nothing in the unit indicated that Danielle had designed a fashion accessory line here or that Courtney had screwed up the business end of it at every opportunity.

I headed back to my car, no closer to learning the identity of Courtney's previous boyfriend. Did Detective Dailey know about him? I wondered. Had they questioned him? Did they consider him a suspect?

Someone other than me would have been nice.

Inside my car, I slurped down the melted remains of a mocha frappuccino. The caffeine and chocolate combo jarred my brain, sending my thoughts scurrying in another direction.

Maybe the first boyfriend had been Mike Ivan. It was certainly a possibility that he and Courtney had been romantically involved—nothing to do with business—and she'd just told Tony those things so he wouldn't be jealous of Mike trying to contact her. Tony—convicted felon that he was—would be the last guy I'd ever tell about a previous relationship.

The mocha frappuccino raced through my brain, waking cell after cell until my thoughts were sliding along quicker and smoother than a top zipper on a Betsey Johnson tote.

Jack had checked into Mike Ivan's background and assured me the guy was legit. I didn't doubt Jack or his info. But he'd only checked into Mike's businesses, not his personal life.

Not so long ago, I'd met a guy who operated in the Los Angeles Garment District. He knew the ins and outs of the place—on both sides of the law.

If I called him, he'd give me the info on Mike Ivan in a nanosecond.

If I called him, he'd think I wanted him in my life.

If I called him, he might be right.

Yeah, okay, enough of those thoughts.

I started my car and pulled out onto Eastern Avenue heading to—well, I didn't know where I was heading. For now, I just wanted to keep moving.

And get in touch with Danielle, of course.

She was probably the only person who knew what had been going on in Courtney's life. I needed to talk to her.

I dug my cell phone out of my purse—a fantastic Ferragamo satchel—and punched in her number again. Just like the three previous times I'd called her today, her voicemail picked up. I didn't bother leaving a message. If she wasn't able to respond to the first three, one more wouldn't matter.

As I drove past Sunset Road, my cell phone rang. I grabbed it, sure it was Danielle finally returning my calls. The I.D. screen read "Executive Travel."

Who the heck were they?

"Miss Randolph?" a woman with a soft British accent asked when I answered. "Rona Davenport here. Executive Travel Agency. I'm contacting you at the behest of Mr. Ty Cameron."

Behest? Only the British could make a word like that sound both regal and comforting at the same time.

"Mr. Cameron has asked me to advise you of an upcoming adventure, if you will, to Dubai," Rona said.

I pulled the phone from my ear, looked at it, then listened again.

"Dubai?" I asked.

Where was Dubai? In the Middle East? I didn't know. I hadn't taken geography yet.

"The annual Dubai Shopping Festival. A month-long event. The city's upscale, most exclusive shops, stores, and boutiques offer lower prices on their high-demand fashions," Rona said.

"A month long?" I asked.

"You'll stay at the elegant Dubai Crowne Plaza, a five star. Full amenities. World-class restaurants. You'll have a driver, of course, and a personal shopping escort. Mr. Cameron has seen to every detail," Rona said, then added, "Provided this meets with your approval, of course. Mr. Cameron was quite explicit about that."

I couldn't say anything. I was too stunned to speak.

"Miss Randolph?" Rona said.

"Yes, I'm here," I managed to say.

"With your permission, I'll e-mail you a complete itinerary," Rona said. "January isn't so far off, after all."

"January?"

"Yes. The Shopping Festival begins in January. Your Mr. Cameron seems to be a long-term planner," Rona said. "Please contact me with questions at any time."

"Okay, thanks," I said.

I hung up, stunned. Ty had planned a month-long shopping trip for us to Dubai? Wow. Just the two of us, together, for all that time? I could hardly take it in.

Only—

Rona hadn't said anything about Ty going. Just me.

But surely he'd go.

Wouldn't he?

CHAPTER 18

Improving oneself always involved risk.

I'm pretty sure I read that somewhere or maybe I heard it in one of my classes. I don't know. I usually drifted off in class. But I couldn't disagree with the statement.

I lay on my bed in the Culver Inn, lights off, television on with the sound turned so low I could barely hear it. The History Channel played what appeared to be a show on thimbles. Honestly, those folks can fill an hour with just about anything.

Improvement involved risk because you had to give up something to get something, I seemed to recall someone saying. That's just the way it was. Yet you could never know at the outset if it would work, if the risk would be worth it.

If you wanted to lose weight, you had to give up food. If you wanted a better job, you had to give up the one you had.

Jeez, that sounded like Taylor's reverse world.

I flipped to the Food Network. An overweight woman was frying what appeared to be a pan of butter.

Ty had offered to pay my tuition and school expenses. He wanted me to go to school full time. Quit my job. College wasn't my favorite thing, but maybe if I went full time I'd like it. Maybe if I knew I could knock it out, get it over with quickly, I'd enjoy it. It was my goal, after all, to get a great job doing something, someplace, where everybody had to do what I said, while I wore great fabulous clothes and carried fantastic handbags.

But that would mean giving up my life as I knew it. My independence. My freedom to come and go as I pleased.

I'd hardly die a thousand deaths if I never set foot inside another Holt's store, so quitting my job wasn't a huge deal. But the money I earned from it—such as it was—was mine. All mine. I didn't have to answer to anyone. I could spend it—or not—as I saw fit.

What would it be like to depend on Ty for everything?

Maybe not so bad, I decided, as I flipped to the Discovery Channel. He'd made all sorts of fabulous offers. The beach house. The Dubai trip—which was a huge surprise. Maybe the kind of surprise I could expect from him often?

Then, of course, there was the money thing.

My bank account would soon be in full-on cardiac arrest. My credit cards needed resuscitating. Not to mention the student loans I would eventually have to repay. Ty could remedy my financial situation.

But did I want to be a resident in that reverse world?

Maybe a psychic could help me decide. I mean, really, another opinion couldn't hurt.

I hauled my laptop into the bed with me and logged on to the Internet.

After my trip to the air force base with Cliff, there seemed no doubt left that I had actually been cursed. I couldn't fight it anymore. I needed to find a way to break the curse—and maybe gain some insight into my future at the same time.

I found the psychic reading sites I'd checked out before and decided I'd give Madam CeeCee a try. No real reason, except that her Web page didn't freak me out quite as much as the others. I punched her phone number into my cell phone and—

Voices in the hallway. A door closing.

I scrambled out of the bed and yanked open my door. Damn. Nobody in the hallway.

How the heck did I keep missing them? Were they some sort of phantom guests?

I went back inside and locked the door, then glanced at my bedside clock. A little after one. They were in early tonight. Three o'clock was their usual hour to call it quits at whatever they were doing that kept them out this late.

Another thought hit me. All along, I'd assumed I'd heard them coming in for the night. But maybe, instead, they were leaving.

Who went out at three o'clock—or one o'clock—in the morning from a second-rate motel in Henderson?

If I'd been anywhere but here in Vegas, I'd have wondered if something illegal was going on with the guests in the room across the hall. But nothing was illegal in Vegas. Gambling, prostitution, topless bars, drinking in public— everything went. The town wasn't called Sin City for nothing.

I walked to the window and pulled back the curtain.

A few lamps burned in the deserted pool area and at the windows on the opposite side of the motel. Two security lights in the maintenance area cast the storage shed and parking area in shadows. I made out the dark outline of a pickup truck.

Okay, that was weird. Why would a pickup be parked there now? The charming and always delightful Whitley at the registration desk had told me no maintenance workers were on duty after nine.

But maybe the truck had been parked there for a while. With the view my room offered, I didn't look outside all that often.

Still, it was odd. I shut down my laptop and crawled into bed.

Maybe Madam CeeCee could explain it.

* * *

The pickup was gone.

As soon as I rolled out of bed the next morning, I looked out the window and saw that the area around the maintenance shed was empty. I had no idea what—if anything—that meant.

I showered, did my hair and makeup, got dressed, and went downstairs to the breakfast buffet, expecting this day to be just like all the others I'd spent in Henderson. It wasn't.

Maya was backed up against the kitchen door and some guy was in her face, giving her hell about something. She just stood there and took it.

No way was I going to stand by and do nothing.

I strode through the tables—most of the diners had the good grace not to stare—and stepped between them.

"Excuse me," I said, ignoring the guy. "These muffins are delicious. Can I get another chocolate one?"

The guy stopped talking. Maya didn't move. She seemed to be held in place by some cosmic force radiating from him.

I put him at late twenties, shorter than me—which, I think, explained a lot—thin, average looking, dressed in an equally average-looking shirt and tie. His jaw was set and his stance screamed I-have-a-little-power-and-I'm-going-to-ruin-lives-just-because-I-can.

I touched Maya's arm. "Are there more muffins in the kitchen?"

She seemed to snap out of it, finally. "Oh, yes. I'll get some."

Maya turned to leave but the guy put his finger in her face.

"You just remember what I told you," he said, then whipped around and stalked away.

I wanted to go after him and mess him over—I don't know how, exactly—but I figured Maya needed me more.

I hustled her inside the kitchen. She collapsed onto the

stool, planted her elbows on the cold, hard, stainless-steel countertop, and buried her face in her hands.

"Who was that jackass?" I demanded.

Seeing her this upset, I was tempted again to go after him. But then I realized—oh my God—Maya was crying.

Oh, crap.

I don't do *crying* well. I never know what to say. Really, my personal skills in highly emotional situations aren't the best.

Believe me, I'm the last person you want steadying you on your wedding day.

"That was Bradley," Maya sobbed, wiping her tears with the backs of her hands.

"Bradley Pennington? The guy who runs this place? *That* Bradley?" I asked.

I hadn't liked him when I'd heard Maya and Amber talk about him. After seeing him in action, I *really* didn't like him.

"He wants to fire me," she said, swiping her palm over her wet cheeks.

"*Fire you?*"

Maya gulped hard. "This is what he does. When he wants to get rid of you, he starts complaining about your work."

I grabbed a handful of napkins from the storage bin on the counter and gave them to her.

"But your buffet is terrific," I said.

"It doesn't matter," Maya said, dabbing at her eyes. "I've seen him do this a dozen times. He'll make things up, give you a hard time, then fire you. The turnover in this place is unbelievable. It's almost like he doesn't *want* anybody to work here very long."

"That doesn't make any sense," I said.

Maya drew in a ragged breath. "I knew this would happen. I knew it was just a matter of time."

"There must be somebody you can complain to," I said,

but I knew there wasn't. The Culver Inn was family owned. Nobody was going to listen to a mere employee— let alone the breakfast buffet caterer.

"How am I going to pay for my classes?" Fresh tears rolled down Maya's face. "How am I going to get my degree? Start my own business? How am I going to *live?*"

Finally, my recessive be-compassionate-in-an-emotional-crisis gene kicked in and I put my arm around her shoulders. She leaned against me and cried harder.

Damn that little Bradley creep, I thought. Somehow, I was going to find a way to screw him over.

"No cell phones on the sales floor, okay?" Fay told me.

I was in men's underwear—the department—sticking bags of white athletic socks on metal display pegs.

And I was in no mood.

I looked up from the address book on my cell phone, which I'd been scrolling through.

"The store isn't open yet, *okay?*" I barked back. "In case you hadn't noticed, *okay?*"

"You're supposed to be working," Fay said.

"And so are you." I pointed to the three U-boats loaded down with unopened boxes sitting in the aisle. "Why don't you go over there and unpack some of those?"

"I don't like your attitude, okay?" Fay said. "I'm going to have to note that in your personnel file."

And the next time I sleep with the owner of the entire Holt's company, I'm going to tell him to fire you!

Damn. I wished I could have said that out loud.

I gave her double stink-eye as she walked away.

"You tell her, Haley," the guy stocking boxers in the next aisle said. "Hey, I've been meaning to tell you. There's an indoor gun range on Tropicana. It would be way cool to go."

I didn't disagree.

I'd been in a crappy mood since I'd left the Culver Inn this morning, and being at Holt's hadn't helped.

Imagine that.

Maya had pulled herself together enough to tend to the breakfast buffet, but I could see that her spirit was broken, her dream crushed, her future in jeopardy.

No way would she get referral business for the other Culver Inn motels in the chain now that Bradley was winding up to fire her. She'd be lucky to scrape together enough money to pay for her fall classes.

I shoved three more packages of athletic socks onto a peg and grabbed more out of the box.

I hated that for her. Maya worked hard. She had a plan, a goal. She knew what she wanted to do with her life. I admired that about her.

But, it seemed, she wasn't getting any help.

I dropped down onto the floor in front of the sock display. I'd exhausted myself with my anger toward that little twerp Bradley.

Jeez, what kind of family business allowed someone like him to run roughshod over decent, hard-working employees? Ty flashed in my head and a wave of guilt nearly knocked the breath out of me.

Ty wanted to buy me a beach house, take over my bills, pay for everything, send me on an international month-long shopping spree.

And Maya had nobody.

Chapter 19

At lunch time, I got in my car and headed down Valle Verde Road looking for a place to eat. I didn't want to eat in the Holt's breakroom, fearing I might actually take out Fay after the run-in we'd had in men's underwear this morning, nor did I want to get caught up in idle chatter and gossip with the other employees.

Almost everyone in the store had gone out of their way to tell me about fun and exciting things I could do while I was in Vegas, but, honestly, I was in no mood for that sort of thing. Right now, only a BFF should be forced to put up with me, or an official boyfriend—and I had neither immediately available.

I spotted a Burger King, hit the drive-through, and found a spot to park where I could eat my lunch in peace. Generally, a burger wasn't a stress-relieving food, but I followed it up with a chocolate milkshake, so that helped.

Now, I had calls to make.

The first was to Madam CeeCee, the all-knowing—and hopefully all-telling—psychic who would advise me on breaking the curse put on me by that freaky old lady in the Santa Clarita Holt's store. I hoped Madam CeeCee's powers crossed state lines.

I scrolled through the address book in my cell phone

and punched in her number. It rang three times, and her voicemail picked up.

Okay, that was weird. Shouldn't she have known I was calling? She was a psychic, wasn't she?

I left a message and my call-back number.

For a few minutes, I watched the traffic whizzing past as I sucked down the last of my shake and debated my next call. I needed information on Danielle Shepherd. She was the only link I had to Courtney's before-Tony boyfriend, a guy who might—or might not—make a viable murder suspect. I wouldn't know until I found out who he was and talked to him.

Danielle still hadn't returned my calls, but looking at it logically—something I usually preferred not to do—that meant nothing. She barely knew me, she had business and financial problems to solve, plus a funeral to plan.

I probably could have let it go and found some other way to learn the identity of Courtney's mystery boyfriend, but that whole whose-TV-was-in-Danielle's-van thing bothered me.

I needed more info on Danielle.

Jack would be the obvious guy to ask. He was already up to speed on the case.

Plus, he was way hot.

I knew he'd help, if I asked.

Plus, he was way hot.

But Jack had actual cases to work—the kind that paid money. Plus, he was way hot—and I had a boyfriend who wanted me to move in with him.

I hate my life.

I scrolled through my address book and punched in the number for Detective Shuman of the LAPD. Shuman and I had history. Nothing romantic. Our relationship was strictly business. But still.

"Shuman."

He answered rushed. All detectives sounded rushed, in

my experience. I think they were trained that way at the academy so people would think they were doing more than they really were.

Maybe I should try that at work.

"How's it going?" I asked.

"Hang on."

I heard noise in the background, the dull roar of too many voices in too small a space. A restaurant, maybe. It dimmed, then stopped.

I imagined Shuman outside on the street wearing a shirt-tie-sport coat combo that didn't quite blend because he'd picked them out himself. Dark hair blowing in the gentle Southern California breeze. Handsome.

"What's new, Haley?"

Shuman sounded friendly now, relaxed.

"Murder," I said.

"I asked what was *new?*" he said, and chuckled.

Some—okay, most—of our history involved murder investigations. We'd had our ups and downs—yeah, okay, mostly because of me—but we'd gotten over our problems.

"I need some background on a woman named Danielle Shepherd," I said. "Can you help me out?"

Shuman didn't answer right away. I pictured him pacing the street, then stopping suddenly.

"Where are you?" he asked.

"Vegas."

"Out of my jurisdiction."

"Maybe not," I said. "Mike Ivan, as in Ivanov, as in the Russian mob in L.A. He's involved."

Shuman was silent.

"Maybe," I added.

Jack had said Mike Ivan ran legitimate businesses, and maybe that was true. But those guys were experts at hiding their illegal activities behind a maze of corporations and offshore accounts.

At least, that's how they did it on TV.

I felt bad for throwing Mike in front of the LAPD bus, so to speak, but they, along with the FBI, DEA, Homeland Security, and most other branches of federal law enforcement probably already had him on their radar.

And if Jack had been misinformed about Mike and he was involved in Courtney's murder, I wanted Shuman to have the info first. I figured it couldn't do his career—and his willingness to help me in the future, of course—any harm.

"Send me a text with what you've got," Shuman said. He was in big-time cop mode now.

"Thanks," I said.

He didn't answer, just hung up. I imagined him frowning his cop frown—which was kind of hot—and heading back into the restaurant.

I spent a few minutes texting him everything I knew, then drove back to Holt's. I turned into the parking lot and spotted Cliff at the corner of the building having a smoke with two guys who appeared to be doofing their way through life, much like Cliff.

The Nevada chapter of the ufology club, obviously.

Crossing the wide parking lot on foot in the blazing mid-day desert heat was preferable to having to listen to the latest on the alien invasion of Vegas—jeez, what's happened to my life?—so I circled the lot with the intention of finding a spot as far away from those guys as I could. As I cruised past the Pizza Hut, I spotted a banged-up white Ford Taurus parked near the door.

I hit the brakes, jumped out, and peered inside.

Worn upholstery. Fast-food bags. Empty drink cups.

Oh my God, this was Cliff's car.

I got into my Honda, crossed the parking lot, and rolled up beside Cliff and his friends.

I buzzed down my window. "Hey, Cliff?"

He looked up, took a few second to react, then ambled

over. The guys with him, Eric and Dwayne, I presumed, hung back, watching me as if I might beam up at any second.

"Hey, Dana, how's it going?" Cliff said, leaning on my open window.

"The police found your car?" I asked.

"No way, man. Like, I don't think they're even looking," he said.

"I found it," I said.

"Whoa, dude." Cliff looked totally confused. "What?"

"It's parked in front of the Pizza Hut," I said.

"No way." He gazed across the parking lot, then at me again. "How'd it get there?"

I didn't need Madam CeeCee to figure this one out.

"Did you drive over for lunch?" I asked. "Then maybe forgot you drove, and walked back?"

"Wow, that is so cool. That is so *Dana*," Cliff declared, smiling and nodding his head. He turned to his friends still cowering beside the store. "Hey, dudes, come here! You gotta meet Dana!"

"Some other time," I said quickly, and drove away.

Jeez, why couldn't I get beamed into another life?

It was a Fendi evening. Definitely a Fendi evening.

After finishing my shift at Holt's, I ran by the Culver Inn and changed into black pants and sweater—always classics—and grabbed my Fendi bag to complete the be-jealous-of-me look I was going for. Nothing less than a Fendi would do tonight. I was going to the meeting of the handbag club and I knew every woman there would bring her best.

Maya had told me the club met at a boutique in a shopping center near the Green Valley Resort and Casino, just a few miles from the Culver Inn. She catered the event. It would have been more fun if we could have gone together. But I was glad she had the work, especially since it looked as if she might lose her job catering the breakfast buffet, if that little weasel Bradley got his way.

I still hate him.

I drove past the resort and casino and into the shopping center parking lot. The District, as it was called, featured wide promenades with benches, lush landscaping, and trees with white lights that fronted all sorts of shops. There were restaurants and bars, and a park with a carousel.

I followed a group of well-dressed women carrying fabulous handbags to a boutique called Fashion Utopia. The window was artfully filled with a wide variety of well-known designer purses, plus gorgeous bags I'd never seen before.

My heart rate skyrocketed.

Where was Marcie at a time like this? She would *so* love this place. I'd have to tell her all about it. Maybe, when her ankle got better, we could come back together.

I hoisted my Fendi higher and went inside.

About two dozen white folding chairs had been squeezed into the center of the store, surrounded by displays of jewelry, shawls, hats, gloves, wallets, totes, handbags, and just about every other fashion accessory you could imagine. Most of the chairs were occupied. Another half dozen or so women were on their feet, working the room.

Everyone was talking and laughing. Everybody had a glass of wine. Spirits were high.

Immediately I spied a Marc Jacobs, a Betsey Johnson, two Michael Kors, an Isabella Fiore, two—no three—Pradas. Gorgeous bags everywhere.

My knees felt weak. Oh my God. What if someone here had a Delicious bag? I'd faint for sure.

At the counter near the cash register, I spotted Maya putting the finishing touches on the refreshments. No canned Cheez-Whiz and Ritz crackers for this group. Trays of shrimp, crab, beef, puffed pastries, cheeses, all sorts of sauces beautifully presented. Impressive. Way beyond the offerings at the Culver Inn breakfast buffet. Maya had a great culinary future—if she got the money she needed to see it through.

"Welcome, welcome!"

A fiftyish woman with platinum blond hair, a deep suntan, white jumpsuit, and gold shoes came at me, arms open.

"I see a new face!" she declared. "I'm Poppy!"

My mom would have loved her—or maybe hated her. I'm not sure. It's hard to predict which way women will go sometimes.

I introduced myself.

"Ladies? Ladies?" Poppy called. The room quieted and everyone turned to us. Poppy gestured at me as if I were a prize on a game show, and said, "This is Haley!"

All the women called out a greeting or raised a wine glass in my direction.

"Majesta is our guest artisan tonight," Poppy said, pointing at a woman across the room.

Majesta—whom I'm pretty sure made up her own name—was swathed in a long purple print skirt and a massive shawl. She dipped her chin demurely. She had an exotic look to her—as an artisan would, I suppose.

"These are her bags. She makes them by hand in her studio. All of them are original works of art," Poppy declared, pointing to the bags arranged at the front of the room. "Aren't they breathtaking!"

Heads bobbed in agreement around the room.

Oh, yeah, they were gorgeous, all right. Floral and geometric patterns in fabrics that, even from across the room, I could see were exquisite.

My palms started to itch. I absolutely *had* to see the linings.

"Your bags are absolutely fantastic," I agreed.

Majesta dipped her head, graciously accepting my compliment.

"She's presenting at the handbag convention! All the major department stores want to buy her collection," Poppy exclaimed, then wagged her finger. "But nooo. We're not going to let her go commercial with these beautiful bags, now are we, ladies!"

The women paused in their wine sipping to nod in agreement.

"You have a complete collection to show at the handbag convention? That's a major accomplishment," I said.

Danielle and Courtney popped into my mind. They'd surely put hours and hours of work into their line, even though it had come to nothing.

"I have friends who had a fashion accessory line," I said, "but just couldn't make it work."

"Did you hear that, ladies? Haley has friends with an accessory line," Poppy called out. "Maybe we can get them here for our next meeting!"

Oh, crap. Why had I referred to Danielle as my friend— I couldn't even get her to return my phone calls. And I certainly didn't want to mention that her business partner was dead. That might spoil the mood.

"Who is she?" a woman with a Chanel clutch asked.

"Maybe we know her," called a woman carrying a Kate Spade.

Every face turned to me, waiting. Jeez, what could I do?

I leaned close to Poppy and lowered my voice. "Her name is Danielle Shepherd. Her partner is—was—Courtney Collins, and she was—"

"*Courtney Collins?*" Poppy shrieked.

The room fell into a stunned silence. Nobody moved. Every eye in the room shifted to me.

Why had everybody stopped talking? Why were they all staring at me? Yeah, okay, bringing up someone who'd been murdered was kind of bad, but it wasn't like I'd done something unforgivable, like mistaken a Gucci for a Prada. And I was carrying a Fendi, for God's sake.

A woman seated in the back row surged to her feet, tipping over her chair, and let out a full-throated, wild-animal, Discovery Channel–worthy scream. She pushed aside a display of jewelry, sending it flying through the air, knocked over a rack of wallets, and bolted out the door.

Oh, crap.

CHAPTER 20

"It's not your fault," the woman next to me said quietly. "Not really."

We were both on our hands and knees picking up the zillion pieces of jewelry strewn across the floor, and she was being nice, which I appreciated. But the mood of the handbag club meeting had been shattered. Behind us, Poppy was doing her best to rejuvenate the group. They were having none of it.

"I'm Rosalyn Chase," the woman said, offering a kind smile. She looked to be in her fifties, maybe, well dressed with short dark hair.

"Who was that woman?" I asked.

"Valerie Wagner. She hasn't been herself in a long time," Rosalyn said quietly. "I was surprised to see her here tonight after . . . everything."

I guessed *everything* had something to do with Courtney.

"She was a friend of—"

"Let's take this jewelry to the stock room," Rosalyn said.

She'd cut me off before I could finish my sentence, so I figured it was for the best. I rolled with it.

The beaded necklaces and bracelets were hopelessly tangled, so we gathered them as best we could. Maya gave me a what-the-hell-happened eyebrow bob from her station by the refreshments, and I gave her a beats-the-hell-out-of-me bob in return. I felt dozens of hot gazes on me as I followed Rosalyn into the stock room at the back of the store.

The tiny area was crammed with shelves and racks loaded with merchandise. A desk sat in a corner. The light was dim and the room smelled sort of musty. I dumped the tangle of jewelry on a shelf and Rosalyn did the same. She pushed the door closed.

I could really go for a bag of Oreos right now.

"Poppy and her big mouth," Rosalyn said, and shook her head. "She should have known better than to blurt out Courtney's name with Valerie in the room."

Or a Snickers bar.

"Valerie owns a little fabric shop near here. Courtney came in frequently, buying things for the fashion accessory line she and Danielle ran. They became friends," Rosalyn said. "Valerie introduced Courtney to her son, Scott. They started dating."

Maybe two Snickers bars.

Wait. Hang on a second.

"Scott and Courtney dated?" I asked.

Jeez, I really need to pay attention to things.

"Quite the whirlwind romance from what Valerie told us at the club meetings." Rosalyn smiled at the memory. "Valerie invited Courtney to bring her accessory line to a meeting. We were all very impressed. Stunning designs. Exceptional workmanship. It was art, more than fashion."

Okay, that seemed weird.

"Danielle didn't bring the collection?" I asked.

Rosalyn shook her head. "I met Danielle later at their workroom. The girls had been selling a few items separately to test the waters, so to speak, and to bring in some money until the collection was completed. I offered to buy some pieces, but Courtney insisted they weren't ready yet. They certainly looked ready to me, though."

I remembered how I'd seen so many different colors of fabric scattered across the workroom they'd used. I guessed Danielle had finally decided in which direction she should take the collection. I wondered why Courtney had insisted on holding it back.

"Danielle saw things differently," Rosalyn said. "She contacted me a few days later and gave me a number of items on consignment. I took them to Laughlin. My sister lives there and manages a shop. She put them in her display window and they sold immediately."

"So what happened between Valerie and Courtney?" I asked.

"I don't know why, but Courtney and Scott broke up," Rosalyn said. She paused and her features saddened. "Apparently, Scott was so devastated he enlisted in the marines to get away. He was killed in Iraq."

"Oh, crap . . . ," I muttered.

No wonder Valerie had freaked out when Poppy had mentioned Courtney's name.

The stock room door opened and Maya slipped inside.

"Are you okay?" she asked.

The fun had definitely gone out of the handbag club meeting for me.

"I think I'll go," I said.

Maya nodded sympathetically. She understood, as an almost-best-friend would.

"I'll walk out with you," Rosalyn said.

We left through the rear door that led to the service alley behind the shops. It was dark back there, with just a few security lamps to light our way.

I'd learned the identity of Courtney's boyfriend before Tony, but no way was he a murder suspect. Maybe, though, their breakup and Scott's death explained why

Courtney had taken up with Tony. Maybe it was a re-bound thing.

"Has Danielle told you what she plans to do with their stock on hand?" Rosalyn asked.

I didn't want to admit that I hardly knew Danielle, that I couldn't get her to return my calls, or that I hadn't even known there was stock on hand, presumably riding around in the back of Danielle's van along with a TV that may or may not have belonged to Courtney.

"I don't think she's decided yet," I said.

"I'd love to buy it from her," Rosalyn said as we turned the corner of the building. "My sister could sell it in her store easily."

My spirits lifted a little, thinking this would be a bit of good luck Danielle could surely stand.

"I'll give her a call," Rosalyn said, "see if she's interested."

"I'll mention it to her, too," I offered. "Maybe I could finally see the collection."

"You've never seen it?" Rosalyn asked, slipping into handbag-lover mode. "It's gorgeous. I've got a couple of items at my house that I was planning to take down to my sister in a week or so. Why don't you come by?"

"Great," I said.

We stopped in front of a greeting card shop. Couples strolled and sat on benches, kids ran around, music floated out from a nearby bar. I pulled out my cell phone and input her address and number. She took my cell number.

"How about tomorrow after work?" I asked.

"Maybe Danielle can make it then, too," Rosalyn said.

We headed for the parking lot. Just as we reached the curb, a Buick sedan shot out of a space and screeched to a halt in front of us. Valerie glared at us out the driver's side window. She looked kind of wild eyed, kind of crazy. Her face was wet with tears.

"Shame on the both of you! Shame on you!"

She pointed her finger at us, and for a minute I was afraid she might put yet another curse on me.

"How dare you be friends with that Courtney! How dare you! After what she did!" Valerie shook her fist. "I'm glad she's dead. I hope she suffered! And I hope you suffer, too!"

Valerie hit the gas. The Buick lurched forward, nearly clipping an SUV, and sped out of sight.

Something jarred me awake. Sort of.

One eye opened just enough to see feeble rays of sunlight seeping in around the edges of my room's curtains. I saw nothing that motivated me to open the other eye.

My ears were already on full alert, though, and I realized my phone was ringing. Not the pleasant, come-hither tone of my cell phone. My room phone.

I rolled over, noted the display on my alarm clock read 5:47, and grabbed the phone. I meant to say hello, but nothing came out.

"Miss Randolph, this is Melanie at the front desk," an entirely too perky woman said.

I wanted to say what-the-heck-do-you-want, but still, nothing came out.

"Could you please come down here right away?" she asked.

I intended to say no-way-in-hell, but that didn't come out, either.

"Miss Randolph?"

"Yeah, I'll be there," I managed, then hung up.

I didn't jump out of bed, of course. This hour of the morning was definitely too early for me.

It didn't help that I'd been up late last night. Marcie had called and we'd talked about what we'd been up to. Her foot was better but not party or shopping ready.

It had taken over two hours to cover everything.

I'd called Danielle last night, too. I thought she'd be

thrilled to hear that Rosalyn was interested in buying more of her accessories for her sister's shop in Laughlin, thereby relieving some of Danielle's financial stress. But, for the fifth time, all I'd gotten was Danielle's voice mail, which was starting to annoy me. I'd left the message about going to Rosalyn's today after work. Maybe she'd get the message and show up.

I pushed myself up and found my cell phone—the warmest thing I'd had in bed with me in a while—under the sheet beside me. I checked for messages.

Nothing from Ty.

Nothing from Madam CeeCee.

Nothing from Danielle.

Nothing from anybody.

Jeez, I used to be popular. What happened?

Despite the desk clerk's insistence that I go there immediately, I took my time in the shower and getting dressed. I mean, what could be so important at this hour of the morning? If the motel had been on fire, surely she would have mentioned it.

When I got to the lobby, Melanie stood behind the registration desk, looking awfully perky and way too cheerful for this hour of the morning, especially given the hideous Culver Inn brown, orange, and green uniform she wore.

Obviously, she was new.

"Yes, Miss Randolph, good morning," she said, when I introduced myself. Her smile broadened. "There's been a little mix-up."

Okay, so this must be something good. And not a minute too soon. I could stand for my luck to turn around. Maybe I wouldn't even need Madam CeeCee.

"It's come to the attention of management that you're not using one of the rooms blocked off for the Holt's Corporation." Melanie's smile stretched even farther across her face. "So we've charged your credit card for the days you've stayed with us."

Yeah, okay, it was early. Way early. Obviously, my brain hadn't had its morning chocolate–caffeine combo fix, so I must have misunderstood.

"You . . . what?"

Melanie kept smiling and nodding. "That's right. Eight hundred dollars, approximately."

"*Eight hundred dollars?*"

"Approximately."

"You charged eight hundred dollars *on my credit card?*" I'm pretty sure I screamed that.

"How could you have done that without asking me?" I'm positive I screamed that.

Melanie kept smiling. "Well, that is the purpose of giving us your credit card upon check-in."

Oh my God. *Oh my God.* I couldn't believe this. Eight hundred bucks—approximately—on my credit card? That's all the available credit I had left. I'd maxed out my other cards shopping and buying that new tire. Now I had nothing left.

What if I had an emergency? What if my car broke down? What if I got sick and had to go to the hospital?

How was I going to buy purses at the handbag convention?

What if I found a Delicious handbag and *couldn't buy it?*

I started to feel light-headed. The lobby swayed just a little.

Oh my God, this was a disaster of cataclysmic proportions. If this didn't prove I was cursed, I didn't know what would.

And why hadn't Madam CeeCee called me back? Shouldn't she have foreseen this disaster? What the hell kind of psychic was she, anyway?

"And, of course, we'll continue to bill you for every day you continue to stay," Melanie told me sweetly. "Or, if that's not convenient, I can assist you in finding a room at another motel in the area, if you'd like."

And how would I pay for it?

I think I screamed that in my head.

Yeah, sure, eventually I'd get my money back from Holt's for the room, but how long would that take? Holt's was a major corporation with a huge accounting department. Accounting departments were always screwing up— I know that because I used to work in an accounting department at a major law firm. I screwed up things left and right, day after day. That's what corporate America was all about.

At this point, I'd be lucky to eat. With my credit cards maxed out, all I had left in the world was the money in my checking account. I'm excellent, kind of, at keeping track of my money—I know if there's a dime in the bottom of my purse—so I knew without hesitation that I had a measly eighty-two bucks in my account as of six o'clock this morning.

Oh, crap. What was I going to do?

Well, I certainly wasn't going to fall apart in the lobby of the Culver Inn.

I pulled myself together and channeled my mother's I'm-better-than-you attitude.

"I demand to speak with the manager," I informed Melanie.

"That would be Bradley," she replied, still smiling as she gestured behind her. Through an open office door, I saw him seated at a desk, giving me a nasty, mustache-twirling smirk.

That little creep. He'd done this on purpose. I'd defended Maya when he'd bitched her out. He knew we were friends. And now he was trying to force me out, same as he was doing to her.

Well, I'd just show him.

I wouldn't leave this place now for anything. They couldn't dynamite me out of that room.

I gave Bradley my I'll-get-even-with-you, triple stink-eye death ray—it doesn't get any worse than that—and left.

By the time I arrived at Holt's, I'd calmed down a little—but only a little—and only because it occurred to me that I would get paid in two days. Two days wasn't that far away. If I could hold out until payday, I'd be okay, for a while anyway.

I clocked in, stored my purse—a delightful Chloe clutch that I hoped the rest of my day would live up to—and walked to the front of the store to check today's assignment.

The jewelry department. It could have been worse—it can always be worse at Holt's. I headed that way when someone called my name.

"Haley? Haley Randolph?"

I turned and saw a guy standing next to a display of T-shirts in the Juniors department. Tall, good looking, warm brown hair, nicely dressed in khaki pants and a black polo shirt.

Oh, wow, had my day suddenly gotten better or what?

I didn't think I'd ever seen him before, but something about him seemed familiar. He grinned and walked toward me.

Oh my God.

Robbie Freedman.

CHAPTER 21

Robbie looked as surprised to see me as I was to see him.

"Is that really you?" he asked, looking me up and down and shaking his head in wonder.

"It's really me," I said, and my heart started to pound a little harder.

I knew I had an official boyfriend who was handsome and wealthy and brilliant, and my heart should have been pounding a little harder over *him*, not this guy. But Robbie was my high school crush. How could I *not* feel this way?

"And that's really you," I said to Robbie, which was really lame.

Just like high school. Jeez . . .

He looked confused and glanced around the store. "What are you doing working *here?*"

Now my heart started to race faster—but for an entirely different reason.

No way did I want Robbie to know I had a crappy sales-clerk job in a crappy department store. I leaned a little closer—he smelled really good—and lowered my voice.

"I'm working undercover," I whispered.

Okay, jeez, what else could I say? I didn't want Robbie—of all people—to know I'd accomplished nearly nothing since high school.

Anyone in my place would have done the same thing. Really.

"Undercover?" Robbie looked impressed. "State or federal?"

What the heck was he talking about—and why was he asking anything at all? Everything about undercover work should be kept on the down-low. Everybody knew that. Had he never watched a movie or TV show?

So what could I say but, "I can't really get into it."

Robbie nodded thoughtfully and I rushed ahead before he could ask anything else.

"What are you doing here?"

"Courtney," he said, as if that explained anything.

Damn. It was just like being back in high school again. Robbie and Courtney, Robbie and Courtney, blah, blah, blah.

Wait. Oh, crap. Did he know she was dead?

Since I'm not good at tiptoeing around a problem and I'm not big on suspense, I just asked. "You heard what happened, right?"

Robbie looked pained as he nodded his head.

"That's why I'm here," he said, waving his arm, taking in the store. "I just wanted to see where it . . . happened."

Okay, Courtney was *dead,* and Robbie was still more interested in her than in me.

I hate my life.

"Where do you live?" I asked, anxious to move on to a Courtney-free topic.

"Reno," Robbie said. "You?"

"L.A."

"Still?" he asked.

L.A. was a fabulous place with lots of great things going on, but the way Robbie said it made me sound like a loser who still lived at home.

Not a great feeling.

"I was surprised she'd moved to Vegas," Robbie said. "Not really her style."

Since it didn't look like I'd get a reprieve from Courtney-Courtney-Courtney, I decided to roll with it and maybe get some info that would benefit me.

"You and Courtney kept in touch?" I asked.

He sighed heavily, as if the memory pained him.

"We broke up the summer after graduation," he said. "Courtney wanted to move to an artists' colony in New Mexico. I wasn't up for it."

Courtney in an artists' colony? No way. She'd nearly driven me—and most everyone else including the teacher—crazy in art class with that stained-glass pattern she used over and over again.

But at least now I knew why she and Robbie had broken up and, apparently, it wasn't because he'd suddenly come to his senses and realized it was me he'd loved all along, and dumped her.

"Courtney always liked that artsy stuff," Robbie said. "She got it from her parents, I think. They never stopped being hippies. She was a scholarship student at Monroe, remember?"

I'd probably known that at some point in high school, but I'd forgotten it.

It hit me then that the bohemian lifestyle might have still appealed to Courtney. She'd been raised that way—right now her parents were off on some trek through Turkey. Her spartan apartment wasn't exactly a tribute to capitalism, and she obviously had no head for business.

Had she wanted Scott Wagner to head out with her on some transcendental journey in search of higher consciousness, or some b.s. like that? Was that the reason they'd broken up?

Realizing you're not really compatible with the person you're in love with could shatter your life. Had Scott been so devastated he'd joined the marines and shipped out to Iraq?

"Have you heard about the funeral arrangements?" I asked. Maybe he'd know, since I wasn't having much luck getting info from Danielle.

"What funeral arrangements?" Robbie asked. "I checked with the police. Nobody's claimed Courtney's remains."

That seemed odd. I thought Danielle would have been able to contact Courtney's parents by now. Maybe they were in some village cut off from civilization or something.

"I guess her mom and dad aren't back from Turkey yet," I said.

An awkward moment passed, then Robbie said, "Any idea who killed Courtney?"

I guess he figured my undercover work here at Holt's was connected to her death.

"No," I said.

"Who would have a reason to murder her?" He looked troubled, and I thought the question was rhetorical. Then he said, "Do you know?"

Something about Robbie's tone made me wonder if maybe he was a teacher now, and I fought off the urge to blab everything I knew about Courtney's death.

A few seconds dragged by with Robbie watching me, waiting for an answer. When I didn't say anything, he finally said, "I'd better go."

"Are you heading back to Reno?" I asked.

"I'm seeing a friend tonight," Robbie said.

I waited, thinking maybe he'd suggest we get together or something. He didn't.

"Good seeing you, Haley," Robbie said.

"Yeah, you too," I said.

Robbie left the store. I watched as he nodded to the security guard at the front door and disappeared into the parking lot.

It kind of hurt my feelings that Robbie hadn't asked for my cell phone number or my e-mail address—which was bad of me, of course, since I had an official boyfriend—but there it was.

Maybe I shouldn't have been surprised, given that he'd driven all the way from Reno—about a seven-hour drive—just to see the spot where Courtney had been killed.

I headed for the jewelry department. Mindless shelf stocking seemed appealing at the moment.

When I turned down the aisle, I spotted Taylor putting bracelets on a display carousel, bobbing her head and smiling even though no one was around. I couldn't hack a morning with her. No way.

Many times in life, instructions are mistaken for directives, commands, or absolutes when, in fact, they are merely suggestions. Through years of careful study and close adherence to my personal this-suits-me-better outlook on life, I've learned to tell the difference. It's an art, really.

I kept walking.

I spotted two girls I'd worked with in housewares stocking flip-flops in the accessories department. I liked the accessories department, I liked flip-flops, and I liked Monica and Kay. They were both about my age and neither one took their jobs at Holt's too seriously. Surely, this was a sign my day was improving.

I grabbed a box from the U-boat and joined them.

"I've got a dentist appointment," Monica was saying when I walked up.

"Are you getting a lip wax?" Kay asked.

Monica grinned. "You bet."

Not exactly the flip-flop-matching-beach-bag talk I'd expected, but this was just as good.

Everybody—except for men, for some reason—understood the importance of a lip wax before a dental appointment. Dentists ranged from not-so-hot, to hot, to way-hot, and if you were a new patient, you didn't always know which you'd get. Regardless, it was no time to look like you had a Chia Pet growing on your upper lip. It was hard enough to look attractive squinting under a florescent light, wearing a paper bib, with a suction hose hooked over your lip like a bass at a fishing derby.

I was just about to chime in with a my-dentist-is-way-hot contribution to the conversation when my cell phone vibrated in my pocket. I yanked it out expecting it to be Danielle or Madam CeeCee—oh yeah, and a call from my official boyfriend might be nice—but it was Bella, my tied-with-Sandy-for-best-friend-at-Holt's in Santa Clarita.

"Want to hear some b.s.?" Bella demanded when I answered.

I love hearing b.s.

She didn't give me a chance to say so.

"Our paychecks are going to be late," Bella declared.

"What?"

"Late," she said again. "Is that some b.s., or what?"

"What—I don't—but they can't—*why?*"

"The time clock blew up. Remember?" Bella said.

Oh my God. I'd forgotten all about it.

"Everything electrical in the store has been shot to hell ever since," Bella said. "Jeanette says we're not going to get paid this week. They're going to double up the payroll next week—if the problem gets straightened out."

This was awful, horrible, terrible—worse than showing up at a function with a tote when you should have brought a clutch.

How was I going to live for an entire extra week without a paycheck? I had eighty-two bucks to my name.

Maybe all of this could have been avoided if Madam CeeCee had called me back. Shouldn't she have known this would happen? I could have applied for another credit card or something.

"When are you coming back?" Bella asked. "This place is too damn boring without you."

That was nice to hear. But there was no way I could leave Vegas now. I didn't have enough gas money to make the trip.

"I'm not sure," I said.

"You doing a lot of gambling?" Bella asked. "Winning some big pots?"

I didn't want to tell her that my curse had followed me here and I didn't dare gamble.

"With no paycheck this week," I said, "I'd better stay out of the casinos."

"Hell, no. This is the best time to gamble," Bella told me. "Throw yourself out there. Take a chance. That's what gambling is all about. Go for it, girl."

Maybe that wasn't the best advice in the world, but it did sound like fun.

"I've got to go," Bella said, her voice low and rushed. "That cow Rita is heading this way. Eat a buffet for me, okay? See you."

The line went dead. I closed my phone.

Jeez, I really missed Bella.

"Haley," Monica called, "I've got a great idea."

I missed Sandy, too.

"We should take one of those jet helicopter tours over the Grand Canyon," Monica said. "Doesn't that sound like fun?"

"Yeah, fun," I mumbled.

I missed Marcie. I missed my apartment and my own bed.

Monica and Kay gave a little cheer and high-fived each other over the flip-flop display.

Rosalyn Chase's home on Elkhurst Place in Henderson wasn't far from the Green Valley Casino, I noted, as my GPS unit sent me in that direction. I'd made arrangements with Rosalyn to meet at her house tonight to get a look at pieces from Danielle and Courtney's fashion accessory line, but now I was thinking I might be a little late getting there.

My financial situation was dire, no doubt about it. So maybe it was time to do something drastic—hit the casinos—as Bella had suggested on the phone this morning.

The image flashed in my head. Me feeding my last quarter into the slot machine, reels spinning, lights flashing, landing on the big-winner combination.

Oh, yeah. I liked that scenario.

Then, of course, just the opposite popped into my head.

Feeding in my last quarter, the slot machine gobbling it up, giving nothing in return.

I didn't like that image so much.

But what was I going to do? I needed money. Where was I going to get enough to live on until Holt's came through with my paycheck next week?

I slammed on the brakes to keep from rear-ending the car in front of me stopped at a traffic light, as an utterly horrible idea came to me: I could return everything I'd bought since I came to Vegas.

The thought was almost too devastating to consider but I made myself do it. I can be strong like that when I have to.

Return everything. The fabulous capris with the coordinating sweaters, jewelry, and sandals. The raincoat and umbrella—yeah, okay, I wouldn't need them until the fall, but still. But what about the new exercise program I intended to start? How could I even consider in-line skating at the beach without those new shorts, T-shirts, and hats? And how would I relax afterwards if I returned those way-hot bathing suits and coverups I'd bought?

I turned onto Horizon Ridge Parkway, my mind racing. There had to be another way. Maybe I could—

Hang on a minute. I had a rich boyfriend.

Ty had offered to pay my tuition, take over my bills,

buy me a beach house, and send me to Dubai—I'm really going to have to find out exactly where that is—to shop for a month with a driver and a personal escort. He could slip me a few twenties to see me through, couldn't he?

And, really, this whole mess was kind of his fault. After all, it was the crappy time clock in the store he owned that had caused this problem. Sort of.

Yeah, okay, not really.

Still, I had no one else to turn to. I would never ask a friend for money. It's the best way to ruin your friendship. And I would drag my dehydrated, fried-to-a-crisp sun-burned body across the desert on my hands and knees to get home before I'd ask my parents for help.

So that left Ty. My boyfriend—my official boyfriend. The one person on the planet who was supposed to be there for me, no matter what.

Hmm. Wonder why I hadn't thought of him sooner.

That probably said something about our relationship, but no sense getting into it too deep right now. I had other problems to solve.

It was one thing for someone—even your official boyfriend—to offer to give you money, quite another to have to ask for it. Asking for money made you look pathetic and weak—which was exactly the way I was feeling at the moment anyway, but still, it changed things. I wasn't sure I'd like those changes.

The GPS unit sent me into a maze of residential streets. Each stucco and tiled-roof house looked a lot like the one next to it—which was the point of a master-planned community, I guess. No grand homes here, just average-size houses with front yards of rock and drought-resistant plants. Everything was clean, neat, and tidy. A quiet neighborhood.

I pulled to a stop in front of Rosalyn's house on Elkhurst. Her place looked as clean, neat, and tidy as everybody else's. No sign of Danielle's van.

If she got here a little later, that would be okay. I wanted to talk to Rosalyn alone.

The one thing I'd never learned about Courtney's death was *why*. Why had she been killed? Who had a motive? Robbie had reminded me of that this morning at Holt's.

I'd found a motive last night—a big one. Valerie Wagner blamed Courtney for her son's death in Iraq, and she certainly looked angry—and crazy—enough to murder Courtney when Rosalyn and I had seen her in the parking lot.

Rosalyn had known Valerie for a while now, so I wanted to talk to her, get her take on the possibility. I wanted to talk to Danielle about it, too, find out if Valerie had come around their workroom at the industrial complex or her apartment, if she'd threatened Courtney.

I really hoped Danielle had gotten the message I'd left for her yesterday and planned to be here tonight. I needed to ask her about Courtney's funeral arrangements, too.

I went to the front door and rang the bell. A few minutes passed. No answer. I rang it again. The neighborhood was really quiet. Only a few cars drove through. No kids on bicycles.

Rosalyn still didn't answer her door, so I got out my cell phone and called the number she'd given me last night. Her voicemail picked up. I left a message. I knocked on the front door again and listened. No sound from inside the house.

It was a nice evening so I figured Rosalyn planned to entertain Danielle and me on her back patio, which was probably why she hadn't heard her doorbell or phone.

I followed the walkway through the gate and around to the back of the house. A nice patio with comfy-looking chairs and a tile-topped table sat under a covered area, an oasis in a sea of rocks. No sign guests were expected, no drinks or snacks. No Rosalyn.

Huh. Well, maybe she was at the store buying food or

something for tonight and was running late. Or maybe something had come up.

Either way, seemed like she would have called me.

Okay, this was disappointing and kind of annoying. I'd really wanted to see some of Courtney and Danielle's accessory line—and find out something new about Courtney's murder.

The curtain covering the patio slider was open about a foot. I cupped my hands around my eyes and looked inside. I got a partial view of Rosalyn's kitchen. No glasses or pitcher sitting on the countertop that I could see. No sign she was preparing for company. I knocked on the door, waited, then knocked again. Nothing moved inside the house.

My cell phone rang. I flipped it open and saw that the caller was Danielle.

Finally.

"Are you coming to Rosalyn's house tonight?" I asked.

"I'm in L.A.," Danielle said. "I'm getting things arranged for Courtney."

"Her funeral?" I asked, thinking that was kind of weird after what Robbie had told me this morning. "The cops said nobody had claimed her body yet."

Static came through the phone and I thought we were going to get cut off, then Danielle said, "I meant I'm making business arrangements. Getting a few things cleared up."

I wondered if she was seeing Mike Ivan. That whole maybe-he's-really-in-the-Russian-mob thing worried me.

"Are you going to Rosalyn's place tonight?" Danielle asked.

"I'm here now. She's not home," I told her, and peeked inside the kitchen again. "Listen, Danielle, I need to ask you something about—"

"I've got to go. I'll catch up with you later," she said and hung up.

Crap.

I closed my phone and headed toward the front of the house again.

So, apparently, Danielle had cancelled for tonight and Rosalyn hadn't bothered to call and tell me. She didn't seem the type but, really, I hardly knew her. I still wanted to see the fashion accessories she had, so what could I do but call her again tomorrow?

I got into my car and drove away.

CHAPTER 22

I hit a McDonald's drive-through and ate in my Honda as I drove back to the Culver Inn. Since Rosalyn had cancelled and not let me know—which irritated me to no end—my plans for the evening had been blown big time.

Normally, this would have been the perfect opportunity to go shopping. But you can't shop without money—which also irritated me to no end.

The gamble-or-don't-gamble-away-my-last-cent scenario flashed in my head again, and that made me think of Madam CeeCee. I pulled out my cell phone as I turned into the Culver Inn parking lot and punched in her number.

Of course, I didn't really have the money to pay her fee now—maybe she knew that and that's the reason she never returned my call—but I had to try again. Maybe she'd do a phone consultation. It's not like I needed a full psychic reading or anything. I only wanted one question answered.

I swung into a parking space and listened as Madam CeeCee's voicemail picked up. Damn. I left another message.

I gathered my trash and was about to get out of my car when Bradley walked out of the Culver Inn, crossed the parking lot, and got into a black Lexus.

I hate him.

And seeing him driving that expensive car made me hate him even more.

What a little weasel. Firing employees for no reason. Throwing his weight around. Being a jackass, just because he could.

If it weren't for his family money, I doubted he'd own that Lexus or manage the Culver Inn. He sure didn't deserve either one.

Bradley backed the Lexus out of the parking spot and pulled away, and because I was irritated with just about everything and everybody at the moment, I started my Honda and followed him. I don't know what I expected to find out about Bradley that I didn't already know, but still.

I followed him onto St. Rose Parkway and my spirits lifted.

Oh, wow, this was so cool. I was tailing a guy just like those hot private detectives do on TV. I wished Marcie was here with me.

I hung back about three car lengths and followed Bradley onto the 215. Lots of traffic was on the freeway, so I was sure he didn't notice me. We transitioned north onto the 15. The Mandalay Bay, the black Luxor Pyramid, New York-New York, and the other casinos on The Strip were on my right, and in the distance to the left rose the Palms and the Rio.

Bradley didn't seem to notice me behind him. No quick lane changes, no evasive maneuvers, no one-finger salutes.

Hey, I'm liking this private detective stuff.

Bradley took the Sahara Avenue exit, so I figured he was headed for The Strip, but he turned left instead of right, headed away from the glitz and glamour of the casinos.

Maybe I could start my own detective agency. Wow, that would be so cool. I could wear great clothes and carry fabulous handbags and hire hot, muscular, good-looking detectives who'd have to do whatever I said.

At Decatur, Bradley turned right. Since we were on the surface streets, I held back a little more.

Did you need a license to be a private detective? A certificate? A degree of some sort? Jeez, I hoped not. That would take all the fun out of it.

Eventually Bradley turned onto Charleston Boulevard and I immediately began to rethink my private detective career.

What the heck was Bradley—and now me—doing in this section of Vegas?

The area wasn't bad, but not the kind of place you'd host a rehearsal dinner, either. Certainly not a location you'd expect someone from the prominent, wealthy, well-to-do Pennington family to frequent.

Mom-and-pop restaurants, bars, gas stations, tire stores. Everything was old, slightly worn, kind of shabby, definitely showing its age. You wouldn't find any of the Vegas high rollers in this neighborhood, unless they were slumming.

Maybe that's what Bradley was doing here, I realized, when I saw him whip into the parking lot of the Shamrock Pub.

No way was I following him in there. I drove past, did a U-turn—which was illegal, but, oh well—and pulled into the parking lot of a laundromat across the street.

The Shamrock Pub was a gentlemen's club, according to the big green sign on its roof, but I doubted anything gentlemanly went on inside. More like pole dancers and topless waitresses.

I didn't want to think about what—ugh, gross—Bradley might do in there.

I guess he was thinking it over, too, because he got out of his car, closed the door, and stood there, looking more than a little out of place in his white shirt and necktie. He gazed around the parking lot, then up and down and across the street.

Yikes! Bradley looked right at me.

I was tempted to duck down but thought that might attract more attention—and, besides, it's not something we cool private detectives would do—and forced myself to sit still.

I never realized this private detective stuff was so nerve-wracking.

Bradley must not have noticed me sitting in the car, because he pulled out his cell phone and made a quick call. I figured he was just meeting up with some of his buddies—hard to believe somebody like Bradley would actually have friends—and they were late or something. After only a few minutes, two biker dudes dressed in leather, sporting tattoos and piercings, approached Bradley.

For a minute I wondered if those guys might beat the crap out of Bradley—which was bad of me, I know—so I pulled out my cell phone ready to call 9-1-1. Even the hottest private investigators need backup from time to time.

But they just started talking to Bradley. Not a get-your-punk-ass-off-of-our-lot kind of thing. Not a hey-let's-party sort of conversation. Just talking. They had the same sort of expressions on their faces that I often saw on Ty's when we were at dinner and somebody from Holt's called him with yet another emergency that would apparently cause the national atomic clock to skip a millisecond and bring on worldwide tsunamis that would wipe out all of mankind if he didn't address it before dessert.

I hate when that happens.

Anyway, Bradley and the bikers talked and nodded, everyone in agreement over something, apparently. Then Bradley got back into his Lexus and drove away. I sat there for a bit watching the biker guys, but they just ambled back into the Shamrock Pub.

Obviously, I'd witnessed nothing that would give me the material for the revenge I desperately wanted and allow me to ruin Bradley's life.

I hate it when that happens, too.

I pulled out onto Charleston Boulevard and spotted Bradley's Lexus two blocks ahead. I followed. The traffic light at the next intersection turned yellow and I could have made it through, but the guy in front of me stopped for no good reason except that the light had turned yellow. I mean, come on, the yellow light just meant get ready to stop—not stop. That's what the red light was for.

Am I the only one who understands this?

By the time I got going again, Bradley had disappeared. I drove around for a while, thinking I might stumble onto him, but no such luck.

So much for my career as a private investigator.

I desperately needed a mocha frappuccino. Yeah, okay, money was tight—really, almost nonexistent—but basic survival needs had to be met. I drove around until I spotted a Starbucks and pulled in.

Inside, I got my frappuccino and, just as I sat down at a table near the window, my cell phone rang. I glanced at the I.D. screen expecting to see Rosalyn's name or maybe even Madam CeeCee's. But it was Ty.

Oh my God. Ty was calling.

My stomach got all warm and gooey just seeing his name.

"I miss you," he said when I answered.

His voice sounded mellow. I imagined myself leaning against his hard chest, resting my head on his shoulder.

Nice.

"I miss you, too," I said.

"I was thinking you needed something to go with the new beach house," Ty said.

My thoughts jumped to light speed. I'd already bought

new bathing suits, coverups, totes, and sandals. Provided I didn't have to return them to keep from starving to death, I couldn't think of anything else I'd need to live at the beach.

"How about a new Mercedes SLK350?" Ty suggested.

My jaw dropped.

"Your choice of colors," he added.

I couldn't think of a single word to say.

"Convertible, of course," Ty said.

Even if I could have thought of something to say, I don't think I could have actually spoken it aloud.

"Haley? Are you there?" he asked.

"Yeah," I managed to say. "I'm just . . . well, I'm over-whelmed."

Ty chuckled softly. "I think you'd look really hot cruising Pacific Coast Highway in a ride like that."

Oh, yeah. I definitely would.

"You know, Haley," Ty said, his voice more serious now, "there's nothing I wouldn't do for you."

Maybe this would be a good time to ask if he'd spot me a hundred bucks.

I didn't have a chance, though. I heard voices in the background, then Ty said, "Haley, I've got to go. We'll look at cars when you get back. I promise."

"Great. I'd love—"

Ty had already hung up.

I closed my phone and pulled in a big breath to steady myself.

Wow, a new Mercedes to go with a new beach house.

The image flashed in my mind. Me in a white—no, black—convertible, top down, wind in my hair—but not so much it gets tangled and I look like a rolling haystack when I stop—wearing a fantastic Stella McCartney sundress—oh my God, I have to shop for sundresses—the gorgeous Pacific Ocean at my fingertips, the hills above Malibu rising beside the highway—everyone who passes me is jealous, of course—and beside me in my black—no, blue—Mercedes is—

Wait a minute. Ty never said he'd be in the convertible with me.

But surely he would.

Wouldn't he?

I didn't want to ruin this fabulous dreamlike scenario with actual facts, so I didn't call Ty back and ask. I decided to put my time to better use.

Sipping my frappuccino, I logged onto the Internet with my cell phone. I didn't use it much for Internet access, except to occasionally check my e-mail or take a quick look at a Web site, because I preferred my laptop. But my laptop was in my room at the Culver Inn and I couldn't quite face that place yet.

I typed Bradley Pennington's name into a search engine and got all sorts of hits. Not on Bradley, but on his family.

Lots had been written about the Pennington family, I discovered as I scrolled through and read newspaper reports and magazine stories. Helen Pennington was the matriarch of the clan, it seemed. I checked out her picture. She looked great. If she'd made it to sixty, I'd be surprised. Dark hair, trim figure, perfect makeup, fabulous suit.

I'd bet she owned a staggering collection of designer handbags.

The most recent magazine article included yet another photo, this one showing her at her massive desk in her opulent Las Vegas office atop the family-owned Corona high-rise office building. This was the nerve center of the Pennington empire, according to the article, which included everything from real estate to manufacturing to mining to restaurants to motel chains.

I read through more articles. No mention of a Mr. Pennington. Guess Helen ran the show.

But she had some family help, another article revealed. Daughter Kaitlin, an attorney; sons Daniel and Conner, both in upper management. Just one big, happy, ultra-smart, mega-successful family.

I finished off my frappuccino as I scrolled to another article, this one heralding Helen Pennington's penchant for seemingly lost causes. She'd donated funds to keep a skating rink open in a not-so-hot section of Vegas. The article also noted her previous contributions to animal preserves, the children's symphony, and youth camps. She was a big supporter of local law enforcement, each year sponsoring a fund-raiser for the police widow's fund.

I kept digging and finally found a small online story reporting the acquisition of the Culver Inns, a generously termed *family* chain of motels in the Las Vegas area. Bradley Pennington, the article noted, had been appointed to manage the St. Rose Parkway motel.

My brain buzzed, coming down from my chocolate caffeine high, and I felt panicky. I needed to figure out what all this information about the Pennington family meant. This was no time to let a frappuccino-free brain cause a lapse in concentration.

Of course, I didn't really need another shot of chocolate or caffeine to figure this out. Nor did I need Madam CeeCee—not that she'd ever call me back, it seemed.

Obviously, Bradley was the screw-up of the Pennington family. If he'd had a college degree, drive, ambition, and good leadership skills, he would have been ensconced in a corner office of the prestigious Corona office building with his brothers and sisters—not running a fleabag motel out in Henderson.

Yet Helen hadn't given up on him. She'd probably encouraged him and cheered him on all his life, and in an ultimate only-a-mom-would-go-this-far moment, she'd purchased an entire chain of motels just so Bradley could manage one. She'd probably convinced herself that if she could just find the right spot for him, not only could

Bradley hold his head up at the Thanksgiving dinner table, he could actually succeed just like all her other children.

You've got to love a mom like that.

I logged off the Internet and shoved my cell phone into my purse.

Hopeless. That's how I felt at the moment. Revenge against Bradley was completely out of my grasp. No way would Helen Pennington let anything happen to her little darling. She surely had a regimen of attorneys standing at attention, ready, willing, and able to fend off any lawsuit brought against Bradley. No matter what anyone at the motel said about him, how much the employees and guests complained, how many people he fired, and how often he had to hire new ones, Helen would stand by her son.

The rest of us were just screwed.

Motel employees would keep being intimidated by Bradley. He'd keep treating everyone like crap. Maya would lose her breakfast buffet contract. She wouldn't get referred to the other Culver Inns in Vegas. Bradley's rein of terror would continue indefinitely.

Why couldn't I have a mom like that?

I got into my car and headed back to the Culver Inn. Honestly, I wasn't sure exactly where I was, and I didn't feel like being ordered around by my GPS, so I headed toward the bright lights of The Strip.

I crept down Las Vegas Boulevard taking in the sights and sounds. Traffic was always near gridlock here, but that was okay with me tonight. I wasn't in a hurry to get back to my room.

In the daylight, The Strip looked kind of gaudy, maybe even a little cheesy. But at night when the casinos and hotels were lit up, it shone like a magical kingdom.

The sidewalks were packed with people, laughing, strolling, looking up wide-eyed at the huge casino buildings. I spotted a few—well, okay, more than a few—

strange-looking people, and I wondered if Cliff and his fellow ufologists were patrolling The Strip tonight.

The fountains danced in front of the Bellagio. The roller coaster clacked on its tracks above New York-New York. Flags waved above the minarets of the Excalibur. The golden lion glistened at the MGM.

I wished Marcie was here. Or Ty.

When I finally got back to my home-away-from-home at the Culver Inn, I'd just kicked off my shoes when my room phone rang.

"Miss Randolph, this is the front desk," a woman said when I answered. "Could you come down here right away?"

Good grief, what now? I wondered.

Then I knew. Oh my God, they'd charged another night's stay to my credit card and the charge hadn't gone through because my card was maxed out. I was going to get kicked out of this place tonight.

No way could I let that happen. I had nowhere else to go.

"I can't really do that," I said, and hung up.

I stood by the phone expecting it to ring again, but it didn't. Whew. Thank goodness. At least I could sleep here another night. And tomorrow?

Well, I'd worry about that in the morning.

A knock sounded at my door.

Oh, crap. The desk clerk with security backup was probably outside ready to evict me from my room.

The knock sounded again, louder this time. I rushed to the peephole and looked out. Two men stood in the hallway. The view was cloudy, sort of distorted, but they looked familiar—

Oh my God. It was Detectives Dailey and Webster. What were they doing here?

"Open up!" Detective Webster called, and pounded on my door again. "We know you're in there!"

I opened my door.

"What's up?" I asked.

I was going for a see-how-calm-I-am-and-that-proves-I-didn't-do-anything-wrong look, but I'm not sure I pulled it off.

"Miss Randolph," Detective Dailey said. "We'd like to speak with you about the murder of Rosalyn Chase."

CHAPTER 23

"Rosalyn is *dead?*"
I blurted that out standing in the doorway of my motel room, and I'm pretty sure it came out sounding stunned—because I *was* stunned.

Detective Dailey's expression softened a fraction, but Webster snarled back.

"Yeah, like you don't already know that?" he demanded.

I looked back and forth between the two of them. Rosalyn was *dead?* Murdered? And the detectives had come *here?* To see *me?* Why would they do that? Shouldn't they be out investigating—

Oh, crap.

"We'd like you to come with us," Detective Dailey said.

He was using his everything-will-be-all-right voice. I'm sure he'd coaxed many a suspect into custody with that tone. But he didn't fool me—not with all the *Law and Order* reruns on TV these days.

Oh my God. They wanted me to go to the police station with them. To be questioned. Grilled. For hours, probably.

Why didn't I have a mom like Helen Pennington? If her little Bradley were in trouble, she could call in attorneys, investigators. She even had friends high up in law enforcement, thanks to her donations to the widow's fund.

All my mom could do was give advice on tiara placement, runway turns, and lip liner. She could tell me how to give a gracious acceptance speech, but, frankly, I wasn't feeling particularly gracious at the moment.

Maybe I could call Jack Bishop. He'd come help me, but what could he do? He operated in Los Angeles, not Vegas.

Detective Shuman would help, but he was an L.A. homicide detective. Dailey might listen to him as a professional courtesy, but that wouldn't keep me out of jail.

Oh my God. Who was left? Who could I turn to who might—

Oh, wait. I had a boyfriend with tons of money and an army of overpriced attorneys who'd like nothing more than to ring up more billable hours courtesy of the Cameron family.

Jeez, why didn't I ever think of Ty first?

No time for deep thoughts right now. I had bigger problems.

Yeah, okay. One problem—staying out of jail.

"What happened to Rosalyn?" I asked, trying for an I-haven't-got-a-clue effect. It came across as pretty convincing—because it was true.

"Let's go someplace where we can talk," Dailey said.

I didn't have to go with them, unless they were arresting me. At least, that's what I thought.

Jeez, I really hoped I was right.

"Here's fine with me," I said, still standing in my doorway.

Dailey's expression hardened again. I knew it didn't suit him, but he didn't push.

"Where were you today?" Dailey asked.

"At work," I said.

They could check my time card and see when I'd punched in and out for the day. Dailey glanced at Webster. He pulled a little notebook from his jacket pocket and flipped pages, then nodded.

I guess that meant they'd already checked my time card. Not a great feeling.

"So what happened to Rosalyn?" I asked again.

"A neighbor got concerned when Rosalyn didn't answer her phone or door. She has a seizure disorder. The neighbor had a house key, so she let herself in," Detective Dailey said. "She found Rosalyn in the bedroom."

"Dead," Webster said. "Stabbed."

Just like Courtney had been stabbed.

Now I kind of wished I'd agreed to go somewhere with them, at least the lobby, maybe, so I could sit down.

"Where did you go after work?" Dailey asked.

I wasn't feeling all that great at the moment.

"Neighbors saw you at Rosalyn's house," Webster barked.

I didn't even want a Snickers bar, or a bag of Oreos—*that's* how bad I felt.

"I was invited," I insisted. "Rosalyn asked me to come over and look at some fashion accessories a friend had designed."

"What friend would that be?" Dailey asked.

"Danielle Shepherd and Courtney—"

"Courtney Collins?" he asked.

Maybe I should stop talking now.

Again, Dailey looked at Webster, who consulted his notebook.

"Nothing like that at the scene," Webster reported, and seemed pleased to announce it.

"But there had to have been," I said. "That's the reason I went."

"So you admit you were there," Detective Dailey concluded.

I really should stop talking now.

"A witness saw you go to the back of the house," Webster said. "You were back there for a while. Long enough to slip in and murder Rosalyn."

"I didn't murder anybody!" I shouted.

Could I trade in my month-long Dubai shopping trip for bail money?

"Look," I said. "I was only at Rosalyn's place for a few minutes—not long at all. Then I left."

"Where did you go?" Detective Dailey asked.

Oh, crap.

I'd been tailing the son of an upstanding, law-abiding pillar of the Las Vegas community. For no real reason, except that I didn't like him and hoped to discover something terrible about him that I could use to help my friend build her muffin empire.

I couldn't tell the detectives that. It sure as heck wouldn't help anything. They'd probably think I was a stalker or something.

"I went for a drive," I said. Yeah, okay, that sounded really lame.

Detective Dailey must have picked up on that, too, because he morphed from good-cop to bad-cop in a heartbeat.

"I don't know what you're trying to pull here, Miss Randolph, but I've had enough of it," Dailey told me. "You showed up in Henderson with some far-fetched excuse for coming here, and your old high school rival just happened to get killed the day you arrived."

"I had nothing to do with that," I insisted.

Dailey ignored me.

"Then I overheard you using an alias with your coworker," he said.

Cliff. That idiot insisted on calling me Dana—how was that my fault?

"You lied about your job to a Reno police officer who came to the store," Dailey said. "You claimed to be working undercover."

Reno police officer? I didn't know any—

Oh my God. Robbie Freedman was a *police officer?*

"You're at the scene of a second murder that's somehow connected to the death of Courtney Collins." Detective Dailey gave me big-time, bad-cop triple stink-eye. "Can you give me one good reason why I shouldn't arrest you right now?"

Oh, crap.

"How about some evidence?" I shouted over the song playing on my car stereo.

Yes! That had shut him up.

I turned onto Sunset Road, last night's standoff in my motel room doorway still playing over and over in my mind. Me being forceful and dynamic, demanding some evidence from the detectives. The look of total defeat on both their faces.

Maybe I should become a lawyer.

I'd showed those guys last night. No way were they going to mess with me.

Yeah, well, okay, I hadn't exactly shouted at the detectives. And, honestly, they hadn't looked totally defeated. But I'd definitely hit them with some undeniable logic—*no evidence.*

How long would it take to get a law degree?

I was on my lunch break—and on a mission—and I still couldn't get the whole incident out of my head. Stocking bras and panty hose for four hours this morning just hadn't taken a lot of concentration. Go figure.

Detective Webster had glared at me like a rabid dog, and Dailey had given me a definite I'll-be-back look as they'd left last night.

Not a great feeling.

But at least they'd left. I was still free to come and go as I pleased—and solve these murders, since the detectives didn't seem to be making any progress.

True, they had no evidence against me. But, unfortunately, I had no proof that I was innocent, either. My word didn't count for anything, obviously, and I didn't even have any electronic backup.

My GPS, when they downloaded it, would show that I'd driven to Rosalyn's house. I hadn't used it after leaving her place, so there was no proof of where I'd been. The detectives could contend that I'd driven right back to her house, once I knew where to find the place, and killed Rosalyn.

The cell phone call I'd received from Danielle would prove I was at Rosalyn's house, which wouldn't do me any good. I'd gotten a call from Ty and used the Internet later in the evening. Since the detectives had already, apparently, checked on the time I'd left Holt's for the day and they'd still come and questioned me, that must mean Rosalyn had been killed shortly before I got there, which meant the call from Ty or my use of the Internet wouldn't help me.

Detective Dailey was probably right that the murder of Courtney Collins and Rosalyn Chase were connected—but not because of me. And the only connection I could think of was the handbag club and Valerie Wagner.

Poor Rosalyn. She was such a nice lady. I couldn't believe she was really gone—or that I'd probably been knocking on her door and all the while she'd been inside dead. Yikes!

I wasn't sure if Dailey knew about Valerie. I certainly wasn't going to mention her to him. Not now, anyway. Not until I checked out something for myself.

I turned onto Pecos Road, searching the store fronts for a house number or, better yet, a sign for Wagner's Fabrics. I'd found Valerie's business address easily enough on the Internet this morning, and now I intended to confront her, see what she had to say for herself.

A big white sign depicting a spool of thread and a sewing needle caught my attention a couple of seconds too late. I braked hard, and swung into the strip mall. Tires screeched behind me. Jeez, drivers really should be more alert.

It seemed like a nice enough location for a fabric store, along with about a dozen other stores and offices all looking clean and well tended. An insurance firm, a bakery, a Chinese restaurant, a gift shop, that sort of thing. I pulled into a parking slot in front of Valerie's fabric store and got out.

A CLOSED sign hung in the bottom corner of her display window near the entrance. I walked closer and checked out the hours posted nearby. The store was scheduled to be open.

I peered inside and saw bolts of fabric, displays of thread, bobbins and notions, cabinets of patterns. Lights off. No movement.

I really hoped Valerie wasn't lying in the back room stabbed to death.

I went to the gift shop next door. A little bell tinkled as I walked inside. The place smelled of scented candles and was crammed full of floral arrangements, dolls, books, kitchen gadgets, holiday decorations, home décor items, and just about every other kind of gift imaginable. Two customers were in the shop, one looking at the greeting cards, the other checking out a display of cat bowls.

"Can I help you?" the woman behind the counter called.

She looked toned and trim, dressed in a no-nonsense sweater set, and was busy packing a set of candlesticks into a white gift box.

"I stopped by to see Valerie, but her store is closed," I said, pointing in the direction of the fabric shop. "Have you seen her? Is she okay?"

"She's not open?" The woman rose on her toes and peered out her display window at the parking lot. "Valerie closed early yesterday. She stopped by on her way out to tell me she was going to visit her sister in Reno. I didn't believe her. Valerie never closes her shop—well, except for when . . ."

I knew she was thinking about the funeral of Valerie's son.

"Scott," I said, nodding sympathetically.

"It's been hard on Valerie," she said.

Hard enough to murder Rosalyn last night, then hide out at her sister's place in Reno?

"I'll catch her later," I said, and left the shop.

I got into my car and headed down Pecos Road again. I had just enough time to grab some lunch and get back to work before my lunch break ended. I spotted a Burger King and pulled into the drive-through.

Of course, I had no evidence that Valerie had killed Rosalyn. She'd certainly looked angry and unstable enough to kill someone—namely, Rosalyn and me—when she'd confronted us in the parking lot after the handbag club meeting.

I didn't know what had set her off that night. Maybe just being back in the boutique and hearing Courtney's name. Maybe she'd gone home and pulled out all of Scott's old Mother's Day cards and lost her mind—not that I blamed her, of course. It certainly wouldn't be the first time someone like Rosalyn had been the target of misplaced anger.

Still, it seemed like one heck of a coincidence that Valerie had closed her shop early on the day Rosalyn was killed, then conveniently gone to Reno to visit her sister.

I pulled up to the menu board and ordered a burger and a chocolate shake—just to ensure good brain function for the afternoon, of course.

Was there another coincidence in this whole thing? I wondered, as I paid for my lunch and drove away.

Valerie had gone to Reno. Robbie Freedman was from Reno. Hmm. Reno was a big place, so it could very well have been just a coincidence. Still, it made me wonder.

It made me think of Robbie.

Robbie was a police officer? He should have told me. I mean, really, those guys should be required to wear their badges at all times. It's just the decent thing to do. Then he'd ratted out me and my *undercover* work to Detective Dailey. What was that all about, anyway?

As I made the turn onto Sunset Road, I wondered about everything Robbie had told me yesterday in Holt's. Had he really driven all the way from Reno to Vegas—four hundred miles or something—just to see the place where Courtney had been murdered? It seemed weird, even if he was a police officer.

I gulped down some of my chocolate shake. My brain cells flashed quicker than the paparazzi cameras on the red carpet, and I remembered that when I'd asked if he was going back to Reno, Robbie had said he planned to spend the night here, visit a friend.

Oh my God. That meant Robbie had been in town when Rosalyn was murdered. Could he have killed her? For that matter, had he driven down and murdered Courtney?

Motive . . . motive. Hang on a minute, I needed a motive. Those TV crime dramas were big on motive.

I took another swig of chocolate milkshake and waited for another explosion of brilliance.

Nothing exploded.

I drove a few more blocks and diligently kept my brain infused with chocolate shake but couldn't come up with one single reason why Robbie might have killed Rosalyn.

Maybe I should switch to chocolate fudge shakes.

Really, though, I shouldn't be concerned that my standard chocolate shake had let me down. I hadn't really found a strong motive anywhere for anyone to have murdered Courtney or Rosalyn.

Yeah, okay, maybe I was getting a little carried away here, but still, Robbie's behavior was weird.

I unwrapped my burger and ate it as I drove. I couldn't get Robbie out of my mind.

If for some unknown reason Robbie had murdered Courtney, maybe that was why he hadn't asked for my cell phone number or e-mail address at Holt's yesterday. I mean, why wouldn't he? I am, after all, *me*. Was it because he really thought I was working undercover in the store, and that's why he went to see Detective Dailey to confirm it?

I finished off my burger as I pulled into a parking space in front of the Holt's store, sucked down the last of my shake, and went inside.

The place was shaping up. Racks and displays were stuffed with clothing. The display team was busy assembling and dressing an army of mannequins. The grand opening was probably scheduled pretty soon. I didn't know. If anybody had told me, I wasn't listening.

As I headed for the employee breakroom, I noticed two guys in the Juniors clothing department putting up framed posters of great-looking models wearing fantastic outfits, none of which would ever be found in the store.

Holt's was not first on anyone's high-fashion list.

Still, something about one of the posters looked familiar. I stopped and looked at the clothing. No, definitely not the clothing—

Oh my God. It was that girl.

I smacked myself on the forehead as I recognized the model in the poster. She was that girl who used to work at the Holt's store in Santa Clarita—I can never remember her name—the one who used to stink up the breakroom heating those frozen diet meals in the microwave. She lost like eighty pounds or something—so I hate her, of course—and she'd gone blonde and ditched her glasses. She'd quit her job at Holt's—so I really hated her then, of course—and, last I'd heard, was trying to get signed with a modeling agent.

Wow, she'd done it. She'd really done it.

I hate my life.

And I still hate her, of course.

Just as I stowed my handbag—a Michael Kors satchel—and punched in, Preston barreled through the breakroom door. His cheeks were kind of pink and beads of sweat glistened on his forehead.

Not a good look.

"Haley? Haley?" he called, even though he was staring straight at me. "Haley, I must speak with you."

"I'm standing right here, Preston," I said.

He puffed up, then glanced at the three employees sitting at the table having lunch, and said, "Outside."

Preston turned around, straight-armed the door, and stomped out of the breakroom.

What now? I wondered as I followed. Then it hit me—oh my God, were Detectives Dailey and Webster here? Had they spoken with Preston? Were they going to arrest me?

I glanced back toward the breakroom. Was it too late to cut and run?

Preston whipped around in the middle of the hallway, wild-eyed and half-crazed, and said, "What were you thinking, Haley? What were you thinking? I asked you to handle one simple project."

I was supposed to handle a project?

"And *this* happens?" Preston said, his voice raising.

Something had happened?

His hands trembled as he pushed his fingers through the little hair that was left on his head.

"The employees—all of them—are expecting everything you promised them," he declared.

I'd promised the employees something?

"Fireworks at the Red Rock Resort. Helicopter rides over the Grand Canyon. A party at some bar at Harrah's." Preston looked stunned, bewildered—which was sort of the way I felt, too.

"I never promised anybody—"

"You most certainly did," Preston told me. "Employees have come to me all morning since the meeting."

There was a meeting this morning? Oops. No wonder the store seemed so quiet.

"They've been telling me what they want to do before our grand opening," Preston said. "They said you told them their suggestions all sounded like a great idea."

Well, yeah, okay, I'd said that—but I thought people were just sharing fun things to do in Vegas. Why would they think I'd have Preston arrange those things?

"I asked you to find a way to reward the employees after the situation with that poor girl's murder," Preston said.

Oh, crap. Now I remembered.

"But I certainly can't do any of those things. There's no room in the budget. They're completely out of the question," he insisted. He pointed his finger at me. "You're going to have to tell them."

"What?"

"Or find a way to pay for those extravagant requests yourself."

"*What?*"

"You handle it. I'm washing my hands of the entire situation," Preston declared, and rubbed his hands together, as if I needed a demonstration.

He expected me to pay thousands of dollars to treat the employees? I'd had to scrounge quarters from the bottom of my purse for lunch.

"We're done here." Preston whipped around and walked off, then stopped suddenly and turned back. "There's someone in my office to see you."

I glanced down the hallway at the door to Preston's office.

Jeez, I really hoped my official boyfriend was in there—

and that he had his platinum American Express card on him.

But more than likely, Detective Dailey—with Webster somewhere just out of sight in case I made a break for it—was in there waiting for me. At the moment, the idea of being arrested didn't seem so bad. Maybe I could organize a tour of my cell block. The store employees would like that just as well as a helicopter tour of the Grand Canyon, wouldn't they?

It least it was something I could afford.

I walked down the hallway and pushed open the door to Preston's office. A man I didn't recognize stood in the corner. Thirty-five, I guessed, not much taller than me, nice build, okay clothes, kind of good looking.

"Haley Randolph?" he asked. "I'm Mike Ivan."

CHAPTER 24

Oh my God. Mike Ivan.

The guy rumored to belong to the Russian mob. The guy with questionable business methods. The guy who'd been looking for Courtney—who was now dead.

He'd come to Vegas. To Henderson. To Holt's. To Preston's office. To see *me*.

Why was he here? What did he want? How had he found me? How had he gotten past the security guard at the door? Why had Preston turned his office over to him?

A zillion thoughts raced through my head—lucky thing I'd had that chocolate shake for lunch—but all I could come up with was—this couldn't be good.

Would it help if I clicked my heels together and repeated, "There's no place like Macy's"?

Mike nodded toward the hallway. "I told the store manager I was a family friend," he said.

He rounded the desk and came toward me. I backed away, into the corner. Mike pushed the door closed.

"We need to get a few things cleared up," he told me.

Oh my God. He was going to kill me. He was going to murder me right here in the store manager's office—which that idiot Preston had conveniently let him use.

Who the hell was doing the hiring for Holt's these days?

Couldn't we get some ex-Navy SEALs, or maybe some Special Forces guys into management positions?

I was definitely taking that up with Ty—if he made it to the crime scene before I drew my final breath.

"I run legitimate businesses," Mike said. "No matter what you've heard, or what your private detective buddy told you, or what the cops say, I run a clean operation."

If Mike had gotten word that Jack Bishop and Detective Shuman had been asking around about him—which I supposed he had or he wouldn't be here—I wondered at just how clean his operation was. Or if maybe he used his family mob connections when he needed them.

I would.

"My family," Mike said, and shook his head as if he'd been through this same thing before, many times. "They go their way, I go mine. That's the way it's always been with us. I can't help what they do. You know what it's like with family."

I knew exactly. The biggest reason I'd come to Vegas in the first place was to escape spa week with my mom and her friends.

Yeah, okay, being related to the Russian mob was way worse than having a former beauty queen for a mother.

"Still, I hear things," he said.

I had to agree that could come in handy, especially when a homicide detective with the LAPD was asking questions about your possible connection to a murder.

"Then maybe you heard that I'm a suspect in the murder of Courtney Collins," I said.

Mike looked sad. "Courtney was a great girl."

"You two dated?" I asked.

"Business," he said. "I'm in import–export. Textiles, among other things."

I'd spent some time in L.A.'s Textile District recently— long story—and knew a little about the place. The culture was very strong there, very diverse. Koreans and Armenians, Latinos, all sorts of ethnicities, lots of unwritten rules. Some places refused to deal with people off the street, others saw everyone as fair game and took advantage whenever possible. It was a twilight economy, lots of cash transactions. Everybody was wary of outsiders, suspicious, and cautious.

But in the end it was business, big business. Everyone hustled, from the guys in the stores to those hidden away in the top floors of the buildings, running the factories. You had to be smart to fit in.

I didn't see Courtney wheeling and dealing down there. She'd need somebody like Mike to handle it for her.

"What did Courtney need?" I asked.

"Fabric. The expensive kind," Mike said. "I'm talking fabric and leather from Florence, Paris, all over Europe. Hundreds of dollars per yard. Courtney needed it for her business."

"Fashion accessories," I said.

"For a very upscale, very exclusive clientele," Mike said.

I knew the sort of items he was talking about. One-of-a-kind pieces, each handmade. More wearable art than fashion. Nothing commercial, nothing mass produced.

"So I guess Courtney owed you money?" I asked.

"She worked some odd jobs, sold some pieces to the shops on Rodeo Drive and in Santa Monica, wherever those types of clients frequented. She paid me when she could. I was okay with that. I don't mind helping out an artist from time to time," Mike said. "Then Danielle showed up."

"Wait a minute," I said. "I thought Danielle started the line, did the designs, and Courtney handled the business end of things."

Mike shook his head. "No way. They were Courtney's designs right from the start."

Okay, that was weird. Danielle had definitely told me differently. But perhaps she'd had her own agenda.

Maybe she thought claiming that she designed the collection herself sounded more prestigious—which, I guess, it did. And she probably hadn't wanted to admit she'd been responsible for the business end of things, since it hadn't gone well.

Or maybe she just wanted to claim the line for herself so she could sell off the few pieces that remained and come up with the cash to pay off Mike and the Eastern Industrial Complex where they had their workroom. They probably had other debts she had to clear up, too.

Or maybe Mike was lying.

"Danielle talked Courtney into moving to Vegas. That's when I stopped receiving money," Mike said. "But that's taken care of now."

Okay, that surprised me.

"Danielle paid you?" I asked.

"She called yesterday, said she'd have the money in a few days. I drove up," Mike said. "Better to do these things in person."

I wondered if that was the Russian mob's standard operating procedure, but thought it better not to ask.

"You came to Vegas yesterday?" I asked. "And you saw Danielle here? Not in L.A.?"

"Last night at Courtney's apartment. Danielle was there with Tony, the boyfriend," Mike explained. "Danielle told me she was coming into some money. Said she'd have everything she owed me in a couple of days."

"Where was Danielle getting the money?" I asked.

Mike shrugged. "She didn't say and I didn't ask."

All I could figure was that Courtney had some life insurance that Danielle expected to collect on. Courtney had no other assets that I knew of.

Mike opened the office door and gave me a hard look. "So we understand each other?"

I didn't understand everything that was going on with

Danielle and Courtney, but I got Mike's message loud and clear.

"You're a businessman, collecting an honest, overdue debt," I said. "Nothing more."

He gave me a curt nod and left.

I plopped down in Preston's desk chair, suddenly exhausted, my head spinning.

Danielle had lied to me last night when she'd called me at Rosalyn's house. She'd told me she was in Los Angeles when, in fact, she was right here in town—according to Mike, anyway.

He'd been in Vegas last night. Tony, whom I'd thought had taken off to parts unknown, was here also. And Robbie Freedman, he'd been in town, too.

Valerie Wagner had told the woman in the gift shop that she was leaving, but had she? She could have easily been here also.

I propped my elbows on Preston's desk and rested my forehead on my palms.

Everybody connected with Courtney's murder had been here last night when Rosalyn was killed. Any one of them could have stabbed either—or both—of them to death.

But why?

It was possible Danielle stood to collect some insurance money from Courtney's death, but I didn't know that for sure. Yet that didn't explain why Rosalyn had been killed, and I knew the two deaths had to be connected somehow.

I sat back in Preston's chair, still stuck on the same question that had bothered me for days: Why had anybody wanted to kill Courtney?

And then, why kill Rosalyn? Why?

As soon as I punched out for the day, I called Detective Shuman in Los Angeles. I wasn't all that happy that his investigation of Mike Ivan, the Russian mob, and Courtney's murder had caused Mike to track me down and show up at Holt's.

Yeah, okay, I knew it had been my idea for Shuman to check into Mike Ivan in the first place, but still.

I got into my car and started it, turning the air conditioning vents to blow in my face while I listened to his line ring. Shuman picked up.

"Great detective work," I said, and managed not to sound angry—well, not too angry. "Mike Ivan came to see me today."

"Are you okay?" he asked.

Shuman sounded concerned. Really concerned. My anger disappeared, replaced by—well, I don't know exactly what it was.

"I'm okay," I said. "How did he find me?"

I imagined Shuman holding his phone up to his ear, frowning his cop frown and thinking.

"He must have called in a favor with someone in Las Vegas law enforcement," Shuman said. "He probably found out who was being investigated in the death of Courtney Collins, then got your name and contact information."

And with that info, he'd put me together with Jack Bishop and Detective Shuman asking around about him.

Maybe Mike was more connected than he admitted.

"What did he want?" Shuman asked.

"Mostly to tell me he was a legitimate businessman," I said. "He'd sold fabric to Courtney and wanted to be paid. That's the extent of his involvement, he claims."

"Might be true. I couldn't turn up anything on him," Shuman agreed. "Struck out on Danielle Shepherd, too."

For a moment, I'd forgotten that I'd asked Shuman to check into her. That whole thing with Mike and the Russian mob knowing my name and where I was working rattled me, more than a little.

"Foster kid, shoplifting as a teen," Shuman said. "Nothing serious."

So much for my idea about Danielle killing Courtney for her insurance money. I mean, come on, you just didn't suddenly stab your business partner to death out of the blue. Right? Something must lead up to it.

"Anything new on your end?" Shuman asked.

I had an armload of suspects but no motive or evidence and, of course, I was now a suspect in yet another murder.

I decided Shuman didn't need to know that.

"Nothing," I said. "Let me know if anything else should turn up."

Shuman was silent for a few seconds, then said, "When are you coming home?"

Something about the way he said it sent a warm shudder through me. Shuman had that effect on me sometimes.

"I'm not sure," I said. "Soon, I hope."

"I hope so, too," he said softly.

A long, silent pause hung between us, then morphed into a mutual we-can't-go-there realization.

"Maybe I'll see you around," Shuman said briskly.

"Yeah, maybe," I agreed, and we both hung up.

Oh my God, what had just happened?

I had to talk to Marcie, my best friend in the entire universe. Only a BFF could make sense of this.

I punched in her number as I backed out of the parking space and headed down Valle Verde Road. Her voicemail picked up. Damn. I left her a message to call me immediately.

Then it hit me. Oh my God, why hadn't I called Ty? He was my official boyfriend. If I was feeling something—and I had no idea what it was—nothing probably—for another man, shouldn't I call my boyfriend for reassurance or something?

Crap. Why did I always think of Ty last?

Chapter 25

The traffic light at the intersection ahead of me turned red with absolutely no warning. Really. I slammed on the brakes.

I was in no mood.

I sat there fidgeting in my seat, tapping my palm against the steering wheel. That conversation with Shuman. What was up with that?

The light changed and I drove forward.

Where was my best friend when I desperately needed to discuss the situation with her? And why—*why*—in a time of crisis did I always think of Ty *last?* It was so irritating.

My cell phone rang. I grabbed it and saw Madam CeeCee's name on the caller I.D. screen. I nearly ran up onto the sidewalk.

Oh my God. If ever I needed my luck to change, it was now.

"Madam CeeCee?" I think I shouted into the phone. "This is Haley."

"Yes, I know." Her voice was calm, quiet. Soothing. "What seems to be your problem?"

Jeez, where to start?

"I'm having some financial troubles—well, okay, a lot of financial troubles," I said.

"I see," she commented.

"But I can still pay you," I said quickly. "The big thing is, well, some lady put a curse on me."

She didn't say anything.

"And I have to find some way to get rid of it," I told her. Jeez, I sounded awfully desperate. "Can you help with that?"

"Certainly," Madam CeeCee said. "Let's make an appointment, shall we? How about November fourth? Two o'clock?"

November? *November?*

Did she honestly think I could walk around with a curse on me for another five months?

"I'll only be in town a few more days. I'm here on business. I'm staying at the Culver Inn on Saint Rose Parkway," I said.

Maybe she knew the place. Maybe she knew how awful it was and would take pity on me, and give me an appointment immediately. I mean, jeez, if staying at the Culver Inn didn't demonstrate a desperate need to have a curse lifted, what did?

"Do you have anything sooner?" I asked.

"Let me check into it," Madam CeeCee said.

The line went dead.

"Hello? Hello?" I'm pretty sure I screamed that into the phone.

No answer. Damn. I tossed my phone into my purse.

What kind of psychic was she? Shouldn't she have known *before* she *called* how desperate I was for curse-lifting assistance, and had an appointment available for today?

I whipped into the parking lot of the Culver Inn and slid into a slot near the front entrance. My cell phone rang again.

Oh my God. That had to be Madam CeeCee with a new appointment time. Or maybe Marcie.

I yanked out my phone. It was Ty calling.

Okay, was this good luck or bad luck?

"Yeah, hey, hi, what's up?" I asked.

I hated to rush Ty off the phone—it's not like he called me all the time—but I didn't want to take the chance of missing Marcie's or Madam CeeCee's call.

"I've got a surprise for you," Ty said, sounding pleased with himself.

Jeez, he'd already promised to take over my bills, buy me a beach house and a convertible, and send me on a month-long international shopping spree. What did he want to do now? Carve my face on Mount Rushmore?

Whatever it was, I hoped he could spit it out quickly.

"I'm taking you to a reception for the designers showing at the handbag convention this weekend," Ty said.

I stared out the windshield at the entrance to the Culver Inn, too stunned to speak.

"You know about the convention, don't you?" he asked.

I meant to say yes, but only a little squeak came out.

"The reception is very exclusive. The fashion elite, industry insiders, some celebrities," Ty said. "It's Saturday afternoon. How does that sound?"

I made a little mewling noise.

"I know you don't have anything to wear with you," Ty said, "so I'm sending a car for you. I've arranged for a personal shopper at Neiman Marcus to have some things ready for you to look at. "

I opened my mouth, but not even a groan came out.

"Would you like me to fly Marcie up so she can go with you?" Ty asked.

I stopped breathing. Really. I'm pretty sure my heart quit beating.

Oh my God, *oh my God*.

Ty was taking me to a reception for the gods and god-desses of the fashion world? I'd rub elbows with them? Talk with them? Get the inside scoop on upcoming trends?

And all of this on Saturday, smack in the middle of the handbag convention, the most fabulous thing that had happened to me—so far—in my entire life?

Oh, wait. No. No, no. No.

The handbag convention. The handbag convention that I'd already committed to work because I desperately needed money so I could eat, because I'd been cursed by a crazy old lady in a crappy midrange department store.

I leaned forward and banged my head against the steering wheel. This couldn't be happening. It could not be happening. Ty had arranged something fabulous—beyond fabulous, really—and it was an event that he actually planned to attend with me. Only I couldn't go.

I hate my life.

"Well, uh, it sounds great, Ty," I said, forcing the words out syllable by syllable. "But, uh, you see, well, I . . . I can't go."

Silence.

I waited. He didn't say anything. For a moment, I wondered if he'd put me on hold or something.

"I thought you'd enjoy this," Ty said. He sounded a little hurt, but more puzzled than anything.

"I would," I assured him. "But, well, I'd already made plans to work the convention."

"Doing what?" Now he was really puzzled.

Ty was a smart guy. He ran a huge chain of department stores, he'd started boutique and specialty stores, and he'd just launched Holt's International. He managed thousands of employees, billions of dollars in assets, in six states and on two continents. Nobody did that by looking only at what was in front of them. Ty's mind was always jumping three, four, or five steps ahead.

I knew he was doing that now. I pictured him dressed in one of his awesome suits, wearing a silk necktie, hunched forward on his desk, pressing the phone against his ear, making that I-can-figure-this-out-and-make-it-my-bitch face.

He's so hot when he does that.

"My friend Maya hooked me up," I said, and managed to put more enthusiasm than I felt into my voice. "We're hostessing. You know, handing out info packets, pointing, smiling."

"Why are you doing that, Haley?" Ty asked in his you've-completely-lost-me voice.

I get that a lot.

"A girl's got to eat," I said, and managed what I hoped was an oh-well-that's-life little chuckle.

"I told you, Haley, I'll take care of you," he said. "You believe me, don't you?"

Of course I believed him. That wasn't the point—or maybe it was.

I didn't want to look pathetic and desperate—which was exactly the way I felt at the moment—but still, I didn't want Ty to know that. I didn't want him to think—to *know*—I was such a colossal screw-up that I couldn't take care of myself.

Yeah, okay, I knew he was my official boyfriend and we were considering moving in together. Under those circumstances, I should be able to tell him anything—yeah, I knew that.

But I couldn't bring myself to ask him for money. Money changed things. It would be like we weren't equal partners. He'd be superior and I would be subservient.

And, yes, I knew that in a long-term, serious relationship, those things shouldn't matter, and there would always be times when one of us would have more or accomplish more than the other. But if I took his money—

or all the other things he'd promised—it would be like I was suddenly less of a person.

Not a great feeling.

"Yes, of course I believe you," I told him. "And I appreciate the thought and all the effort you put into arranging everything. It's great. Really. But I've already committed to working the convention. My friend is counting on me, so I really can't back out. It wouldn't be right, and I just can't do it."

Silence.

I heard nothing. Not a sigh, a groan, a grumble. Nothing. I had no idea what Ty was thinking—or maybe he'd just put me on hold.

So, okay, I couldn't take him up on his offer of a lifetime, but maybe I could salvage something.

"Could you get me a Delicious handbag?" I asked. "I've looked almost everywhere in Vegas and haven't found one yet."

"You won't find one in Vegas," Ty said. "Stores are withholding them until after the handbag convention."

Anger whipped through me quicker than a supermodel sliding into a silk slip dress.

"What?" I demanded. "You're kidding."

"It's one of the grand prizes in the raffle at the convention," Ty said.

A Delicious handbag was a grand prize in a raffle—and I had a curse on me?

Just my luck.

I didn't ask Ty if he was still coming to the convention. Maybe he wouldn't want the fashion elite, industry insiders, and celebrities to know his girlfriend was handing out info packets.

I hate my life.

"I've got to go," I said, and hung up.

My whole life was a mess—a complete mess. The only

thing I knew for sure was that I was working as a minimum wage grunt at the handbag event of the century when I could have enjoyed it, being pampered at every turn, in the lap of luxury, getting face time with the rich, fabulous, and famous—not to mention my way-hot official boyfriend.

Somebody was going down.

I glared out my windshield and spotted Bradley's Lexus in the parking lot.

This was all that rat-weasel's fault, I decided. If he hadn't charged all those nights to my credit card and maxed it out, I could have blown off working at the convention and gone to the reception with Ty.

I got out of my car, slammed the door, and stomped into the lobby of the Culver Inn. Maya sat on one of the chairs near the registration desk. I'd never seen her here in the evenings, only at the morning buffet. Her arms were folded and she was tapping her foot against the floor.

"I'm here to pick up my final check," she said.

"You're kidding," I said. "Bradley really fired you?"

Maya looked up at me and I saw tears pooled in her eyes. "I'm done."

"That little bastard," I muttered.

She nodded toward Bradley's office door behind the registration desk.

"He told me to be here at four," she said, "and I've been sitting here waiting for him all this time."

"He knows you're here?" I asked.

"He knows."

Okay, now I was really mad. I'd been mad before I walked into the lobby. Now I had somebody to take it out on.

I stormed around the registration desk. The girl on duty—yet another new clerk—called to me but I ignored her. I pounded on Bradley's door, then yanked it open. He was reared back in his chair, his feet up on his desk, flipping through a magazine.

"Have you got Maya's check, or not?" I demanded.

Bradley swiveled in his chair and threw me a smirk. "No. Tell her to call me tomorrow. I'll have it for her then. Maybe."

I was so angry I could have slapped that grin right off his face. It took everything I had to hold back. I left the office and slammed the door.

Maya walked over. "He doesn't have it, does he?"

"No," I said, and managed to keep my anger in check.

She drew in a deep breath, steeling her emotions. "At least I'll get paid for working the convention. Arlene usually gets our checks to us in a week."

A week? One whole week more before Maya—and I—would get money?

"I'll pick you up Saturday morning," Maya said. "We'll ride to the convention together."

"Sure, okay," I said, but I wasn't really paying attention.

She left. I walked outside. It was blazing hot and the wind had kicked up. In the distance, I saw the tops of the casinos on The Strip.

I thought about hitting the slots, taking a chance on winning a boatload of cash, even though I knew I shouldn't. But money wouldn't break my bad mood. Not now. Only one thing would do that—getting even with Bradley.

I had an idea of how to do it. It was a long shot, but hey, isn't that what Vegas was all about?

The scary part was that only one person could help me with it. I pulled out my cell phone and placed a call.

"Yeah?" Cliff answered.

He sounded cautious and for a minute I thought he'd forgotten who I was. Then I realized he didn't recognize my name on his caller I.D. screen.

"It's Dana," I said.

"Oh, yeah. Hey, Dana, how're you doing?"

"Listen," I said. "I need you to bring your ufology field investigation kit and come over right away."

"Whoa, dude, what's up?" he asked.

"I located a whole colony of aliens."

CHAPTER 26

"Whoa, dude, is this like illegal or something?" Cliff asked.

We were in the third floor stairwell of the Culver Inn, outside the door that led to the hallway my room was on. Our voices echoed off the concrete walls and steps. It was dusty and hot in the airless passageway.

"We're in pursuit of scientific truth," I said. "Isn't that covered in your ufology mission statement?"

"Yeah, well, I guess," Cliff said.

"Okay, then, let's go," I said, and clapped my hands together.

"Are you sure they're aliens staying in there?" he asked, nodding toward the adjoining room.

Of course there were no aliens sleeping off an all-nighter in the room on the other side of the wall. There were no aliens anywhere. But it was the only excuse I could give Cliff to get him to come over and do this for me.

Yeah, okay, I'd lied. What was the worst that could happen to me? I'd get cursed or something?

"There's only one way to find out for sure," I said, and gave him my move-it-will-you eyebrow bob.

Cliff dug through the big toolbox he'd brought over—

his ufology field investigation kit—and pulled out an electric drill.

"Hey, hang on a second," he said.

He didn't say anything for a minute. I figured he was waiting for whatever thought had shot through his brain to circle back around.

"Like, uh, what if the noise wakes them up?" Cliff proposed. "What if they all take off?"

Good grief.

"This breed of gray aliens doesn't sleep," I said. "They put themselves into suspended animation for a designated time period."

"Yeah?" he asked, looking unconvinced.

"I saw it on the History Channel," I told him.

He nodded. "Oh, yeah, well, okay then."

Cliff gunned the drill a couple of times. It was really loud in the stairwell.

"Hey," he said, grinning really big. "This is like, you know, like the real Dana and Fox."

"*X-Files* isn't real, Cliff," I said. "It's a TV show."

"Yeah, I know," he said, as if that only made it better.

"Drill," I said, and tapped the wall. "Right here."

I'd selected a spot on the common wall between the stairwell and the room across the hall from mine. Cliff started drilling.

It was a long shot, but something was going on in the rooms in this wing of the motel. Something illegal. Something Bradley knew about. I'd thought about it every way I could, and that was the only thing that made any kind of sense.

There was no other reason for the rooms to be off-limits to guests. Nothing else explained the voices in the hallway, the late-night visitors, the mysterious pickup truck I'd seen parked near the maintenance shed. No explanation for the huge turnover in employees that assured nobody would be around long enough to question anything.

Cliff pulled the drill bit out of the wall and stepped back.

"Okay," he whispered. "We're in."

He knelt down and dug through his field investigation kit until he came up with another tool.

"A borescope. See, it's got a camera on the end," he said, and fed the tiny tube through the hole he'd just drilled.

I waited, bouncing on my toes, using all my strength to hold back and not rip the thing out of his hand and look through the gadget first.

"*Whoa, dude!*" Cliff said. He jumped back, his eyes huge.

Oh my God. There weren't really aliens in there, were there?

He looked at me, grinning and nodding his head big-time. "This is *way* better than aliens."

I peered through the eyepiece into the interior of the room.

Oh, yeah. Way better.

Cliff yammered all the way from the third floor to the parking lot, but I wasn't listening. I just went with him to make sure he got out of the motel immediately.

I'd cleaned up the drywall dust from the floor of the stairwell—okay, I'd just spread it around and mixed it with all the other dirt and dust up there—while Cliff plugged the hole with something that looked a lot like gray Play-Doh. He didn't seem to know exactly what it was and I figured I could go on living without knowing.

"You'll hook me up when you get, you know, all the details?" Cliff asked as we stood next to his Taurus.

"You bet," I said.

I had no intention of telling Cliff anything, but, oh well. That's the way it had to be. He'd have to live with it—if he even remembered I was supposed to give him the info. I waited until he drove away, then walked back into the Culver Inn plotting my next move.

"Miss Randolph?" someone called.

I spotted a woman in the lobby standing beside a couch, eyeing me.

Wow, she looked fantastic. Classy, elegant. Mid-forties, I guessed, full-on hair, makeup, and nails, dressed in a cream-colored YSL suit, four-inch Jimmy Choo heels—oh my God, was that a Delicious handbag tucked under her arm?

She walked over, poised, calm, sedate. "I'm Madam Cee-Cee."

"I love your handbag." I think I moaned that.

She smiled pleasantly. "I know."

For a moment, I was so stunned at seeing the Delicious, I didn't remember that I'd told her where I was staying. And how did she know who I was? Was she just an awesome psychic, or had the desk clerk described me?

I preferred to think she was an awesome psychic.

"Where did you find it?" I asked, my gaze still glued to her handbag.

"It was a gift," she said softly.

"I'm dying for one of those." I'm pretty sure I moaned that, too.

"I know," she said. "Please, let's sit."

We settled onto the couch. Now that she was right in front of me, I couldn't let her leave without telling me how to break this curse. But I couldn't mislead her. What if she put another curse on me?

"Look, like I told you on the phone, I'm having some financial difficulties right now," I said. "But I'll have money very soon."

"I know," she said softly.

"And I'll pay you every cent of your fee,"

"Yes, I know that, too," she assured me. "Now, tell me about this curse you're under."

"Some crazy old lady waved her finger around and called on the powers of the universe to curse me," I told her.

Okay, it sounded kind of lame when I said it out loud, but Madam CeeCee didn't seem to think so.

"And why did she do this?" she asked. "What precipitated her actions?"

I thought back, trying to remember everything that had happened that day in Holt's. I'd been serving Bolt, the energy drink. The old lady was in the women's department and had asked for help with the bathrobes, then got mad when I couldn't—okay, wouldn't—help her.

"She said American girls—meaning me, I guess—had everything," I said. "She said we gave nothing in return and that we were selfish."

Madam CeeCee considered this for a moment.

"Of course, now I understand." She nodded and smiled. "To lift this curse, you must simply perform a selfless act."

Oh, crap. A selfless act?

That wasn't really *me*. Hardly the sort of thing I did best.

"That's it?" I asked.

"Yes," she replied, looking altogether pleased with herself.

"Are you sure?" I asked. "Don't you need to look in a crystal ball? Check my aura or read my palm?"

"That's not necessary."

Okay, I didn't want to seem ungrateful but, jeez, there

had to be a better way—better for me, that is—to get rid of this curse.

"You can't shake a dead chicken at me instead?" I asked. "Chant something, maybe?"

"The universe doesn't work that way," Madam CeeCee said. "You've gone too far in one direction and been selfish. Now you must go the other way and do something selfless, so the cosmic forces will balance."

Oh my God. That's exactly what Taylor had been blabbing on about with her reverse world theory.

Maybe there was something to it.

"Exactly how selfless does this act have to be?" I asked.

I mean, really, no need to go overboard, provided I could actually pull off something selfless.

"How large is your curse?" she asked.

Oh, crap. I was screwed, all right.

"You have another question," Madam CeeCee said.

Something had definitely been on my mind for days—well, longer than that, actually. Hopefully, she'd give me an answer I liked better than this selfless-act thing.

"I've got this boyfriend," I said. "I'm not sure he's the right one for me. Can you tell me?"

Madam CeeCee frowned a little, leaned back, and looked me up and down. A full minute crawled by while she just stared.

"All I can say is you've met the man who is your destiny," she told me.

"Who is he?" I asked.

Madam CeeCee got to her feet. "You already know him quite well."

I got up. "Yeah, okay, but what's his name?"

"Look in your heart. You'll find your answer there."

She smiled and walked out of the motel.

How could she just leave like that—without giving me his name?

I knew a lot of men. I knew a lot of men quite well. Did that mean it was Ty? Or some other man like—

Oh my God. Could she have meant Detective Webster? Or Cliff?

Oh, crap.

It was a Louis Vuitton day. Definitely a Louis Vuitton day.

I'd called in sick at Holt's, using the touch-of-the-stomach-flu excuse—it's a classic—then loaded up some shopping bags and headed to the mall.

After carefully calculating the prices of the items I'd bought for myself since arriving in Vegas, I selected a few and returned just enough to buy a totally awesome DKNY business suit and accessories.

Returning clothing—especially the fantastic clothes I'd bought—went against everything I stood for, but hey, I could be strong when I had to be. Besides, I could always return the suit and buy those items again.

So here I stood in the lobby of the ultra-chic Corona office building, heading for the elevators. The guard at the security desk gave me a nod as I walked past. I hadn't expected any trouble.

Not only was I wearing a fabulous black suit, semi-sensible shoes, my hair in a no-nonsense up-do, but I'd channeled my mother's I'm-better-than-you attitude, which had gotten me through many a tough situation.

At least Mom was good for something.

I took the elevator up to the top floor, got off, and approached the receptionist's area. The office was huge, opulent, decorated in neutrals with desert landscape watercolors on the walls. Floor to ceiling windows across the room offered an incredible view of the vast expanse of the desert. I'm pretty sure I spotted the Chrysler Building on the horizon.

"May I help you?" the receptionist asked.

She was an older woman, well dressed, perfectly groomed, wearing an earpiece, and seated at what looked like the helm of the space shuttle.

I walked over and ratcheted up my I'm-better-than-you attitude another notch.

"I'm here to see Helen Pennington," I told her, and gave her my name.

She consulted her computer screen, and said, "I don't see an appointment scheduled."

"I don't have an appointment," I told her. "But Helen will want to see me."

The receptionist's heavy brows drew together. "I'm sorry, but Mrs. Pennington can't see anyone today without an appointment."

I'd expected this. In fact, I'd hoped for it.

I gave her an understanding smile, and said, "Would you give Helen a message for me?"

"Certainly," she said, picking up her pen and looking relieved that I wasn't going to be any trouble.

I was about to make her day, big time.

"Tell Helen I'm here to talk with her about her son Bradley growing marijuana in the rooms of the Culver Inn," I said.

Her hand froze over her notepad. She looked up at me.

"That boy of hers is really quite clever," I said. "The grow rooms were located in a wing of the motel that he wouldn't allow guests to use. Gardeners, if you will, came up the fire exit stairwell at night from the service area. The utility companies wouldn't alert law enforcement to excessive use of water or electricity because Bradley wasn't putting any water in the pool and, as I said, nobody was using the rooms in that wing."

The receptionist's eyes got wider.

I pointed to her message pad.

"Did you get all of that?" I asked.

"Perhaps you should discuss this with Mrs. Pennington in person," the receptionist said. "I'll send you right in."

I love being me.

CHAPTER 27

This is what heaven was like.

At least, I hoped so.

Handbags. Tens of thousands of gorgeous, magnificent, beautiful handbags spread out before me, offered by the most talented, gifted designers on the planet.

My knees shook, my palms got sweaty. Really.

Jeez, where was Marcie when I needed her?

I stood in humble reverence at the entrance to the Mandalay Bay ballroom, the vendor room for what was billed as the first annual—please, God, let there be more—handbag convention.

The convention center had been built with large crowds in mind—extra-wide corridors, scattered seating areas with comfortable-looking couches and chairs, and hospitality tables with plastic cups and pitchers of ice water. The lighting was soft, giving the oak wood trim a warm feel. The orange, gray, and beige design in the carpet looked classier than it sounded.

Maya and I had arrived at our designated time this morning along with dozens of other workers, and had been given pale blue oxford shirts with "*hospitality*" embroidered over the pocket in red, along with I.D. cards on lanyards.

Arlene had given us long-winded instructions that,

really, I tried to listen to, but I'd drifted off. But before her speech turned into *blah, blah, blah,* she'd stressed the importance of security at the event, and the number of uniformed and plain-clothes personnel in place, plus the eyes-in-the-sky that Vegas was known for.

With a ratio of approximately seven handbags for each woman expected to attend—a pitifully low figure, in my opinion—I could see why they expected trouble.

The two-day event was set to kick off in a few minutes. Throngs of women—accompanied by a few bewildered men—formed a line that stretched through the foyer and out of sight, anxiously waiting to get inside. Lots of laughter, talk, and giggles. Spirits were high.

In my arms was a stack of glossy convention brochures detailing the layout and schedule of events. I, along with a half dozen other girls, was supposed to pass them out as the women filed past. Hopefully, we wouldn't get trampled in an all-out stampede of women who wanted to be the first to see the newest handbags—not that I blamed them, of course.

After all the brochures were distributed, we were supposed to take up a designated position and remain there to answer questions and offer assistance.

Yeah, right.

Next to the ballroom, down an adjoining corridor, were three breakout rooms. Two held exhibits and displays, the third was a hospitality suite manned by a security guard and open only to the upper echelon.

I'd have to find a way to get inside, of course.

When I'd awakened this morning, I told myself this would be a fantastic day because, really, I didn't know when the next great thing might roll my way. My finances were in shambles. Somehow I was going to have to come up with a fabulous event for the Holt's employees—out of my own pocket, apparently. So far I hadn't thought of one single selfless thing to do that might break the curse I was under. I was on the radar of the Russian mob and, of course, a suspect in two murders.

The only good thing that had happened to me lately was my visit to Helen Pennington yesterday and, really, that wasn't so good. When I told her about Bradley's grow rooms at the Culver Inn, she'd cried—which took all the fun out of ruining someone's life.

Oh, yeah, and Ty. He was one of the good things in my life—if I could just remember that.

Outside the ballroom doors a few feet away stood a security guard. Tall, broad shoulders, close-cut hair, he wore a suit with a subdued tie and had one of those earpiece things coming out the back of his collar and going into his ear. He stood straight, feet braced apart, hands folded in front of him.

So far I hadn't seen him move a muscle, but his eyes swept back and forth watching for trouble, obviously ready to put the smack down on any unruly handbag buyer without hesitation.

The noise level escalated and the crowd of women surged forward as the velvet rope holding them back was removed. They hit the long registration desk on the other side of the foyer, forked over their money, and got a lanyard in record time, then headed for the vendor room.

I think I know how General Custer felt.

"Smile," Maya called from her position nearby.

I plastered on a smile and handed out brochures as the women filed past. Most were dressed as if they'd come to play hard—comfy shoes, stretch pants, light jackets. Others were Vegased out with big hair, full-on makeup, tight jeans, and fake boobs squeezed into tight T-shirts.

Almost everybody had brought out their big guns, handbag-wise. Designer purses of every shape, size, and color on the market.

This was my place, these were my peeps.

The line passed by us and I smiled—though I'm sure nobody noticed—and handed out brochures at a furious pace, then the attendees spread out through the aisles like hot lava careening down a volcanic hillside.

"Let's go check it out," I said to Maya, once everyone had gotten past us.

The security guard's gaze shifted to me.

I ignored him.

"We're supposed to stay here," Maya said.

"How can we give great service if we don't get the lay of the place?" I asked.

Yeah, okay, it was just an excuse to go see everything, but so what. No way could I stand this close to all those designer purses and not see every single one of them.

"I guess you're right," Maya said.

The ballroom was huge, the ceiling high. You could fit three football fields or something in the space—they'd told us the measurements at this morning's meeting, but I'd drifted off. The carpet was a gold pattern that might have looked cheesy anywhere but Vegas.

A maze of vendor booths was set up featuring the newest, latest, classic and best-selling bags. Totes, shoulder bags, clutches, satchels, hobos. Leather, fabric, beads, bows, feathers. A rainbow of colors, patterns, and textures galore.

Other booths carried suitcases and trunks. A few had pet carriers along with designer collars and bedding. Some catered to the younger set with purses for kids and teens, and diaper bags for babies.

I wanted to lie down and roll around in them, but I was going to work here for two days. No sense in doing all the fun stuff right away.

"Look, they're raffling off some bags," Maya said.

In the center of a booth atop a tall pedestal and encased in what was no doubt bulletproof glass sat two Judith Leiber handbags. My heart skipped a beat. Light shone down from above—and it wasn't just the overhead lighting, because I also heard angels sing. I swear.

Maya grasped my arm. "Oh my God. Judith Leiber."

Judith Leiber bags weren't simply purses, they were art. They transcended fashion. Each bag was exquisitely and lovingly made with only the finest fabrics and trims, and—as if the human heart could stand any more—Austrian crystals.

"I'd kill for one of those," Maya swore.

I had a Judith Leiber. I'd earned it the hard way—long story—and treasured it beyond belief. That, of course, was no reason not to have another one.

Just when my pulse had started to settle down, I spotted two Delicious handbags in display cases nearby, ready to be raffled off.

Oh my God. Delicious bags and Judith Leibers both in the same place. How much could my overstressed senses take in one day?

Women crowded the booth buying raffle tickets as quickly as they could get their money out of their wallets.

"Let's buy a ticket," I said.

Maya grimaced and said, "Wow, fifty bucks a ticket. That's pretty steep."

A blonde standing next to us carrying a Marc Jacobs satchel turned. "The Judith Lieber bags are valued at over seven grand—each. They're special editions just for the convention."

The woman next to her with a terrific Chanel tote said, "Have you seen the message board by the entrance? Offers for up to ten thousand dollars to buy one of them from the raffle winners."

Maya's eyes lit up. "Ten grand?"

"I'm buying a ticket," I said.

Of course, I didn't have fifty dollars to spare—I barely had fifty dollars at all. After leaving Helen Pennington's office yesterday, I'd gone back to the mall and returned the business suit. But instead of repurchasing the items I'd exchanged it for, I'd had the clerk credit my Visa card. Then I'd raced to an ATM and gotten a cash advance so I'd have spending money for today.

And what better way to spend it than on a raffle ticket? This was Vegas, after all. Plus, it wasn't exactly gambling, was it?

Maya drew a big breath. "Okay, I'll buy one, too."

We eased through the crowd of women, put down our money, and bought our tickets. I checked my number. It ended with twelve, my lucky number. Cool.

"Darn," Maya said, eyeing her ticket. "The drawing is at noon. I'm scheduled to work the registration table then. What are you scheduled for?"

There was a schedule?

She pulled out one of the papers Arlene had given us this morning, which looked familiar, kind of, and checked it.

"You're working the info kiosk by the Kate Spade booth," Maya said. "You'll be close by when the numbers are called. Here, take my ticket so, if I win, you can claim it right away."

As I buttoned her ticket, along with my own, into the pocket of my shirt, a face on the other side of the raffle booth caught my eye. It was a man, which was odd enough at this event, but he looked familiar. When he turned to speak to the woman beside him, my breath caught.

Mike Ivan. What was he doing here?

I fought off full-on panic mode. Did he somehow know I was here? Had he decided I was a threat to him, after all? Or was he just here with his wife or girlfriend or whoever, to see the handbags?

"Let's check out the exhibits," Maya said.

"Great idea," I said.

We made our way to the ballroom doors and out into

the foyer. I felt the security guard's eyes on us as we walked by.

We turned down the hallway that led to the three break-out rooms. The Breakers Room, farther along the hallway, was the hospitality suite to the rich and famous.

According to the signs outside the other doors, the Reef Room held exhibits of vintage bags and purses of historical significance. In the Lagoon Room, authorized dealers were on hand to determine the authenticity of questionable purses, and to clean and repair handbags. Authors were selling and autographing books related to fashion, and artists at easels waited to paint your face onto the body of a supermodel dressed in designer clothing—and holding a fabulous purse, of course.

"Let's check out the vintage bags," Maya said, and I followed her into the Reef Room.

The lighting was subdued. Accent lights beamed down onto glass cases that displayed vintage bags and accessories spanning over a century. Striped travel bags from Fendi, sold in the 1980s. Fabulous Chanels from the 1950s. A Louis Vuitton Noe bag from 1932. French clutch bags created with precious jewels and damask in the early '20s. A metal mesh bag, labeled 1910.

There were bags on display that had been carried by celebrities and royalty alike. Grace Kelly, Princess Di, Cher. Another case held purses used by first ladies Nancy Reagan, Bess Truman, and Jackie Kennedy.

By the time we'd looked at most of the exhibits, I'd calmed down and convinced myself that it was merely a coincidence that Mike Ivan was here today. I mean, jeez, he couldn't be upset with me for anything, could he?

Still, I thought it best to avoid him.

"Haley, come look at this," Maya called. I joined her at the display case. "Isn't this the company you work for?"

Inside lay a vintage handbag, circa late 1890s, beaded,

trimmed with feathers, featuring a jeweled clasp. The Wallis bag, according to the sign. Beside it was an artist's sketch of a five-story department store in Los Angeles with the words HOLT'S DEPARTMENT STORE written in cursive on the sign above the front door. Next to it was a very old black-and-white photograph of a rather handsome man posing beside a lovely young woman.

Oh my God. This couple were the founders of the Holt's Department Store. Ty's ancestors. And the bag was one of the first items they'd carried.

I studied the couple, looking for a family resemblance. The man's jaw, I decided. It looked hard and determined, just as Ty's looks most of the time.

"We'd better get back," Maya said, glancing at her watch.

I followed her from the room and just as I turned the corner, I saw Ty walk out of the Breakers Room, the hospitality suite.

"I'll catch up with you later," I called to Maya as she walked away.

My stomach turned all warm and gooey, just as it always did when I saw Ty. He looked tense and grim, but handsome in his suit, and sort of like the man in the old black-and-white photo. His gaze passed right over me, then bounced back, and he smiled. Ty's got a great smile.

He threw his arms around me in the middle of the hallway, causing people to stream around us, and held me close. He kissed me. It felt good.

"I didn't know you'd be here today," I said.

"Business," he said, and nodded toward the hospitality suite.

"I just saw your great-great-great-great-grandparents or something," I said.

He looked lost for a moment—I get that from him a lot—then nodded. "The exhibit. It's usually at the corporate office."

"I love that Wallis bag," I said, then realized where I'd heard the name before. "Is that why you named your boutiques *Wallace?*"

Ty pulled out his phone and glanced at the caller ID screen as he said, "Marketing suggested the spelling be changed for the stores."

I was about to ask another question when he answered his phone.

I get that a lot, too.

I stood there trying to look like I was working in case Arlene happened by, yet not so available that somebody would stop and ask me an actual question—it's a delicate balance—when I noticed two men in expensive suits and a young woman come out of the hospitality suite and head toward us.

Oh my God. It was Danielle. What was she doing here?

The three of them were smiling and engaged in heavy conversation as they walked by. She didn't notice me.

"Ty?" I tapped his arm. He covered the mouthpiece and looked at me, as I pointed down the hallway. "Do you know that girl? Did you see her in the hospitality suite? Danielle Shepherd?"

"Yes," he whispered, then turned back to his phone conversation again.

"What was she doing in there?" I wanted to know.

I mean, jeez, if Danielle could go into the hospitality suite, certainly I could go in, too.

"Hang on a minute," Ty said into his phone, then turned to me. "She sold her line to one of the national chains."

"What?"

"It was a small acquisition," Ty said. "A hundred grand, I think, for a—"

Ty kept talking, but I quit listening.

Oh my God. Danielle had sold her accessory line to a major national chain of department stores, and raked in a hundred thousand dollars in the process?

I hate my life.

Well, at least now I could see her collection—before it was on the shelves of a zillion department stores nationally. No way would Danielle be here today, closing a deal, without having her line on display.

Ty had turned back to his phone conversation, so I tapped his arm again, gave him a little wave, and left.

As I headed toward the vendor room, I pulled out the brochure I'd shoved in my back pocket, flipped through it to the back, and found the alphabetical listing of vendors. The place was so big, the room had been drawn out on a map with grid coordinates. I located Danielle's booth, near where the fashion show would take place this afternoon, and headed that way.

She'd gotten a prime location between Coach and Prada, and the walkway was jammed with buyers. I figured if I had to wear this dorky uniform today, I may as well use it to my advantage.

"Excuse me! Excuse me!" I called as I pushed my way through the crowd. "Official business! Please stand aside!"

When I made my way to the display cases, I stopped still in my tracks. I couldn't move. Someone bumped me from behind. Another woman murmured a rude remark and pushed past me.

A cold chill washed over me as I stood there taking in the displays of tote bags, cosmetic cases, scarves, gloves, hats, every fashion accessory imaginable.

I knew who killed Courtney.

CHAPTER 28

It was that stained-glass pattern. The same pattern Courtney had done a gazillion times in art class back in high school. It was used in every piece of the accessory line.

Danielle hadn't designed this collection. Courtney had.

My mind raced—and I hadn't even had any chocolate this morning.

Courtney was the artistic one of their partnership. Mike Ivan had been right. Danielle had lied when she'd told me Courtney handled the business end of things. That must have been Danielle's responsibility all along.

Another thought zapped me—motive. The one piece of this murder puzzle I'd never really found. Danielle had killed Courtney to claim the collection as her own so she could sell it.

Yet another thought zapped me—I hate it when that happens.

Why wouldn't Courtney have gone along with the sale? Surely she could have used her share of the money.

Maybe Danielle wanted it all for herself, I realized. But why be greedy enough to kill Courtney, the goose that laid the golden stained-glass design, so to speak. Fashion lines could go on for years, generating income for decades.

"Can I help you?" the young girl behind the display case asked.

She was young, blond, and looked as if she didn't really want to be there—can you imagine? I didn't recognize her. I figured she was just somebody Danielle hired to man the booth today.

"Where's Danielle?" I asked.

She shrugged. "No clue."

As much as I wanted to confront Danielle myself, I knew I had to call the cops. My spirits lifted a little. Oh yeah, it would feel way good to tell Detective Dailey and that annoying little mutt Webster that I'd solved their murder for them.

I forced my way through the crowd and headed for the ballroom exit, deciding how best to handle this. Since it was Saturday, I didn't know if the detectives would be—

Hang on a minute.

Mike Ivan was here. Somehow I doubted he'd coincidentally attended the handbag convention because of his love of designer satchels and totes, on the heels of Danielle closing the deal on the sale of the collection.

He'd told me she'd promised him the money she owed him, and said she'd have it shortly. That's why he'd come to Vegas.

I flashed on the image of my disintegrating bones blowing around in the hot desert wind after very-possibly-connected Mike Ivan did away with me for screwing him out of his money by reporting Danielle to the cops before he could collect from her.

Not a great feeling.

I turned in a circle and rose on my toes, scanning the room. Mike wasn't in sight. The place was so huge, so packed with people spread out over so much space, the chances I'd spot him were very small. I had to find a way to contact him.

I pulled out my cell phone—which I wasn't supposed to

have on me, but, oh well—and called Jack Bishop as I hurried out of the ballroom toward a quiet area of the foyer. The security guard still stood by the door watching the area like a well-dressed Terminator.

I paced impatiently while the call went through. I had to contact Mike quickly, get this handled before Danielle concluded her business and left. With that kind of money available to her, she'd leave town for sure. Who knew how long it would take law enforcement to find her?

"I need Mike Ivan's phone number," I said when Jack picked up.

I heard music playing softly in the background, then shut down.

"Where are you?" he asked.

I turned around, watching the crowd as it flowed in and out of the ballroom and down the hallway to the breakout rooms. The security guy was still there. No sign of Mike.

"At the Mandalay Bay," I said. "Look, I know who killed—"

"I'll be there in twenty minutes," Jack said. "Sit tight."

"Twenty minutes?" I asked. "You're in Vegas?"

"On my way to Henderson to kick somebody's ass," Jack told me. "You wait—"

"I can't wait!" I'm sure I shouted it.

The security guard at the entrance of the ballroom turned his attention to me. I swung away.

"Text me Mike's number," I said to Jack, then hung up.

"Excuse me?" someone called.

I turned and found two women swathed in polyester with fanny packs fastened around them, looking at me expectantly.

"Where's the Ed Hardy booth?" one of them asked.

Jeez, what was it with old ladies and Ed Hardy–wear?

I had no clue where the booth was, but my Holt's training kicked in automatically.

"Go all the way to the back of the ballroom, then turn left," I said in my I'm-a-trained-professional voice.

It works every time. The women headed into the ballroom.

A group of four women honed in on me with a where's-the-bathroom look on their faces. I turned sharply and walked away.

I mean, really, people should make an effort to figure things out on their own.

My cell phone chirped and I saw that Jack had texted Mike's number. As I punched it into my phone, the security guard left his post beside the ballroom doors and headed my way.

"Yes?" Mike Ivan said into my ear.

I heard the cacophony of sounds behind him and figured he was still in the vendor room.

"It's Haley," I said. "Listen, I'm at the handbag convention. Something's happened. I absolutely have to talk to you right this minute."

"Where?"

He hadn't hesitated. I guess with his lifestyle, he had to be ready to make a move on a moment's notice.

Either that or he was sick of looking at handbags.

I didn't know the layout of the Mandalay Bay beyond the convention center well enough to suggest someplace out of the immediate area. Besides, I wanted to stay close in the hope I could spot Danielle.

"Meet me in the Reef Room by the Jackie Kennedy handbags," I told him. Somehow, it seemed appropriate.

Mike hung up without saying anything. I guess that meant he'd meet me there; I wasn't really up on possibly-connected-to-the-Russian-mob communications.

I headed for the hallway leading to the breakout rooms. The security guard cut diagonally across the foyer to intercept me, but my long pageant legs and my well-honed ability to dodge Holt's customers—it was like having superpowers, really—allowed me to stride away well ahead of him. I slipped into the mass of people in the hallway and wove my way into the Reef Room. Mike Ivan stood next to the Jackie Kennedy handbag display.

"Did you get your money from Danielle?" I asked. Okay, I kind of just blurted it out, but I was in a hurry and more than a little stressed.

He looked at me as if it were none of my business, which it wasn't, but that wasn't the issue at the moment. Still, better to explain, I decided.

"Danielle murdered Courtney," I said. "I'm going to call the police but I want to make sure you got your money from her first."

Mike seemed surprised, but I didn't know if it was because I'd said Danielle was a killer or because of the money thing.

"I collected from her this morning," he told me. Then he looked disgusted and shook his head. "I always liked Courtney. It was Danielle? You're sure?"

"Absolutely. Look, I've got to go."

Mike said something, but I didn't hang around to listen. I wanted to find Danielle, make sure she was still here. I only knew one place to start looking.

I hurried back down the hallway, through the foyer, and into the ballroom again. The security guard at the door gave me a hard look, which I ignored.

Jeez, I guessed that if I was his biggest problem security-wise, the convention was in good shape—except there was a murderer on the loose in here somewhere.

For a few seconds, I thought about telling the security guard, but decided against it. In the time it took me to explain everything—then get him and probably his supervisor to believe it—Danielle could be long gone.

Squeezing through the crowd, I made my way back to Danielle's booth. The same young girl was there, showing a cosmetic bag to a customer.

"I need to talk to Danielle," I said.

The customer glared at me for interrupting. I flashed my conference ID lanyard as if it were a police badge and she backed off.

"She's not here, like I said," the girl told me

"Where is she?" I asked.

She huffed. "Like I should know."

"Haley?" someone called.

I spotted Danielle about six deep in the crowd behind me. She looked at the stained-glass collection, then back at me. Neither of us said anything, but I knew we were having the same thought. She'd known all along that once I got a look at the line, I'd know it was Courtney's work, not hers.

Then she surprised me by calling, "It's not what you think," over the heads of the people between us. "Let me explain."

She walked away. I followed her through the ballroom and into the foyer. She turned left and finally stopped in front of the massive windows that let in natural sunlight—which was really weird inside a Vegas casino—and offered an awesome view of the Luxor Pyramid, the Mandalay Bay Hotel, and its huge swimming pool.

Danielle turned abruptly and faced me. Hers was hardly the expression of somebody who'd just gotten a hundred grand. Nor did she look as if my knowing she'd murdered Courtney was troublesome in the least.

Either she was playing it really cool, or she had a knife in her purse that she intended to stab me with.

I glanced back at the entrance of the ballroom. No security guard.

Just my luck.

"Courtney designed the collection," I said, just because I wanted to get my accusation out there first. "You murdered her so you could pass it off as yours and keep all the money for yourself."

Danielle drew herself up straighter and stared out the window for a moment, then cut her gaze to me. "You shouldn't act like you're all that, Haley. None of this would have happened, if it weren't for you."

"Me?"

"I was standing right there when Courtney got your Facebook message and learned you were coming to town and wanted to hook up," Danielle told me. "She couldn't wait for you to get here. That's why she went to the Holt's store to meet you first thing that morning. But not for the reason you think."

I didn't say anything.

Her expression darkened. "Courtney told me how you didn't really like her back in high school, how you used to make fun of her artwork. She was thrilled to show you what she'd developed it into, and explain how she was an artisan now, selling her line to only the most exclusive clients."

Okay, that didn't make me feel so great.

Danielle drew in a breath, gazed out of the window for a minute, then turned to me again. "You were right. Courtney was an idiot."

That didn't make me feel any better.

"A complete idiot," Danielle said, her voice rising a little. "I told her about the kind of money we could make going commercial, selling the collection to a department store—and I was right. But no. Oh, no. Courtney insisted she was an artisan. Each piece had to be handmade. Stitch by stitch."

"So you, what, went with her to Holt's that morning? Followed her?" I asked. "Either way, you were inside the store with her. You slashed her with the box cutter. Left her in the dressing room to die."

"What was I supposed to do?" Danielle demanded. "It was the perfect opportunity. You were coming to the store. She'd told me how you didn't like her, how some guy you wanted to date went out with her instead. I couldn't let that moment slip by and not make the most of it."

"You set me up," I said. Hearing Danielle admit to it hit me hard. "That's why you didn't want me to see the collection. You knew I'd recognize it as Courtney's work."

Danielle just stared at me.

Then I flashed on something else. "You killed Rosalyn Chase."

She didn't say anything.

"You lied when I talked to you that night. You claimed you were in L.A., but you were really here," I said, then I thought of something else. "That's why you called me at Rosalyn's house. You wanted to make sure the police would know I was there when they looked at my cell phone records. You did that to try to cover up the fact that you'd murdered her."

"Which was also your fault," Danielle pointed out.

I guess, in a way, she was right. I was the one who'd called Danielle, told her I was going to Rosalyn's house to see the collection, and asked her to meet me there. I'd given Danielle the motive and the occasion to commit a second murder and, once again, make me the scapegoat.

Danielle had been so cold and calculating. Stealing Courtney's work, lying to cover up everything, murdering two people, then cashing in on the sale.

But maybe I shouldn't have been surprised. Detective Shuman had told me Danielle had been raised in foster homes. She'd been picked up for shoplifting as a teenager. No emotional grounding. Stealing in order to have the things she wanted. I guess this wasn't such a big leap after all, especially with a hundred grand at stake.

"Why did you have to murder Courtney?" I asked. "She could have designed more collections, kept your business going for years."

Danielle huffed irritably. "I got her out of Los Angeles,

up here, away from people she knew, where I could control things better. She was so weak-minded. But she *refused* to design anything else. She insisted it was her *signature*. Stained glass, stained glass, *stained glass.*"

"I'm going to call the cops," I said, "and turn you in."

She shrugged indifferently. "Call whoever you want. I'll be long gone before they get here."

Danielle let out a scream, then charged me, hitting me in the chest with her shoulder and knocking me backwards. I went down hard on the floor and saw her running through the foyer. I scrambled to my feet and went after her.

"Help!" Danielle screamed. She stopped in front of the security guard at the ballroom entrance. "Help! She's trying to kill me!"

The security guard whipped around. Danielle took off running again. I continued after her, did a little sidestep to avoid the guard—but he matched me move for move. He grabbed me around the waist and yanked me off my feet.

I kicked hard and made contact with something. He loosened his grip. I slithered away. The guard caught my arm. Something ripped. I pulled free and charged after Danielle.

She had on pumps and a dress, I wore Sketchers and pants but, damn, she could run. I followed her out of the foyer, then saw her jump onto the down escalator. It was packed with women. She bumped them aside as she made her way down.

"Official handbag business!" I shouted as I squeezed my way through the crowd of women.

Ahead of me, Danielle reached the lower floor and sprinted off to her right. I made it off the escalator a few seconds later and followed.

Around the corner in an open area, I saw Danielle stop. I looked past her and saw Detective Webster confronting her, with Detective Dailey not far behind.

I stopped, ready to cut her off if she ran my way. The security guard appeared next to me and wrapped his meaty hand around my upper arm.

Danielle looked at me and the guard, then at the two detectives. She must have recognized them from their interview after Courtney's murder.

"Detective Dailey," she called, pointing at me. "This is all her fault. None of this would have happened, if not for her."

The two homicide detectives surrounded Danielle, their gazes bouncing from her to me.

I pulled my arm away from the security guard and jogged closer. Her eyes were wide, half crazed.

"Tell them why it's my fault," I said to Danielle.

"Because she came here," she exclaimed. She faced the detectives, gesturing wildly at me. "If she hadn't come here, there would have been no one to take the blame for Courtney's death. I could have let her live."

"She killed Rosalyn Chase, too," I said to the detectives.

"What else could I do? I had no other choice." Danielle exclaimed. She flung her hand toward me. "Arrest her!"

Neither of the detectives made a move toward me, so I figured they were satisfied with her confession.

"I guess that settles things," I said to Detective Dailey. "I'm out of here."

"Not so fast," he said. "We're not finished with you."

CHAPTER 29

The employee locker room at the Mandalay Bay was nicer than you'd think. I, for one, was particularly glad to be in it after spending a couple of hours in the security office.

Detectives Dailey and Webster had been there, along with hotel personnel, asking me questions, wanting me to repeat my story over and over again. I wasn't sure who'd called them, but I figured it must have been Jack Bishop, or maybe Mike Ivan.

The detectives seemed okay with the motive for Courtney's murder being a disagreement over a fashion accessory line. Greed was hardly breaking news for law enforcement. They had considerable trouble, though, grasping the concept of just how a fashion accessory line had led me to solve the murders.

Jeez, what's with men sometimes?

When I'd finally gotten them to pull up the Monroe High School Web site and check out the archives, they'd spotted Courtney's stained-glass pattern right away and matched it with the accessories they'd brought from Danielle's booth in the vendor room.

Detective Dailey had also admitted they'd lifted a partial fingerprint from inside Rosalyn Chase's house. In itself, not enough to positively I.D. Danielle as the killer, but enough to add to the mounting evidence against her.

By then I'd had all I was going to take and told them I was leaving. No one stopped me. No one thanked me, either. I didn't care. I was just glad to be out of there.

Maybe I didn't deserve their thanks. I'd been wrong about Valerie Wagner. Guess she'd really just gone to Reno to see her sister, after all.

That made me think of Robbie Freedman. He'd really come all the way to Vegas, made that long, hot trip just to see the place where Courtney had died. That probably meant he'd really cared for her a lot back in high school. And that he hadn't cared for me at all.

Not a great feeling.

No way could I go back to working the handbag convention now, I decided, as I pulled off the pale blue shirt Arlene had given me to wear. It was dirty and the sleeve was ripped, thanks to the wrestling match I'd had with the security guard.

I pulled the red top I'd worn this morning out of the locker I'd been assigned for the day, put it on, and grabbed my purse—a super little Chloe tote. I took a few more minutes to brush my hair and touch up my makeup, then I dropped the blue shirt into the trash can as I walked out the door. Arlene could just take it out of my pay.

I was tired, a little sore, and still had to explain everything to Jack Bishop. He'd gotten here about the time I went into the security office. I'd told him what happened and he'd promised to wait. He'd want a full story of what had happened.

Oh, crap. Ty.

I stopped and rolled my eyes at nobody. Jeez, I'd completely forgotten about Ty. Again. I hadn't called him or anything.

Of course, he probably didn't even know anything had

happened. I imagined he was in the hospitality suite talking over a business deal, waiting for the afternoon reception to begin.

I glanced at my wristwatch. Nearly noon. Maybe I could catch up with him and spend a few minutes before he—

Hang on a second. The raffle would take place in a few minutes.

My spirits lifted considerably. If I won one of the Judith Leiber bags, or the Delicious, it would prove my luck had changed—and I wouldn't have to perform a selfless act. All I had to do was—

Oh my God! The tickets!

I rushed back into the locker room, snatched the shirt out of the trash can, and whipped the tickets out of the pocket. Whew! Thank goodness.

By the time I made it into the vendor room, the crowd around the raffle booth was packed almost twenty deep. I wedged my way into the group, getting as close to the booth as I could.

A woman with bright red hair stood on a little platform with a microphone, ready to pull a ticket stub from the metal hopper. She had on white pants so tight she must have been beamed into them, and would likely need the Jaws of Life to get out of them.

"Okay, ladies, are we ready?" she called.

A cheer went up.

I looked at Maya's and my tickets. I repeated the numbers over and over in my mind, throwing good thoughts out there—I figured it couldn't hurt—emphasizing my lucky number, twelve.

She spun the hopper, opened the cage, and pulled out a winning ticket. She hesitated a moment—which made me want to go up there and strangle her—and called out the number.

A scream rang out on the other side of the room. A nearly hysterical woman pushed her way to the booth and was awarded one of the Delicious handbags.

Yeah, okay, one of them was gone, but that didn't mean I couldn't win the next one. Or one of the Judith Leiber bags.

Jeez, I really wished I'd thought up a selfless act before the raffle started.

"Here we go again!" the redhead declared. She cranked the hopper, pulled out another winning ticket, and read off the number.

Wasn't solving a murder considered a selfless act? I wondered. I mean, jeez, it's not like I got anything out of it.

Oh, yeah, wait. I wasn't a murder suspect anymore.

Crap.

"Okay, ladies, one of you has this number!" the redhead announced. "Who's got it?"

The woman next to me punched me in the side and said, "That's your number! You won!"

What? *What?*

"Read it again!" somebody shouted.

She read the number off once more and, suddenly, a light shone down from above, I got dizzy, angels began to sing. I swear. My lucky number twelve had come through for me!

"I won! I won! I won!" I screamed, jumping up and down, waving my ticket in the air.

The crowd cheered as I waded through the mass of people to the booth. My head spun and my knees wobbled as one of the assistants opened the case and removed one of the Judith Leiber bags.

Oh my God. I'd won a Judith Leiber.

She wrapped it carefully, placed it in a carrier bag, then presented it to me.

My spirits soared. This was fabulous, tremendous, stupendous, and way cool. I couldn't wait to tell Marcie—and Maya.

I clutched the bag to my chest, ready to fight to the death if anyone tried to take it from me, and left. I stopped at the door and listened to the other two winning ticket numbers that were drawn—just in case—but no such luck.

I couldn't complain. Wow, my luck had changed. And I hadn't even done anything selfless.

That Madam CeeCee. What kind of psychic was she, anyway? Maybe I should call and tell her that her curse-breaking advice was jacked up.

I expected to find Maya at the registration desk. Instead, I saw Jack. He spotted me and walked over.

"You okay?" he asked.

Jack had sort of a biker thing going today—which looked really hot, of course. Jeans, black T-shirt, boots. I figured he wanted to know everything that went down with the detectives and Danielle's arrest, but first things first.

"I'm fabulous—beyond fabulous," I told him, clutching the carrier bag to my chest. "Where's Maya?"

"Taking somebody to one of the exhibits." He nodded down the hallway, and shook his head. "She works hard. Too hard for what she gets out of it."

His tone made me wonder if something else was going on.

"What are you doing back in Vegas?" I asked.

"I heard about Maya getting fired by that ass, Bradley," Jack said. His expression darkened. "So I drove up here to kick his butt."

My spirits lifted a little more. "Cool."

"Not so much," Jack said. "He wasn't there. Doesn't work there anymore. Left the state, apparently."

Up went my spirits even further. So Helen Pennington

had removed her little darling from the Culver Inn, as she'd promised. Not a bad compromise, considering what I'd agreed to keep quiet about.

Jack's frown deepened. "That wouldn't have gotten her the tuition money she needs—but it sure as hell would have made me feel better."

Despite the old Disney movies, most women didn't really want to be rescued. They just wanted a man who'd stand up and do the right thing—but it was still nice to know a guy who'd kick somebody's butt for you.

"Haley, are you okay?" Maya asked, joining us at the registration desk. She looked at my shirt. "Aren't you going to finish out the day? What about tomorrow?"

I figured Jack might have told her about the whole Danielle-Courtney-murder thing that had just gone down. Or maybe not. Either way, I didn't want to get into it.

"I'm not feeling all that great," I said, hoping she'd let it drop so I could show her the fabulous Judith Leiber bag I'd just won.

"Do you need a doctor?" Maya asked. "I know a free clinic you can use. They're really nice there, and the wait isn't usually more than a few hours."

"It's nothing serious," I told her.

"Are you sure you can't work?" she asked. "You're going to miss out on a lot of money. Nearly a hundred dollars."

She was concerned I'd lose a hundred bucks, and here I stood with a purse in a carrier bag worth thousands.

"I'll be okay," I said, which wasn't really true, but I sure as heck wouldn't admit to it in front of Jack.

"I'll explain things to Arlene," Maya said. "I'll make sure she understands so you can work for her again."

Wow, was that a BFF thing to do, or what?

"Did you buy something?" Maya asked, pointing to the bag.

I squeezed the Judith Leiber purse a little closer, held it

against my heart for a few seconds. I knew I had to do the right thing.

I hate it when I have to do the right thing.

"It's from the raffle," I said, and held out the carrier bag. "You won!"

Her mouth fell open. Her eyes bulged. She looked at me, then at the carrier bag, then at Jack, then back to me again.

"I . . . I won?" she whispered, as if she were afraid to say it aloud.

"You bet," I said. "It's one of the Judith Leiber bags."

"Oh my God. Oh my God! *Oh my God!*"

Maya grabbed the bag and clutched it with both hands. I couldn't help smiling. Neither could Jack.

Her eyes widened. "I'm going to sell it."

"*What?*" I gasped. "This is a *Judith Leiber*. A special edition. One of a kind."

"I'm going to sell it to one of those people on the message board who wanted it," Maya said. "And then I can pay my tuition and I can buy my books for next semester. I can give some to Mom so my brothers can go to camp this summer. And I'll even have some left over that I can save to start my bakery."

I guess I couldn't argue with that.

"You should contact the Culver Inn and see about getting your catering job again," I said. "I've got a really good feeling they'll hire you back, plus have you cater for the whole chain."

"Do you think so? Oh, wow, that would be so cool!" Maya said. "I've got to check out the message board."

"I'll go with you," Jack said, and grinned. "In case you need backup."

They walked away and I saw them smiling and talking. Nice.

Ty flew into my thoughts and I wished he were here with me right now being my backup. But he wasn't. He was off somewhere taking care of yet another business matter, something that was—as usual—more important to him than me.

Call me crazy, but I wanted a boyfriend I could count on to be around.

Of course, a beach house and a convertible would be nice, too. So would enough money to pay my bills.

Then I saw Ty striding through the foyer toward me. Tall, handsome. My heart fluttered a little at the sight of him.

His killer grin grew into a killer smile as he stopped in front of me and presented me with a flowery gift bag.

"For you," he declared.

I dug through the white tissue paper and pulled out a Delicious handbag. I gasped so hard I lost my breath for a second.

"Oh my God!" I launched myself into his arms. He held me tight, then looked down and we kissed. One of those long, warm kisses.

"I can't believe you found this," I told him. "How did you manage it?"

He just gave me a knowing grin and said, "Look inside."

Oh my God. The lining. Everybody—well, women— knew that the lining of a purse was crucial to the success of the bag. How did Ty know that?

I opened the bag, but instead of checking out the lining, I saw an envelope tucked away.

"Open it," Ty said.

I did. Inside was a platinum Visa card with my name on it.

Ty smiled, looking quite pleased with himself.

"I don't need your money," I said.

"Yes, you do."

I couldn't argue with him. He was right. He'd known it

all along. That's why he kept tempting me with a beach house, a car, a shopping trip.

But Ty hadn't stopped there. His mind had skipped ahead. He knew that as long as I needed money, I'd need him.

"What kind of man would I be if I stood by and did nothing while you struggled with your bills?" Ty asked.

I couldn't argue with that.

"The beach house, the convertible, the shopping trip, it's a lot," I said.

"Then forget about them," Ty said quickly, dismissing them with a wave of his hand. "We'll take one big thing at a time. We'll go slow. Move in with me and let me take care of you."

I shook my head. "I don't know."

"I need you, Haley. I need you in my life, every moment I can possibly get you in it," Ty said. "I know I'm distracted and gone a lot. I wish it could be different, but it's not. So let's make the most of the time we have. Move in with me. You'll see. I can make things better."

He looked honest and sincere, a little desperate even.

I handed him the Visa card. He didn't look happy about it, but he took it.

"Let me think about it," I said.

Ty looked relieved. "Good."

"Oh, wait," I said. "There's something you can do for me right now."

"Anything," he promised.

"Give a two hundred dollar gift card to each of the employees in the Henderson store," I said. "And not a Holt's gift card. One from someplace nice."

He looked at me as if I'd lost my mind, but he simply said, "Sure."

Ty looked at his wristwatch. "I have to get back to L.A."

"You're not staying for the reception?" I asked.

"Something came up," he said. "Come back with me."

I almost protested but, really, I'd had enough of Henderson, Vegas, and the opening of the Holt's store. If Preston had a problem with me leaving before the grand opening, he could take it up with Ty.

"Can we go out for dinner tonight?" I asked as I carefully put the Delicious back into the gift bag. "I want to take my new handbag out for a spin so everybody can see it and be jealous."

"Whatever you want," he said.

Ty pulled out his phone and made a call as we walked past the wedding chapel and restaurants, then stopped suddenly near the entrance to the buffet. His tone changed and his expression morphed into the this-will-be-a-long-call look I'd seen more than a few times across the dinner table.

Nearby, just steps away, was the casino. Rows and rows of brightly colored slot and video machines glowing in the dim light, their *pinging* and *ponging* a siren song that lured in thousands.

Mike Ivan stepped in front of me. Yikes, where had he come from?

He leaned closer and said, "I won't forget what you did," then walked away.

Oh my God. What did that mean? Was it a good thing, or a bad thing?

Jeez, I really hope I haven't been cursed again.

I turned to the casino once more. I hadn't gambled at all since I'd been here. Marcie had advised against it, and I'd gone along with her advice.

Madam CeeCee had told me I must perform a selfless act to break the curse. I hadn't done that, yet I'd won that awesome Judith Leiber handbag. Of course, I'd given it away, so I didn't know if that constituted good or bad luck—

Hang on a minute. I'd given my raffle prize to Maya. That was selfless, wasn't it?

Only one way to find out.

I was leaving Vegas now, and how would I possibly know if the curse had been lifted unless I tried my luck?

Ty was still on his cell phone, so I ventured into the casino. The sights, the sounds, drew me in. I eyed the machines, waiting to feel a connection.

"Trying your luck?" Jack asked as he appeared beside me.

"Where's Maya?" I asked.

"Working," he said.

"Did she sell the bag?"

"Didn't you hear the screaming?" Jack asked. "I'm heading home."

"Me, too," I said, and turned my attention to a bank of slot machines. I eyed them. The Lucky Star machine called to me—I swear. A giant, neon yellow star shot out of the top.

I dug into my pocket and came up with a five dollar bill. Okay, so I wasn't exactly a high roller.

I settled onto the stool in front of the Lucky Star. A tiny old lady sat next to me wearing a ball cap covered with gold sequins, her cane propped against the machine she was using.

"I've got the Beemer," Jack said, easing a little closer.

I fed the five into the slot machine.

"The blue convertible?" I asked. "Cool ride."

"Want to ride with me?" he asked.

I tapped the max bet button on the machine, then hit the spin button. It chimed, the three reels spun, stopping on a star, then a moon, then a comet. The readout announced I'd won a quarter.

Hmm, not exactly the kind of luck I'd hoped for.

"Haley?" Ty walked up and gave Jack a sharp look.

I hit the spin button again.

"The car is waiting," Ty said.

The reels spun. The first one stopped on a star.

"You can drive," Jack told me.

The second reel stopped on a star.

"The corporate jet is waiting," Ty said.

The third reel stopped on a star.

An alarm went off. Bells clanged. A whistle blew.

"Heaven above!" the lady next to me screamed. "You won the big jackpot!"

"What?" I eyed the machine, not really understanding what was happening.

"Look! There!" She pointed to a display at the top of the machine, hopping up and down in her chair. "You won almost fifty thousand dollars!"

"*Fifty thousand dollars?*" I screamed.

"Yes!" she cheered.

Oh my God. I'd won that much money? I couldn't believe my luck.

I whirled to Ty and shouted, "I won!"

But he didn't look happy. His shoulders sagged and he looked absolutely defeated.

"Oh, crap," I heard him mumble.